The Adventures of Jaguar Jack

By
Dana Taylor

Prologue

Unknown Beast does dwell,
Unleashed power from depths of hell,
Unchecked 'til Warrior does wake,
United with power of Saint

Paradisio Island, somewhere in the Pacific

Time collided. Jaguar Jack Campbell froze in place on the jungle floor. He shook his head, disoriented. An explosion of buried images from the past flashed in his psyche.

Jagged teeth.

Earth crumbled around him as he burrowed into an animal's den.

A gagging smell.

Roars and screams.

A taunting voice—*Coward, coward…*

Then, a white bird dove toward his face, arrested his attention, and brought him back to the present. The bird circled, squawked, and zoomed ahead. Tail feathers urged him to follow.

Fully in charge of his senses once again, he glanced over his shoulder at the black feline pursuer and grinned.

Then Jaguar Jack ran like hell.

He jumped over fallen branches, dodged infested insect mounds, and scrambled around the huge trunks of trees that formed the canopy of the rain forest.

"Rroww!" The big cat's howl echoed in the humid air.

Jack sensed the angry feline gaining on him. The sleek jaguar rounded a gigantic trunk, too close for comfort.

You can't outrun a cat, mate, and she's not losing interest. Better come up with a plan ... and fast.

A gnarled kapok tree caught his eye, perfect for a man to catch a foothold and make a natural ladder to the green universe above. He zigzagged away from the tree, ripped the buttons of his shirt open, and tore the garment off his back. He threw the sweat-drenched shirt into the branches of a prickly bush, ran through dense underbrush, and doubled back toward the kapok.

The ferocious jag passed the kapok, following Jack's path, and stopped at the discarded shirt. She sniffed and pawed it, then circled the bush for traces of the man.

Jack hurled himself onto the rough-ribbed wood behind the stalled cat, gashed his naked chest as he found hand holds to climb toward the leafy ceiling. A flock of startled parrots lit out from tangled foliage as he reached the first limbs twenty feet in the air. Splashes of bright red and blue filled the sky as they surged to another roost. Their disturbed chirps caught the cat's attention.

Jack grabbed a thick branch thirty feet up, sturdy enough to hold his weight. Rope-like muscles of his biceps bulged as he hefted himself skyward. He swung his leg over the branch and gazed below. Sweat dripped off his forehead, but his breathing remained steady. Excitement sped his heart beat. Playing tag with cantankerous kitties really got the juices going.

The perturbed black cat circled the base, tail whipping in the air.

"Rrooww!" She let her roar rip.

Even from thirty feet above, Jack glimpsed the glint of long, carnivorous fangs in the cat's mouth.

"I'm up here, darlin'. What's the matter, afraid of heights?"

The cat howled again, as if in reply to his taunt, and stretched her long body, claws digging into the coarse trunk. Her hind legs added a powerful climbing force the man hadn't possessed.

Jack lingered on his resting spot a moment, admiring the sheer grace of his pursuer as she conquered the climb with instinctive precision. Her yellow eyes targeted him with a killer's intent.

"All right, Jack," he muttered. "Best be moving on."

He scampered higher into the dense canopy of intermingled trees. A coiled green snake, camouflaged in the greenery lifted its head. Its tongue flicked to sense the identity of the intruder.

"Sorry, mate, I need a diversion." Jack grabbed the hefty snake and aimed for the rising black feline. *Splat*, the snake's body hit the cat in the face. The surprise assault caused her to momentarily lose her grip and slide a couple of feet, catching her rump on a branch. She lost sight of Jack long enough for him to grab hold of a sturdy vine and swing Tarzan-style to a neighboring kapok. Hugging the trunk, he used his legs to hold and release the tree in the efficient manner he'd learned from his native friends. Ms. Furious Feline continued her upward motion, not realizing her quarry now traveled in a downward mode on another trunk.

Jack glimpsed welcome terra-firma and jumped the last few feet to the ground. He leaned a broad hand against the trunk and saluted his wayward pursuer with his other hand. "It's been fun, sweetheart."

High above, the cat screeched her frustration again. "Rrooww!"

She sprawled on a strong limb, panting, much of her fight lost in the chase.

The camera crew materialized out of the jungle."Cut! That's a wrap, Jack."

Mulligan, the tall, balding cameraman, checked his equipment. "I think I got a lot of good shots. Taking off the shirt was a great move. That ought to push your ratings up a couple points."

Catching his breath, Jack grinned. "Always happy to oblige."

A white cockatoo circled in for a landing on Jack's shoulder and cooed bird love talk.

Jack patted the silken feathers. "Lorelei, my own sweet girl."

Mulligan shook his head. "You had me worried for a moment back there when you froze. I was afraid you were going to turn it into a wrestling match. You cut it close, pal."

A cloud of apprehension passed through Jack. *What the devil had happened in that moment?* The world had blurred, reality distorted. A bad dream escaping from his subconscious. Lorelei rubbed against his cheek. *Better not to think about it.*

Auntie Edith handed Jack a clean shirt. "The cat really wanted to rip your heart out. I almost gave the signal to hit her with the tranquilizer gun. If she'd have come one foot closer to your back, I'd have done it. You have no idea how angry she was."

Jack shrugged his wide shoulders into the shirt. "Oh, I have a pretty fair idea. I may not be able to read their minds like you do, but I saw into her eyes. Bloody scary."

Edith pursed her pixie lips. "You loved every minute of it and you know it."

Jack reached out and mussed his aunt's short-cropped cap of gray hair. "By God, you're right. Did you see the way she put her head back and yowled? Gorgeous sight. Hey Mulligan, did you get that shot of her howling?"

"Got it," he said as he removed Jack's body mike.

Jack gazed up. The jag still roosted in the tree, posing now with queenly disdain. "What's she thinking?"

Edith focused her mental beam on the cat. "She's thinking, 'next time, next time.' You better keep your guard up. This one is more intelligent than most. She'd love nothing more than to rake her claws across your naked back."

Jack reared his head and laughed. "I seem to have that effect on so many females."

Edith continued her mental exchange with the jag. "I've told her to stay put or we'll have to shoot her. She's really annoyed. I also told her not to worry about her cubs. You hadn't meant them any harm."

Jack walked to the base of the jag's tree. "So long, darlin'! You don't know it, but I've just made you a television star."

The cat's tail snapped in irritation.

Jack wrapped his arm around Edith as they began to walk away. "That bit of excitement really worked up my appetite. Let's get back to camp and you can grill me a deer steak."

"Of course, luv. Then promise me we can leave this godforsaken island."

Jack halted a moment and listened to the wild noises—birds, monkeys, insects. He stood trying to hear…something. What was it that drew him back to this place again and again, even when he had no desire to return? He shivered slightly. Ghosts walking over his grave or some such nonsense. He shook off the foreboding.

"You got it, Auntie. Hey, Mulligan, is there any beer left?"

Jack and his crew took a leisurely stroll back to their jungle camp.

Another working day in the life of Jaguar Jack Campbell, star of television and movies, international celebrity, daredevil extraordinaire.

And unbeknownst to him, soon to be undercover agent for the United States of America.

* * *

Across the island, massive paws pounded the jungle floor and charged up the volcanic mountain. The true ruler of Paradisio reached the apex of his domain, above the tree line, balanced on the lip over churning lava in the bowels of the earth. Lightning struck the ground around him. He rose on hind feet, higher and higher, monstrous bear claws attached to a huge lion body.

His strength was increasing; he could feel it. Through the air, he sent his roaring message. Invisible thought waves rippled from the vortex of his island prison to weak minds across the continents.

Hear me. Come to me. Destroy the unbelievers. Great will be your reward.

His time was coming. He would break free and roam the earth once more.

Chapter One

Desert Flats Marine Base, California

Major Maggie Savannah whipped her shiny, black Mercedes into an available parking place, efficiently turned the vehicle off and gathered her purse and briefcase. Her gaze roved the sterile military buildings, set off by occasional palm trees. A high desert wind blew, filling the air with particles of sand and stinging debris. She opened her door and prepared for the blast of dry heat. Seven years she'd been coming back to this hellhole for assignments. Turn left at Barstow, and drive until you hit total desolation. She'd never liked it—for the miserable landscape, the lack of entertainment during her brief furloughs and, well, other reasons, too.

She slammed the door and marched into the fray toward the yawning doors of the front entrance.

Click, click, click. Her smart pumps tattooed a beat as she nodded to acquaintances rushing down busy hallways in the military maze. Tense faces passed her, each chest adorned with a security badge. Since September 11, the casual air of complacency had been replaced by wary urgency. Each day brought unknown demands, challenges, changes in plans.

"Hey, Maggie, wait up!"

Maggie pivoted toward the owner of the familiar voice. She recognized Derby Crane, five-foot four computer nerd for whom she held grudging respect. Derby sidled up to her and tilted his head back to gaze into her face through his thick, black-rimmed glasses.

"Beware, little man, you're still on my list." She sent him a cutting glance.

Derby chuckled. "Hey, I didn't tell you to call the new supply officer a 'pompous, pinheaded prick.' But I admired your alliteration."

"You egged me on because you were afraid of him, and you knew I wouldn't keep my mouth shut."

"They don't call you Maggie-the-Mouth for nothing. I loved watching his face turn beet red. I swear smoke floated out of his ears."

"Yeah, well the next time you want somebody dressed down, find another mouthpiece. Maggie-the-Mouth is out of business." She resumed her steady stride.

"That'll be the day," Derby muttered.

He dashed to catch up. "I heard the General was pulling you in on this one. You kicked ass in that Yemen hostage situation."

Maggie's jaw tightened. "It could have gone better."

Her team had gotten the oil company employees out, but her contact and friend, Jordanian born Al-Jabbar, had been shot and killed. And Ahmed Saeed had gotten away. Being raised military, Maggie knew the inevitability of casualties, yet it didn't make death any easier. A month in the Bahamas had given her a great tan, but she still felt like shit about Al. He was one of the good guys. He'd given up any semblance of a normal life to infiltrate terrorist cells. Now, he had no life at all.

She shook off her blues and asked Derby, "So, what's up?"

"I don't want to spoil the General's fun," Derby said as he reached for the door knob to the head man's office. "Ladies first."

Maggie sailed into the reception area and spoke to the long-time assistant. "Is he ready for me, Lois?"

"Is anyone ever ready for you, Maggie?"

"I love you, too, Lois."

Maggie didn't wait to be announced into the General's office. Derby followed in her wake and came to attention beside her. The General talked on the phone behind his mammoth mahogany desk. He gestured his visitors at ease and to take a seat.

Maggie sank into a fine leather chair, crossed her long legs comfortably, as she surveyed the familiar room. The rich paneled walls were covered with photographs and citations; flags stood at attention in the corner. Her gaze traveled to the family photos on the desk. The tall General had his arm around his diminutive wife, all snuggly and happy. She looked so dainty and perky.

Next, Maggie took in the General's daughter. Strong chin, wide hazel eyes framed by Brooke Shields eyebrows. Full, fluffy red hair framed her face in the picture. Straightforward expression, no coy shrinking violet, she.

The General hung up the phone and addressed his guests. "Major Savannah, you're looking well, all things considered."

"Thank you, sir."

"Care for a piece of Mississippi Pie? Dotty sent it over this morning."

Mississippi pie. Cripes, her weak spot. "Sure. Dish some up, Derby, while we listen to what the General has cooked up for us."

Derby eagerly scurried to the sidebar and cut three pieces of gooey pie, found fresh milk in the mini-fridge and poured three glasses as the General began to fill them in on the assignment.

"Three months ago a missionary Bible translator was taken hostage on the Pacific island of Paradisio by the Sons of Allah, under the leadership of a Bangkok prostitute's son named Moktar. As islands go, Paradisio is big—about the size of Texas, inhabited by scattered tribes of unfriendly natives. Paradisio has never developed much civilization, due to its lack of a decent harbor, and its tendency to get hit by killer typhoons on a regular basis. Still, it appears to be a haven for terrorists and pirates who can disappear in the mandrake groves. They blend into the tropical forest hidden from the satellite surveillance that photographs the island."

Maggie dipped her fork into the corner wedge of the decadent chocolate confection. "So, Bible translators are a big military priority nowadays?"

"They are when the translator is the only child of the head of the Ways and Means Committee of the United States Senate."

"Ah, the plot thickens. Is this a male or female child?"

The General pulled out an 8 by 10 photo of a fresh faced, all-American girl. "This is Hannah Smith. Twenty-eight years old, committed to translating the Bible to natives in their native language. The young lady received 'the call' to Paradisio and overcame every obstacle thrown in her path to get there. She's been working in a remote village for three years without gaining much attention. But, the professional kidnapper, Moktar, made the connection to the Senator and grabbed her."

"What are their demands?" Lord, how that marshmallow danced on her tongue.

"Two million dollars."

"In their dreams."

"We can't find them from the air. They are camouflaged too well. We've sent in two teams on the ground who've come back riddled with nasty venom-tipped darts, courtesy of the locals. Neither team got close to the kidnapper's camp. We can't go in and blast away the villages on our way to the camp. Besides, according to the national government there, Americans can only train local troops, not carry out military operations. We've come up with a covert operation that should work if the right person heads up the team. Maggie, I think you're that person."

"Interesting. So how do I get past the natives with the darts? Offer them a few beads? Free trips to Disney World?"

"No, you're going to put them on TV."

Maggie cocked an eyebrow. Now she'd heard everything.

The General explained there was one white man who had regular access to the island. He'd made great friends of native headmen and had even cleared a landing strip for his private plane. The guy shot segments of his popular television show there.

"Surely you've heard of him, Maggie—Jaguar Jack Campbell?"

Maggie shrugged her shoulders. She wasn't much for TV. Real life concerned her.

"You've never heard of Jaguar Jack?" Derby's voice squeaked in amazement.

"Excuse me for living, no."

"He's on the cover of all the tabloids. His reality TV show, *The Adventures of Jaguar Jack*, turned the Adventure Channel into a major cable player. McDonald's has Jaguar Jack action figures in all its Happy Meals this month," Derby explained.

Maggie stood up and leaned across the wide desk toward the General. "Are you trying to tell me that you want to include a civilian in this operation? No way! It was inept, scared shitless civilians that got Al-Jabbar killed in Yemen. In Panama a civilian attaché from the Embassy got those hostages all shot to hell. Every operation that has included civilians has been nothing but trouble."

The General's face hardened. "Major Savannah when I issue an order, you *will* follow it."

Maggie and the General engaged in a silent staring match until she sighed, ran her fingers through her wavy hair and settled back in the chair. "Cripes. I want another piece of pie." Derby hopped up to oblige.

The General's expression softened. "I know you had a rough time of it in Yemen. Al-Jabbar was a good man. The information he acquired in his undercover work saved a lot of lives. There must have been a breach of security. I read the report. There wasn't anything you could have done to prevent it."

"Yeah, I know. Shit happens." Maggie slouched in her seat.

The General's leather chair creaked as he leaned back. "This Jaguar Jack character will be your cover to getting into the jungle. You'll pretend to be part of his crew. An expert brought in on special assignment. You'll have electronic equipment to signal to the satellite when you find the camp and send the coordinates to Derby. Then we can send in a commando force by air. You will be able to give us the lay of the land. We'll maintain voice contact with you with some of the new equipment he's come up with."

Derby grinned with excitement. "I can hardly wait to see how well it works. There's some atmospheric interference in rain forests that makes transmission difficult. But I think I've got it licked."

Maggie eyed him suspiciously. "Let's hope it works out better than the pantyhose body mike. The buzzing sensation was highly distracting."

The General stood and walked around his desk. "I've got a meeting at 1400 hours. We can discuss this further at dinner tonight, Maggie." His calloused hands reached out to meet hers and pulled her up into a bear hug. "It's good to have you with us, even for a few days."

Maggie rested her forehead on her father's shoulder. She whiffed in the familiar scent of his aftershave and felt five years old again. She leaned back and gazed into hazel eyes that matched hers, only his had years of crinkles around the edges.

"I suppose Mom has lined up dinners with eligible bachelors?"

"Some things can't be avoided, Sugar."

"Cripes."

General Savannah kissed her cheek and headed for the door. "I'll see you later. Clean up the dishes, Derby."

"Yes sir," Derby said, as he started KP duty.

Maggie paced the room. "So, is Jaguar Jack excited about being part of a military operation? Is he planning on filming it for sweeps week or something?"

"Actually, so far his communications with us have been somewhat negative. We've been trying to set up a meeting with him. I believe his last reply to us was 'Stick it in your ear.'"

***

The evening news reported a suicide bomber in Afghanistan blew himself up on a bus filled with women and school children. Terrorist leader Ahmed Saeed sent out a message over the radio promising more such incidents and calling followers to join the Jihad. A cloud of fear spread across another village, increasing the spiritual power of a mythical creature on a tropical island thousands of miles away.

Chapter Two

Maggie crossed the living room of her parents' desert home. She gazed out the huge picture window to the backyard. A sparkling pool, surrounded by potted plants against the dramatic arid backdrop, looked so inviting. The wind had died down. Lord, wouldn't a swim feel good? Slanted late afternoon sun cast long shadows of the finger-like palm fronds across the lounge chairs. Glancing at her watch, Maggie knew her mother would put up a fuss if she jumped in the pool and appeared for dinner dressed in sweats with damp hair pulled back in a ponytail.

Dotty entered the room holding a tray of beverages. "Maggie, come in here and sit down. I'll pour you a nice glass of tea. I want to hear about every little thing you've been doing."

Maggie inhaled a deep breath, turned around, and faced her mother. Dotty leaned over the coffee table, clinking ice in tall frosted glasses, serving tea, strong and sweet. Just the way they loved it in the south, the deep, deep south. Maggie quit putting sugar in her tea years ago, but with her mother, sugar was not an option. Like so many things.

"Bright, new upholstery, Mom," Maggie said as she joined her mother in the living area. She couldn't spit out a lie declaring she actually liked it.

"It was time. I just loved this floral, simply had to have it," Dotty said as she scooted back on the crimson and yellow cushion.

Maggie settled into a Queen Anne chair, marveling as always, that her mother looked like a living doll. Barely five feet tall, Dotty's shoes didn't touch the carpet if she leaned against the back of the sofa. The room smelled like Dotty's perfume—gardenias galore. With petal soft skin, a halo of silver hair, and delicate features, Maggie's mother epitomized Southern femininity. And despite the Frank Lloyd Wright architecture of the house, she'd managed to bring a dash of the antebellum South into the California desert. Floral upholstery and an explosion of ruffles and doilies made Aunt Pittypat's escape from the Yankees invading Atlanta seem imminent.

"You've let your hair grow longer," Dotty observed. "It's very becoming. I'll bet the men in the officers' clubs gather round you like flies to honey."

Brother, it sure didn't take her long to get to her favorite subject. "Sometimes I buy a round and shoot the breeze with the guys."

"Have you been seeing anyone special?" Dotty sipped her tea.

"Mom, I've been kinda busy, what with one hostage situation after another. It hasn't left much time for roses and romance."

"You can't be on assignment *all* the time. Have you worn that darling dress I sent you? When I saw it, I knew you'd look as fresh as a Georgia peach."

Maggie grimaced. "It looked like walking wall paper with those huge flowers all over it."

Dotty's face drooped into familiar wounded martyrdom. Maggie wanted to kick herself. Why couldn't she just fib and say she loved it?

"I'm sorry, Mom. It was thoughtful of you to send it. The package followed me halfway around the world. I don't have much occasion to wear girlie clothes. Besides, they always make me feel like I'm pretending to be someone I'm not."

"Now that's ridiculous." Dotty's lips pursed into a perfect bow. "You're a striking woman. All you need to do is gild the lily a little bit like women have been doing since the beginning of time. You should let your guard down once in a while, and allow the charming side of you to shine through."

These conversations always made Maggie want to rip her hair out. She settled for running her fingers through it. "We've been down this road before. I don't simper and coo. Face it, Mom. Your Southern Belle gene went defective in me. I take after my Daddy, a total straight shooter."

Dotty waved her hand in dismissal. "You don't know yourself at all. You're so much more than a military machine. I'm your mother. I know you better than you know yourself."

"Okay. Whatever." Maggie stood up. "I'm tired. I think I'll take a short nap before dinner."

"Certainly, sweetheart, you just freshen up. I've invited the most charming intelligence officer to join us."

"Boy, you just don't give up, do you?"

Dotty's dimples winked. "Never. I have my campaigns too. You be sure to blow dry your hair, and wear that lovely blue dress that's hanging in the closet. And, for heaven's sake, try to curb that straightforward tongue of yours tonight." She leaned forward, a gleam in her eye. "He could be Mr. Right."

Maggie shrugged. "Right." She paused near the hallway. "Is there still a TV and DVD player in the guest room?"

"Yes, Sugar."

"Good, Dad gave me a few discs of Jaguar Jack's adventures to watch."

"Jaguar Jack, that Australian animal mad man? Whatever for?"

"Research. Seems I'm going to make Jack an offer he can't refuse."

***

Maggie sat on the satiny flowered comforter; her feet tangled in a frilly pink dotted Swiss dust ruffle. Hot air from the blow dryer teased her flame-colored hair into soft swirls as she watched Jaguar Jack wrestle alligators and catch snakes on television.

She had to admit the man was damn good looking. Jeez, that smile must have cost a fortune. Dark hair and broad shoulders filled the TV screen.

Wowie-kazowie. Okay, cool it girl. Don't turn into another Jaguar Jack Junkie. The man probably has less brains than his cockatoo.

"Isn't this a beauty?" Jack said as he held the venomous snake behind the jaw with one hand and cradled the long body with his other. "Its emerald color provides a perfect camouflage in the canopy. An unsuspecting tree frog hops by and zap! He's a tasty lunch. This lovely parrot snake just waits for the rain forest to deliver its next meal right to his mouth. Now, that's what I call fast food."

Maggie shook her head at the weak pun. Boy, this guy was corny. Cocky and corny. For a big guy, he touched the animals with amazing tenderness. *Wonder how he touches the female of his own species?* She shook off her silly daydreaming and got back to business.

Opening the profile on Jungle Man, she read his vital statistics: 35 years old, 6' 1", son of Phillip Campbell, world-renowned Australian zoologist. Mother killed when he was eight years old. Circumstances unclear. Maggie frowned at that.

Her attention returned to the file. Jack grew up traipsing the world's forests with his father. Active in Green Peace and various environmental watch groups. Got arrested once for liberating laboratory animals. Collects Biblical-era artifacts, predominately weaponry.

Something very interesting snagged her attention. "Hold on, what's this? *Spent six months in an Australian psych ward when he was nineteen.* Wonder what that was about?"

Records sealed. *Drat.* Went on to Harvard. Active in the college drama club where he learned to love the sound of applause. Joined forces with a college chum to film the first segments of *The Adventures of Jaguar Jack.* Blues eyes, black hair and devil-may-care attitude found a wide audience. From children to grownups, the world loved Jaguar Jack Campbell.

Personal life: a string of photogenic women hung on Jack's arms at gala events of the rich and famous. No marriages or engagements.

Faithful sidekick: Auntie Edith Campbell, also known as the Auntie Animal Psychic. Has segment on every show where she reads the minds of the animals.

Maggie stopped at that sentence. "Animal psychic?" Good grief, this guy had a regular carnival act going. She laughed out loud.

She dug deeper into the material, searching for a weak link, a chink in Jack's armor to assault and bring him over to her side. If the TV hero wasn't willing to cooperate out of the goodness of his heart, she'd have to rely on other techniques. The long arm of Uncle Sam provided a plethora of power plays. She could threaten the IRS, freeze his assets, plant bad publicity. Whatever it took, Jaguar Jack was a marked man.

The screen went blue. So much for *The Adventures of Jaguar Jack.* Maggie sighed. Time to face the music and see what ghastly, frilly frock hung in the closet. Plush carpet pampered her toes as she crossed the room and slid the mirrored door open. She blinked. Rather than the expected floral disaster suitable for a 5-foot-two, eyes-of-blue kewpie doll, a simple, velvet sapphire cocktail dress waited on a padded hanger.

Maggie reached out and ran her fingers down the soft material. Tasteful, beaded trim highlighted the neck and cuffs. Something like yearning punched her gut. Oh, God, how she'd like to look and feel beautiful just for one night. Maggie-the-Mouth transformed into Cinderella.

With sweaty palms, she grabbed the hanger and hoped the dress cast a magic spell.

Half an hour later she stood before the full length mirror staring at her reflection. *Who is this person, this imposter? What have you done with Maggie the Marine?* Lord, who was she trying to kid? She liked to stomp in combat boots. She hated anything fake, and this image in the mirror was not the real Maggie. But part of her wanted it to be.

"Magnolia! Cocktails are served. Come meet our gentleman caller." Dotty's voice chimed across the house.

Maggie nearly tore the pretentious dress off and slipped into slacks and a comfortable shirt. But the look of disappointment on her mother's face would stab her with guilt. And her father's scowl of censure would feel like a second blow.

"Suck it up, Major Savannah, you can play the Southern Belle once a year," Maggie said to her reflection. The "gentleman caller" was probably a pot-bellied, balding pencil-pusher trying to make points with the General.

She entered the living room. The visitor had his back to her, talking to Dotty and the General at the wet bar.

"Oh, here she is now," said the General.

The officer pivoted in her direction, all six feet two of him in dress uniform, full head of sandy hair and soft brown eyes to die for. His gaze roved over her in frank male approval.

Play it cool. You can do this. He's a man. You're a woman. Play the part.

Dotty spoke with proper hostess elegance. "Colonel Matthews, may I introduce our daughter, Magnolia?"

Without thinking, her military training kicked in and she saluted. "Major Maggie Savannah, sir."

Well, hell, so much for feminine mystery.

Colonel Matthews smiled and bowed slightly with his greeting, "Ma'am."

Oh my God, that homespun word held the glory of Dixie, peaches and plantations, the South-will-rise-again in one long inflection. Matthews epitomized the ultimate Southern gentleman, too handsome for comfort. She flushed as if she'd just chugged a shot of Jack Daniels.

General Savannah popped Matthews on the back. "This is Colonel Chris Matthews. Sharpest anti-terrorism specialist I've seen on the base. He'll be heading up your next assignment."

Dotty maneuvered her tiny body between her daughter and their guest, slipping her arms into theirs and leading them to the seating area. "Oh no, we are not talking shop this evening. This is a social occasion, and I won't have constant conversation of massacres and car bombings." Dotty effectively forced the two on the love seat. "Colonel Matthews, I understand your family is from Georgia."

"Yes, ma'am. My folks still live on what's left of the Matthews plantation. The family graveyard goes back to the 1700's. Of course, my father commutes to Atlanta where he works as an investment banker, but he still runs a little cotton and tobacco on the land."

Dotty's eyes fairly glittered as she sighed a swoon. "Oh, did you hear that Maggie? A man with a pedigree."

Maggie envisioned generations of Matthews men leading the hounds, gentlemen farmers asking debutantes for a dance, damning that upstart Abe Lincoln for interfering with states' rights. She looked into the fabulous face of Christopher Matthews, and blabbed the first forthright thought that came to mind.

"Comes from a long line of slave owners, huh?"

Chapter Three

A few days later, Maggie sipped coffee in the base cafeteria, reading over data regarding Paradisio's terrain. A live volcano. *Swell.*

"Interesting reading, Major?" Chris Matthews' fair, friendly face gazed down at her, a coffee cup in his hand.

Cripes. Just the man she'd been avoiding one-on-one. Team meetings were going okay, plans coming together. But the sour taste of the dinner-party-gone-bad lingered. Fear of repeating another gauche statement had left her tongue-tied the rest of the evening. Dotty played the perfect hostess while shooting her surreptitious signals to lay on girlie charm she didn't possess, and never would.

"Colonel Matthews," Maggie nodded. "Just reviewing the aerial recon, sir."

"Mind if I join you?"

Yes. "Of course not."

Matthews slid across the table from her. "I need to apologize for the other evening."

"*You* need to apologize? I'm the one who flapped off about slave owners and had the mother shoving me down your throat."

"I sensed I made you uncomfortable." He leaned back against the red vinyl seat.

She laughed. "Boy, you are a gentleman deluxe." If she had any brains at all, she'd work at flirting with this guy. She tried on her mother's southern accent. "I most graciously accept your totally unwarranted apology. And I promise never to allow my mother's matchmaking schemes to include you again, sir."

Chris smiled. "Maybe that's my loss."

Maggie blinked, nonplussed. "Really?"

"I've been watching you this week, Major Savannah. I appreciate your style and respect your abilities. I think I'd like to get to know you better."

"Wow. I generally scare the fellas away with my forthright ways. You must be made of sturdy stuff, Colonel."

"You'd be surprised." He warmed up her coffee from the carafe, an unconscious gesture of inbred civility. "Call me Chris."

"Call me Maggie." They toasted coffee mugs, a step toward friendship. These days she could use a friend. She liked his warm, open smile. "Not to change the subject, but what's your take on getting Hannah Smith out of the jungle alive?"

Chris' expression turned serious. "Well, it's a sure thing we won't count on the IMA, the local military. The last group of hostages were all killed in crossfire before Moktar and his men disappeared into the underbrush. A quick, covert operation is the only way to guarantee getting Hannah out alive."

"Are we stringing the kidnappers along with negotiations for ransom?"

"The U.S. government doesn't negotiate with terrorists, as you know. But, Hannah's parents have been contacted and are pursuing every lead. Moktar has collected about twenty million dollars in ransoms in the last five years."

Maggie whistled. "Twenty million…all going into the terrorist organization coffers, I suppose."

"Mostly, except what lines Moktar's pockets. Money to pay a suicide bomber's family $25,000 has to come from somewhere."

"What a crazy world we live in. There's just no end to the bad guys."

"It's imperative you and Campbell find the targets as soon as possible." Chris stirred cream into his coffee. "I'll send in a team to apprehend Little Miss Muffet. As I've said before, our main concern in this operation is getting her out alive. Then we'll hunt down Moktar. By the way, I've gotten some new intel you'll be interested in. He's taken on a new partner—Ahmed Saeed."

A flash of angry heat swept over Maggie. "That golden-tongued murderer. He's the kind of snake that gives the Taliban a real bad name."

Silence hung between them as Maggie fought back images she'd been trying to forget.

Chris took her hand. "Sorry. I know Saeed took out your partner."

Bitterness clouded Maggie's mood. "Then he went on the radio and bragged about it across the Arabic world." Remembering the ranting voice of Saeed sent chills up her spine.

"We won't let him win this time." He gave her fingers a reassuring squeeze.

She gazed at their joined hands. No rockets seemed to be going off, but she sensed a steady strength in Matthews.

"I think you're going to be a good man to have at my back, Colonel."

"Believe me, Maggie, nobody wants you to succeed in this mission more than I."

***

The drive down the coast helped to clear Maggie's mind and set her agenda straight. Attaining the cooperation of Jaguar Jack Campbell, Aussie adventurer, headed the list. She hoped he had more for brains than bat guano.

Briefings with Chris Matthews, Derby, and the rest of the team had yielded a workable plan to rescue Hannah Smith, code name Little Miss Muffet, and clean out the nest of terrorists once and for all. Capturing Ahmed Saeed would be high priority. The Arab's bold Internet broadcasts were galvanizing the disgruntled Third World.

Maggie should have been focused, raring to go as she usually was on a new assignment. But she struggled for the first time in her life with malaise. And loneliness. Chris Matthews had reached out in friendship. Was she interested in something more? Could she figure out how to send the right signals? What would it have been like to have a romantic farewell?

Chris: "It's so hard to let you go, Sugar."

Maggie: "Then make me stay."

Chris: "If that plane leaves the ground and you're not on it, you'll regret it. Maybe not today, maybe not tomorrow, but soon. And for the rest of your life."

Maggie: "But what about us?"

Chris: "We'll always have Barstow."

Screech--the fantasy halts when you've got Barstow instead of foggy Casablanca like Bergman and Bogart.

Standing in the stark headquarters hallway, he had shaken her hand to say goodbye. "Good luck, Mag-Pie. I want both you and Hannah Smith out of that jungle safe and sound. Watch your backside." His eyebrows knit. "I mean it."

Genuine concern shone in his brown eyes, but she sloughed it off. "I'll be fine, Matthews. Go play with your satellites."

She liked Chris, but did she have the guts to attempt the woman/man thing? He had a steady, dependable quality that appealed to her. But she didn't know how to go from soldier to siren. And as the song says, *You Can't Get A Man With A Gun.*

She sighed, rolled down the window and let the ocean air fill the car. The Pacific on her right, and the jagged hills to her left, should have been view enough to keep her attention. But her mind wandered with a kaleidoscope of images.

First, warm-fuzzy fantasies of Matthews, and then the harsher memories of Al-Jabbar's last moments came into focus. Those awful seconds when everything went wrong, everything in slow motion. Al slammed by bullets before she could take Saeed down. Running through the desert just seconds too late, she watched a smirking dark face rise in the helicopter. The bastard had the balls to salute her as he flew out of sight. The memory came back, making her pound the steering wheel in frustration.

Now, she was being given another shot at the network that had been responsible for Al's death. She had to get her act together. Their plan was solid. It just required the cooperation of one carefree, cocky television star.

Chapter Four

Maggie waited in Jack's room at the plush seaside resort. He was attending a glitzy awards banquet in Century City—Fabulous Phony-Baloney Awards, or some such crap as that. She'd acquired the adjoining suite and easily let herself into his domain. Elegant upholstered furniture filled the room. She explored the area for hints of the man beneath the star image. His closet revealed high dollar clothes, shiny shoes. An array of Australian bush hats. A taste for Hawaiian sport shirts. Figured.

In the back of the closet she came across a burlap bag tied with twine. Maybe he kept his porn under wraps. Sitting cross-legged on the carpet, surrounded by his suits and the scent of men's cologne and shoe polish, she opened the bag. She pushed back the burlap.

Well, blow me down.

Her hand curled around the hilt of a tarnished sword. Black with age, ancient engravings tantalized the tips of her fingers. The warrior in her marveled at long-forgotten battles. What stories could this link to the past reveal? Momentarily awestruck, she held the artifact with reverence. Did she feel a slight hum of energy in the metal?

She snapped out of it, and shoved the sword back in place. She remembered Jungle Boy's fetish for Biblical war toys.

She returned to the living room, flopped on the couch, and made herself comfortable. The room featured all the standard issue luxuries you'd expect for the rich and famous. An ornate empty birdcage added an exotic touch.

She watched Jack on the live telecast accept an award for Hottest Hero. Beyond the sexy black hair and wide shoulders, he radiated charisma. Jack's masculine star quality couldn't be denied. His slanting smile charmed the audience as he caressed his award. He scanned the crowd for familiar faces; winked at the latest crop of starlets. A cockatoo perched on his shoulder as he made his acceptance speech.

He thanked the usual people, and then turned to the bird showing off his trophy. "It's a beaut, don't you think, Lorelei?"

"Crikey, mate!" squawked the bird.

Jaguar Jack kissed the bird on live TV, and millions of women around the world wished they were cockatoos.

Afterwards, Maggie sat on the balcony, watching the moonlight reflect off the pounding waves. Dressed all in black, sitting still as stone, no one noticed her in the shadows. She didn't know how long a wait it would be. Jack might be hitting three parties or spending the night with a shampoo commercial star.

But Maggie was patient. She would get her man.

About midnight the hallway door opened, and light poured into the dark room. From her vantage point on the balcony, she watched through the slits in the shutters. Jack and a female companion stumbled in, arm in arm, probably full of celebratory champagne.

"Come in, darlin'," Jack said. "Make yourself comfortable. I need to see to Lorelei for a moment."

Maggie swiveled her head until she saw the bird resting on Jack's forearm.

The short blonde spoke in true high-pitched bimbo fashion. "I think Lorelei is just adorable. I had a parakeet once. My cat ate it." Her red lipstick mouth pouted at the memory.

"Oh, rotten luck," Jack said while tending his bird.

The cockatoo squawked.

"Yes, I know, sweetheart, you're ready for a treat." Jack crossed to the mini-bar and opened the fridge. "You've been a real trouper tonight." He pulled a bowl of grapes out and placed them on the counter.

The blonde wiggled her butt across the room. "Oh, can I feed her? Will she bite me?"

"Nah. She's very polite. Of course, *I* might bite you." He leaned over and laid a big smooch on the blonde's lips.

"Grape! Grape!" the cockatoo called.

The lip-locked humans pulled away from each other, laughing. Jack placed grapes in the blonde's hand. "Here, darlin', just hold your hand out flat and she'll nip them right out."

The woman followed his instructions and Lorelei obliged, standing on the bar eating each grape held out to her. "Ooo, she tickles!"

Jack sidled behind the woman, and pressed his front against her kewpie-doll behind. "What's your name, again, sweetheart?"

"Tara."

"Tara…lovely name. Scarlett O'Hara…Gone With The Wind… Yes, you have the same kind of Vivien Leigh star quality," he said nuzzling her neck.

The girl turned around, having finished feeding the bird. She eased her arms around his neck. "I got called back for a mascara commercial last week."

"You have fascinating eyes. They'd make love to the camera."

As Jack came in for his own close-up on the beguiling Tara, Maggie wondered if she should walk in and break up this little tryst before it got too hot and heavy. Voyeurism wasn't her bag, and the thought of watching them groping each other made her feel like she'd eaten bad seafood. On the other hand, tipping off Tara to her presence might be a mistake. Breaches in security had a way of coming back to bite you.

Jack and Tara tumbled onto the couch in a tangle of loose limbs, on their way to casual coupling. Maggie bit back impatience, and decided to take a seat on the balcony to wait for the bimbo's departure.

A white streak of feathers darted into the night air. Maggie discovered, much to her dismay, that Lorelei was a guard bird.

Painful pecking on the top of her head, accompanied by cockatoo screeches, caught the female commando completely by surprise. Maggie stumbled around the balcony, slapping at the beak and talons that continued attacking her head. She knocked over a table and three chairs, and finally fell to her knees. She rolled, raised her two arms in the air and captured Lorelei in a strangle hold. Strong wings fought under her grip; woman versus feathered fury.

Jack's Aussie drawl sounded deadly serious. "Drop me bird, lady, or by God, I swear I'll shoot you."

Maggie glanced over her shoulder, and found herself staring into the barrel of a .35mm pistol held in the steady grip of blue-eyed Jaguar Jack Campbell.

Spitting a feather out of her mouth, Maggie said, "Cripes. Call the damn bird off and I'll let her go."

"Come here, Lorelei." Jack emitted a soft whistle. Maggie released her hands and the winged creature flapped in the air, circled, and headed for a roost on Jack's shoulder. Maggie rose from her crumpled position and stared coolly at Jack.

"Mystery lady in black." Jack examined her with an appreciative eye.

Tara tiptoed behind Jack and asked, "Who is she?"

"I expect she's another Jaguar Jack groupie. Though she seems a bit long in the tooth for this kind of thing. I often have teenagers hiding in me closets and under the bed."

Maggie smiled. He thought her a zealous fan. Fine, that would work. Or something like it.

She strolled up to Tara until she knew her height would intimidate the miniature starlet. "Take a hike, sweetheart. Jack and I have a little reminiscing to do. Your party is over."

Tara shot a confused look to Jack, who immediately put himself between the two women. Maggie felt a twinge of intimidation as she gazed up into his irritated midnight blue eyes.

He spoke through thin lips. "See here, lady. I don't know what your game is, but I'll give you thirty seconds to clear out of here or I'll call security."

Maggie sighed. "Jack, I'm very disappointed in you. Trying to pretend you don't know who I am after all we meant to each other in… Casablanca."

"What the bloody hell are you talking about?"

Maggie peeked around his shoulder at Tara. "Men can be such bastards. He'd have forgotten your name by morning. Quick, Jack— what is her name?"

His blank expression said it all. "Uh…Scarlett?"

"See? Do you really want to screw a man who can't even remember your name? We spent an entire week together in North Africa making love and shooting footage of lions and crocodiles, and now he claims he doesn't know who I am. He promised me a job with his production company and when I showed up at the airport, his plane had already left. No note, nothing."

Tara slapped Jack on the back of the head. "Creep." She turned and walked to the sofa and found her shoes. "I'm outta here. I've had my fill of users."

Jack crossed back into the room. "Wait a minute. She's making all that rubbish up."

Maggie crossed her arms and leaned against the door post to the balcony. "Give it a rest, Jack."

"Scarlett, don't listen to her," Jack said, following the blonde.

"My name is *Tara*, you jerk," she said as she pulled open the door. "I didn't want to make love with a bird watching anyway."

"Crikey, mate!" Lorelei screeched.

Tara slammed the door shut.

Jack wanted to skewer the gorgeous female intruder, who was laughing in his famous face. He held the gun in his best Clint Eastwood stance. "You're obviously some kind of mental case. Doesn't this gun in my hand make you the least bit nervous?"

The woman pushed away from the wall and walked directly to the weapon, putting her hand over it. "It might, if you had taken the safety off." She took the pistol out of his hand and placed it on the mini-bar counter. "You wouldn't have intentionally shot me, but you might have-- accidentally. Besides it's hard to take a man seriously with a cockatoo on his shoulder."

He ran fingers through his dark hair. "Who the hell are you?"

"Major Maggie Savannah, United States Marine Corps, at your service."

She leaned against the bar and crossed her arms. A challenging female, not at all his usual fare.

Jack stared at her with ice-blue resentment. "Maybe I should just give Lorelei the signal to go after you again."

Maggie reached over, calmly picked up the pistol, flipped off the safety and leveled it on the bird. "Try it. But it would be a shame to have her bird bits splattered all over this lovely room."

Lorelei squawked and fluttered, "Crikey, mate!"

He muttered, "You said it, baby," and walked Lorelei to the safety of her cage. She flapped in as he covered the wired haven with a fancy flamingo designed material and said, "Go to sleep, sweetheart. You've had a long day."

The bird cooed and settled down.

Jack turned back toward the sheila Marine, who had put the gun away and taken a seat on a comfortable cushioned chair. Lorelei's bowl of grapes rested in her lap, and she seemed to be enjoying them very much. Jack studied the brazen redhead in the way he observed wild creatures in the rough.

Her strong jaw and emerald eyes conveyed a cagey intelligence that far surpassed the vacant stare of sex-kittens like Scarlett…or Tara, or whatever the blonde babe's name had been. Maggie moved with the unconscious sensuality of a large cat, loping long limbs with retractable claws. And, blimey, those full breasts and mahogany mane caught his male attention. He might have yielded to his attraction if she wasn't from the bloody military.

"Listen Major, I don't know what you and your superiors are selling, but I'm not buying. I stay as far away from military types as possible. I've seen the aftermath of military campaigns all over the world, and I want nothing to do with it. So, why don't you leave Lorelei a few grapes for her breakfast and clear out of here."

Maggie laid the grapes aside, reached behind the chair and pulled up a briefcase. From it she drew out an 8 by 10 glossy of a young woman that she tossed on the coffee table. "This is Hannah Smith. She's being held captive on the island of Paradisio and you're going to help us get her out."

Paradisio again. Would that bugger island never get out of his life?

Jack hitched his hands on his hips. "I don't like being bullied either by a cantankerous elephant or a long-legged female Marine."

She crossed her legs and batted her eyelashes. "Gee, if I say, 'please,' does that mean you will cooperate?"

"No." He stood his ground, reining in his irritation. "I'm not scheduled to go back to Paradisio until next year. I'm due for a shoot in the Amazon in three days. Surely, with all the resources of the American military machine you can get your Miss Smith off the island without my help."

"Unfortunately, we're not supposed to be there at all, according to local law. They are a little shy of Americans taking over their islands after their days of colonialism. We're supposed to be training their local IMA forces, but those guys couldn't catch a turtle crossing a road. So this operation is strictly covert."

She rose from her seat and crossed to the wet bar, in search of munchies. "We've already sent in two teams to track down the kidnappers' camp, which is moving on a daily basis. The teams returned with a backside of poison darts, courtesy of the locals. We need to quietly locate the captive, signal her position to a rescue crew and get the job done. No big time military operation, Jack, to ruin your precious ecology or kill any of Lorelei's feathered cousins." She tossed chocolate-covered peanuts into her mouth.

Jack paced the room. He knew why they wanted him. He could get past the unfriendly villages and the IMA. He'd spent years on the island with his father, when he was a kid, living with natives. His mother had been killed on Paradisio, was buried there. Something about that vague memory always gave him a headache.

Jack froze. Unbidden images flashed in his brain. *Lightning... running...fear, oh God, he was afraid...*

Maggie snapped fingers before his face. "Hello? Earth to Jack."

Jack blinked and turned toward her. "Look, the people on Paradisio have no love for the American military. About sixty years ago you blew their original islands all to hell testing the first A-bombs. You ruined their fishing grounds, and set them off on desert islands that couldn't support the population. You tried to enslave them with American culture, Coca Cola and Spam. Fathers saw their sons turn into lazy, fat, alcoholics waiting for the next supply ship of American junk food and beer. They had a bitter dispute about it and split into factions. The ones that didn't want to be eating at the American trough loaded up their canoes and left. They found Paradisio and have been clinging to their native ways ever since. If they find out I've helped the Americans mount a military operation on Paradisio, I'll be a *sbano*, a no-good traitor. Sorry, sweetheart, you'll have to find yourself another way in." He yanked the tie out of his collar and flung it on the coffee table.

Maggie tossed her head in a manner that sent a shimmer through her red curls. "You seem to think you have a choice in the matter. We're going to Paradisio. You're going to hire me on as one of your crew members, and you can shoot an episode of your Jungle George TV show while we track down Hannah Smith."

Jack walked around the bar, threw some ice in a glass and poured himself a drink. "You're beginning to annoy me, darlin', even with your lovely long legs and sunset-colored hair. I'm not a member of the Army, Navy or Marines and you can't order me around. I haven't broken any laws and the IRS already bleeds me dry, so rack off. You haven't got anything hanging over my head."

She leaned across the bar. "No? How about we pull the grant money on your father's little research project in Papua, New Guinea? The one he's been working toward his whole life. I think I can get him permanently kicked off the island if I pull a few strings."

Jack froze, his voice a low rumble. "You bitch."

Her lips turned up in a cat-smile. "Hannah Smith's father is Senator Smith, Chairman of the Ways and Means Committee that appropriated the funds to Operation New Leaf. I think one phone call telling about your unpatriotic attitude will put an end to Daddy's pet project."

He felt like a mouse caught in the grip of a boa constrictor. "You damned arrogant Americans, pushing everybody about like you own the planet."

Maggie bristled at the familiar accusation, placed both hands on the counter. "Listen, Jack, we 'damned arrogant Americans' are spread all over the world putting our lives on the line to keep the peace, which allows pretty-boy stars like you to have your Hollywood parties and trot around the globe making stupid television shows."

A vein throbbed along Jack's dark temple. "My show serves a significant purpose promoting important ecological issues."

"Let me tell you something, buddy, if the terrorist networks flourish, there won't be much ecology to worry about. Those guys will drop poison gas on their own grandmothers and not care if oil spills all over a pristine wilderness as long as they earn their way into some fanatical version of heaven. The operatives on Paradisio are pouring millions of dollars into the hands of terrorists from Baghdad to Malaysia, and I intend to see them stopped. So let's just cut the crap. Call your crew. Tell them there's been a change in plans and tomorrow we're off to Paradisio or your dear old Dad is out on his ear in Papua, New Guinea."

Jack slugged back a gulp of whiskey, paced the room and finally punched a hole in the wall with his fist. *Damn, bloody, bitchy seppo.*

Maggie strolled to the adjoining door to her room. "I'll see you first thing in the morning, Jack. You'd better put some ice on that hand. It's going to hurt like hell."

Pain and irritation sprang open the psychic door of Jack's mind he usually kept shut. But now, in this moment, he welcomed the beam of insight that would allow him to glimpse Maggie's weakness. In an instant, he knew where to throw a dart. "I was hoping to spend the night with a soft woman and end up with a hard-ass soldier. Is it worth it? To give up every shred of femininity to become a fighting force for Uncle Sam?"

Maggie paled. Echoes of her mother's accusations reverberated with Jack's parting shot. *Suck it up, Savannah.* She kept her voice steady. "Get some sleep, Jack. I'll be back at 0700."

***

On a faraway island a sleek beast reveled in his growing global influence. His ability to manipulate with lies and temptation increased. He laughed at the fall of priests over sexual misconduct. Each disillusioned parishioner weakened the Other and made the creature stronger. Passion for money spread like a virus around the world, bringing hopelessness and confusion. He sucked energy from people with no spiritual fortitude. He remained physically trapped on the island, but his spiritual territory spread. And soon he would be completely free.

Chapter Five

Hannah Smith lay on a cot in a small tent listening to the outside voices, harsh male exchanges of shouts and orders. Sweat dripped between her breasts, and she thought longingly of her family backyard pool in Virginia, another life away.

What's a nice girl like you doing in a place like this?

Hannah sat up. "Hey, Felipe! I'm burning up in here. Agua, por favor!"

For some reason, they'd had her penned in her tent all day. She didn't know what was worse—moving through the nearly impenetrable jungle, slogging in stagnant water—or being cooped up in an airless enclosure.

And she couldn't strip down like for a day at Virginia Beach, or even dress in short sleeves as she'd done in the Acaba village. Being surrounded by Muslim terrorists meant adjusting to a different culture, a whole new world view.

The day she'd been kidnapped had started out as so many others of the past two years. Morning rituals, quiet time, preparing a simple breakfast before her faithful followers showed up to work on the Acaban Bible. It had been through a series of "coincidences" and "miracles" that an American girl had been allowed to enter the hostile territory and live among the Acabans. Her call to Paradisio had been so overwhelming, so definite, she'd closed down any other possible avenues of life.

At first the Acabans didn't believe she was actually a human being. They'd never seen blond hair and blue eyes. Some weren't sure she could see with such colored eyes.

She'd learned so much in three years, endured so many physical, emotional and spiritual challenges. From her rudimentary understanding of Acaban, she had developed an alphabet. From there her ultimate goal, the work of perhaps a lifetime would be to give the Acabans a Bible in their own language.

Beyond that, the power of love was changing the Acaban culture. When the headman Ysway embraced the Christian message, a new day dawned for the Acaban people. Cannibalism of other tribes, for one thing, became outlawed. Twelve-year-old girls no longer endured repeated rapes as acceptable social behavior.

She'd begun to think the worst was behind her. Then, the Sons of Allah marched into the village. Acaban knives and darts were no match for the assault rifles of the terrorists. Two young native men were killed before Ysway and Moktar of the terrorist band came to an understanding.

Hannah had watched the action with her students in her makeshift school. Suddenly she knew—the terrorists had come for her. Catching phrases of the Spanish that had become a second language for most of these islands, her stomach trembled. Ysway nodded his head and began a ponderous walk toward her. Anxiety gripped her chest as she realized she'd be leaving with the men holding the guns.

She turned and fled to the back room that served as her living quarters, trying to think straight, trying to lift a coherent prayer, find a spiritual connection. But she was afraid. Her hands shook as she quickly stuffed a duffel bag. Her mind seemed to disconnect, short circuited by fear. She stood frozen in the center of the tiny room, and the only prayer she could muster was *Help!*

Then it came. The Voice, the Presence. Whatever you want to call it. The internal guidance whispered from another dimension. *Put on a long skirt, long sleeve blouse, cover your head with a scarf.*

She followed the silent instructions, understanding from earlier training how important modesty was in the Muslim world. Her well-being could very well depend on keeping her arms and legs covered.

Ysway stood tall and thin in the doorway. "Bright Bird, you must go with the dead-eyed men," he said in the Acaban tongue she could finally understand.

Would she ever hear this language that had become so precious to her again? Ever be called by her native name, Bright Bird, again? Hannah had smiled when her students christened her with the name. With her yellow hair and busy ways she reminded the villagers of that noisy bird of the forest.

She swallowed down her tears, nodded, and slung the green duffel bag over her shoulder. When she stepped off the steps onto the dirt lane, armed men surrounded and prodded her on the beginning of a new journey.

The irrepressible Hannah forced down her fear. *Okay, Lord, this is another fine mess you've gotten me into.*

Now, three months later, she'd been playing some kind of jungle shell game, hiding with the Sons of Allah in one camp after the other. The inept IMA military force of the mainland government chased them, fired on them. But once night fell, all skirmishes came to an end. The IMA definitely lacked conviction about bringing down the Sons of Allah. To Hannah, it seemed almost like war games. Flying bullets sent her heart and feet racing but she'd noticed everyone appeared to be very poor shots—like the bad guys in action movies. Guns blazed, pounding her eardrums, but very few got injured on either side. Still, her frayed nerves took their toll. Crying became a daily occurrence, an outlet for fear and exhaustion.

Camped high in the mountains near the ocean, she hadn't seen IMA in several days and everyone seemed more relaxed. She didn't know whether to be relieved about the lack of crossfire or worried that she'd never be rescued. Moktar repeatedly told her ransom negotiations were going well, and she'd be going home soon. *Home.* Where was that? She'd felt so called to the Acabans. Her work was unfinished, barely begun really.

She couldn't understand the change in God's plan.

At first she tried to reach out to her captors with her Christian beliefs, but soon saw the folly in that. Ignorant boys taken from poverty-stricken island cities found camaraderie in the Sons of Allah. They followed the rituals of cleansing and prayers, spoke of being on jihad. Yet it appeared none of them had ever read the Koran. Many couldn't read at all. Their beliefs seemed to be more the product of brain washing than spiritual insight.

They had no respect for the words of a woman. Only her high potential for ransom money kept her from being claimed by one of the men. Moktar saw to that. The bowlegged, Asian leader viewed her as a valuable commodity and, thereby, made sure she remained fed, watered, and reasonably sheltered. Like a prize cow.

Three other women started out as kidnapping victims and ended up as reluctant wives. They kept their distance from Hannah, but once in a while brought her special food, if something became available. Any variation from boiled rice was cause for celebration. After a supply boat landed, she knew God answered prayers when she received a packet of M & M's.

Which reminded her, she was hungry and thirsty. "Felipe! I'm not kidding. Agua, por favor! And how about some lunch?"

Her teenage guard opened the tent flap and entered with a canteen of water and a banana leaf holding rice. Tattered clothes he had long ago outgrown covered his skinny limbs. Filthy rags wrapped his head.

He handed her the food and water. "Aquí."

Her Spanish had improved in the three months of her captivity. And she didn't even think twice anymore about eating rice with her fingers. "So what's up? Why have I been cooped up all day? What's all the commotion about?"

Felipe appeared nervous. "Visitors."

Before she had a chance to ask more questions, Moktar strolled into the tent. The short guerrilla leader had an amazingly friendly manner for a cold-blooded murderer. He liked his job. Being a mercenary and kidnapping people suited him. He enjoyed his role as head honcho. It was rumored he occasionally got off the island and took glamorous gambling vacations.

"Ah, Miss Smith, I hope you have been enjoying a day of rest. Would you please come with me? A very important visitor would like to meet you."

Hannah wiped her fingers, grabbed a scarf and covered her head. She walked between Felipe and Moktar into the humid jungle camp. A small, fetid breeze brought mild relief to her over-heated body. Beams of dappled sunlight penetrated the dense leafy canopy above. She noted with surprise the amount of clearing that had been carved out of the undergrowth. The camp bustled with activity. A wild boar, smoked in a pit, filled the air with the smell of gamey, roasting flesh. Tarps pitched at odd angles served as tents for Moktar's motley soldiers.

Near a makeshift seating area of fallen logs mingled a contingency of visitors, obviously Arab from their robed appearance, only slightly the worse for wear from having traveled through the jungle. A young man pointed at Hannah and the turbaned middle-aged leader turned and faced her. He possessed the penetrating eyes of the true believers. His gaze roamed over her, registering disdain and disgust.

"Miss Hannah Smith," he said in accented English. "I am Ahmed Saeed. You have heard of me perhaps?"

Hannah shook her head no. "I'm sorry. I have been working with the Acabans for three years and have little contact with the outside world."

"Ah, yes, spreading your American religion." He pointed long fingers toward a bumpy fallen tree truck. "Sit down, and I will tell you why I hate America."

Chapter Six

Maggie's phone rang at dawn. She rolled over in the luxurious hotel bed, opened one eye to spy the time and picked up the receiver. "Maggie Savannah."

"Rise and shine, Mag-Pie. Have you made contact with your target?"

Maggie ran her fingers through her tousled hair and sat up. "And a good morning to you, Colonel Matthews. Yeah, I bagged him last night. Piece of cake."

"That's my girl. So, what do you think of America's Hottest Hero now that you've met him face to face?" Chris' honey voice led her to a fantasy of sipping mint juleps beneath the mimosa trees.

"He's a lightweight. I'll bet he has a stunt double doing all that daredevil stuff, and he merely hams it up in front of the camera." She didn't mention the killer blue eyes, strong stubborn chin, or muscle-bound chest. "He's probably still getting his beauty sleep. I'll have to rouse him out of the rack. These Hollywood types have an army of handlers who bring them breakfast in bed, and read the comics out loud."

"He's not one of us, but you'll make the arrangement work. I have confidence in you."

"Thanks, Colonel. I won't let you down." *It won't be another Yemen.*

"When this assignment is all over, I'll treat you to a twelve course meal on a floating restaurant I know in Manila. How does that sound?"

There he goes again, offering friendship and the chance to explore something more. Maybe I'll wear a dress and take another stab at the girlie thing. "Sounds swell."

"Good, be sure and check out the equipment Derby sent along. I'll be in touch, Mag-Pie." He clicked off.

Maggie sank into the voluminous pillows, and imagined herself at a romantic dinner in Manila with Chris Matthews. Could she go from soldier to siren? Where did a girl learn to be a *femme-fatale*? In the meantime, she needed to get the Australian heartthrob off his bloomin' arse.

After a shower, Maggie blew dry her hair and donned khaki slacks and a black blouse. She headed toward Jack's room to make coffee at his wet bar. She hoped the promise of caffeine would stir him from his slumbers. She opened the adjoining door, expecting a quiet atmosphere. Instead, Jack paced the room talking on his cell phone.

"Bill, you're my agent and publicist. You're supposed to know everybody and be able to get anything done. Yeah…I know it's the bloody U.S. Marines. That's what I've been telling you. It's blackmail, it is…" Jack sighed. "All right, all right, I know when I'm licked. If this red-haired sheila gets eaten by a boa constrictor or mauled by a jaguar, it won't be my fault. Probably doesn't have the first notion how to survive on walk-about."

Maggie loudly cleared her throat and crossed to the bar where coffee sat, hot and steamy. She caught Jack's eye and realized he'd known exactly when she'd entered the room. She had a childish urge to stick her tongue out at him, but went for a lofty look instead. She'd show him survival techniques the Aborigines had never dreamed of.

She poured herself a cup of coffee as Jack said goodbye to his agent. He walked to Lorelei's cage and talked over his shoulder to Maggie. "Pour me one, also. Two sugars and extra cream."

"Do I look like I'm wearing a maid's uniform to you? Make your own coffee." She sat down on a high bar stool.

Jack drew Lorelei out of her cage. The bird immediately took her comfortable spot on his shoulder and cooed.

He walked the length of the room to Maggie's side and entered her personal space, towering over her as she sat on the stool. "See here, Major Savannah, if I've got to go along with this little charade then we're going to set some ground rules. If you're going to be a member of the Jaguar Jack crew, you're going to have to fit in and obey orders. You're going to come on board as my new assistant. Nobody's going to know you're a damn Marine and get my arse in a sling on Paradisio. And if you think that filming in the rain forest is a day trip to Disneyland, you've got another think coming. It's dangerous, sweetheart, *real* dangerous, and I can't have a disobedient prima donna General's daughter putting my people at risk."

"I am not a prima donna General's daughter!" Maggie's eyes flashed green fire.

"Oh no? That's not how I heard it. I've been up all night trying to get my neck out of this noose and I've learned quite a bit about you, *Magnolia* Savannah. I don't want my camera man shot in the crossfire like your mate, Al-Jabbar, in your last mission."

Maggie slammed her coffee cup on the counter. "That was not my fault. If Al hadn't been dealing with a hysterical civilian, he'd be alive today." She knew it was true, but still felt a pang of guilt that somewhere she'd missed an opportunity to save him. And the impotent fury of watching Saeed slip away burned in her gut. "How did you get that information? It's classified."

Jack shrugged. "I have my sources. You just better 'get with the program' as you Yanks put it. If you're going to be my assistant, you'd better act like my assistant." Holding his ground over her, he leaned closer. "That means doing what I say. And, when I say I want me coffee with two sugars with extra cream, you'd better fix the bloody coffee. Am I making myself clear, sweetheart?"

Maggie knew the importance of a chain of command, knew the importance of maintaining a cover. Still, kowtowing to this pseudo-hero turned her rebellious. She grabbed the coffee pot, slopped the dark liquid in a cup, tossed in two teaspoons of sugar and a generous dollop of cream. The spoon clanged against the sides of the mug as she stared at Jack with insubordination.

She thrust the mug toward him. "Here, don't burn your tongue, Mister Jaguar, sir."

Jack accepted the hot cup and laid it aside on the counter, never taking his gaze from Maggie's face. The pupils of his eyes flared, making them a midnight blue. He roved across her features, deeply delving. His hand reached up and slowly explored the contours of her cheeks and down her chin with his fingers. Hypnotic eyes and touch mesmerized her, much as she'd seen him fascinate a female puma on his TV show.

Whoa, Maggie, watch your defenses, don't fall under his charismatic spell.

In a mercurial switch, his voice murmured with a melodious rhythm. "Interesting. Tough talk on the outside, but softer layers below the surface."

Maggie's breath hitched. His mysterious manner threw her off-balance. Was this some kind of new line? "Are you hitting on me, Jack?"

His lips turned up slightly. "Just exploring. It's something I do. When I decide to 'hit on you,' as you put it, you'll know it."

She swallowed and swiveled away from him. Feeling warm and unsettled, she dug for bravado. "Well, don't bother. I don't like this situation any more than you do. A pseudo-Hollywood hero isn't the partner I'd choose to go after terrorists. But I'm stuck with you."

His eyes darkened. "We're stuck with each other. Let's hope you prove a better partner for me than you were for that poor bloke, Al-Jabbar."

They glared at each other until the door popped open. Maggie recognized Aunt Edith Campbell from the TV show. Wearing a brightly colored bird motif blouse tucked into turquoise stretch pants, Edith possessed a squat middle-aged body accented by a bubble butt. Her choice of clown-like clothes crowned by a straw hat over wiry gray hair had made her a popular sidekick on Jack's TV show. Even without her purported psychic abilities, she made great television. Top off the eccentric character with an engaging English accent and the ability to peer into the minds of lions and tigers and bears, and oh my, did the ratings climb.

Edith held the door open and spoke to someone down the hall. "Quit dawdling, luvie, Mummy's come to visit Uncle Jack."

A primate screech echoed from the hallway. Maggie blinked when a spider monkey charged into the room, leaped over the back of the furniture, and catapulted to a spot near her elbow on the bar.

Maggie hurriedly pushed away from the bar, knocked over her stool and bumped into the back of the couch.

Jack shook his head. "A bit clumsy aren't you? First knocking over all that furniture last night, and now bouncing things around in here."

"Cripes, I'm not used to cockatoos and monkeys attacking me."

"Well, get used to it, darlin'. This is just the beginning."

Edith held the monkey like an errant toddler. "Sorry if Mr. Jiggs startled you. He's just ready for his breakfast."

Maggie watched in fascination as the monkey and the bird ate from the fruit plate. Dressed in a cute checked vest and matching hat, Mr. Jiggs made short work of a juicy plum, working his sharp teeth around the purple orb, manipulating it with deft little fingers. When he finished, he picked a grape and held it out for Lorelei. They appeared to be companionable creatures. Maggie shook her head, gingerly reached behind the monkey and took her coffee to a distant chair.

Edith crossed around to the seating area, joining Maggie. "I'm Edith Campbell. Thought I'd introduce myself as Jack seems to have forgotten his manners."

Jack had been deep in thought. "Oh, sorry. This is my new assistant, Maggie Savannah."

Edith's eyes widened. "New assistant? Are you firing me, Jack?"

Jack crossed to Edith and embraced her in a warm hug. "No, of course not, Auntie. It's just Miss Savannah here came so highly recommended. *I couldn't have refused her even if I'd wanted to.*"

The last phrase delivered with such tension turned on Edith's psychic antenna. Something was going on here.

Her attention swiveled to the cool redhead sipping coffee, perched on an arm of a chair. "So, Maggie, you've got a lot of experience with animals? Are you a zoologist, perhaps?"

Maggie nearly choked. "No, my background has more to do with survival in the rough."

Jack smiled until a dimple graced his cheek. "I thought it might spice things up a bit to have a sheila taking on some danger once in a while. You're not scared of jumping on a crocodile's back, are you, Maggie?"

"Piece of cake." She hoped.

Jack appeared nonchalant as he crossed back to the bar. "I've decided on another change of plans, Auntie. We're scrapping the Amazon and going back to Paradisio. This is mating season for the jalunga lizards. We should be able to get some great footage of those prehistoric creatures."

"Not Paradisio again, Jack," Edith groaned. "You promised we wouldn't have to go back for a long time."

"Guess I lied, Auntie." He searched a cabinet for a clean mug and prepared tea for Edith.

Edith sighed and assessed the situation. She'd protected him from the truth of Paradisio often enough. She guessed she could do it again. She glanced between Jack and Maggie, felt undercurrents and tried to hone in on them. Too bad people were so much more complicated than animals. She could pick up any creature's fears and desires except humans. People simply didn't know what they wanted most of the time.

Whoever this Maggie Savannah was, Edith sensed a strong will covering up a layer of vulnerability. Oh, yes, and some confusion.

Edith settled down on the couch. "Don't worry, my dear. I'll be able to read any animal's mind that you may encounter and I'll warn you if it means any harm. Why, I remember an orangutan that appeared quite friendly, but really had murder in his heart. He'd been terribly mistreated by some poachers, and had barely gotten away with his life. He'd gone a bit bonkers, don't you know, and I told Jack, 'Don't trust that orangutan. He's up to no good.' And sure enough, he nearly ripped Jack's arm off."

"Auntie's saved my cookies more than once. Wouldn't go on a shoot without her." He carried a steaming cup of Earl Grey to Edith. "And she's almost as popular as Jaguar Jack. We sold 100,000 Auntie Edith dolls last week."

Maggie stared at the pair with undisguised skepticism. "That psychic stuff seems like so much hooey to me. At least you don't run a 1-900 number, offering to talk to people's dead pets at five dollars a minute."

Edith remained undaunted by doubters. "I can see you're out of touch with your spiritual side. We'll have to work on that. By the way, what's the name of the German shepherd that's standing guard at your feet? He's very protective of you. He passed over some time ago, but I don't think he leaves your side very often."

The blood drained from Maggie's face. "Rex... I had a German shepherd named Rex."

"Ah, yes, Rex, that's it. Rex says you get into a lot of trouble. Keeps him hopping, you do. Says he has to constantly warn you about danger." Edith's attention was diverted to Mr. Jiggs. "Oh, dear, get down from that chandelier, you naughty boy. Uncle Jack doesn't want to pay any repair bills." Edith trotted after the monkey.

Maggie dropped from the chair arm to the cushion. Memories flashed in her mind when she'd suddenly known something was coming her way. Occasionally, she'd even imagined she'd heard a bark of warning in her mind from her dear old companion, Rex.

Jack crouched in front of Maggie and looked her square in the eye. "What's the matter, luv, cat got your tongue?"

"This isn't just a zoo, it's a nut house."

Jack lifted one dark eyebrow. "That's about right. And now you're one of the inmates. Welcome to *The Adventures of Jaguar Jack*."

***

A massive feline creature released the spirit of revenge from his jungle prison. An angry young man in India received it. In a crowded Indian marketplace, an attractive young woman examined silks at a merchant's stall. Behind her, the man whispered her name. He'd teach her a lesson for rebuffing his advances. His face would be the last thing she'd ever see. The acid he flung in her eyes burned, maimed, and melted her delicate features.

And fear and darkness continued to creep across the land.

Chapter Seven

The crew assembled at LAX and boarded the Lu-Lu Bird at 1500 hours. Jack loved taking off at sunset and flying into the west, chasing the sinking sun. His corporate jet was a regular home away from home, specially outfitted for his traveling needs, decorated in jungle decor. Comfortable private beds for Aunt Edith and himself occupied the back private quarters. Over-sized chairs flattened out into individual cots for the film crew. Even Mr. Jiggs and Lorelei had their own space.

Jack served as co-pilot for take off. A certified pilot himself, he enjoyed experiencing the rush of land disappearing under the plane from the cockpit vantage point. Life brimmed with one thrill after another, if you knew how to keep a look out. The plane surged over the LA basin through the layers of brackish sky to the pure blue above the smog line.

Jack craved a new adventure in the wild. Freedom. Away from the teeming crowds of the city. All those warring thoughts and energy fields swirling in the air. Jack had to maintain a protective mental shield to prevent being bombarded with the thought patterns of strangers. Like Auntie, like nephew.

But Jack hated his psychic gift; generally tried to ignore and close it off. Six months in the psych ward had given him some survival skills. Thank God he had a therapist who understood what had happened to him. Otherwise, he might still be living in a padded cell.

He shook off the past and focused on the present. The crew had been away from the field, editing for a couple of months. Jack was itching to return to the spongy jungle floor, maybe tangle with a python or two. He longed to relax his mind and explore the secrets of the rain forest. The Amazon would have been pure joy. But he wasn't winging toward South America.

Destination: Paradisio. His island. The mists of his childhood beckoned to him. No matter how many continents he explored, fate seemed to bring him back to Paradisio. Each time they'd filmed a segment there, he'd felt a combination of challenge and terror. Images flashed in his mind, memories he wanted kept buried. Certain parts of the island terrified him.

Fearless Jaguar Jack Campbell. Ha!

And now he was returning against his will, on a fool's errand, taking on crazy terrorists. Plus being bossed around by the bloody Ms. Terminator. Why couldn't the Americans fetch their own hapless missionary? It was a damned inconvenience. The Lady Marine's lush looks distracted him. Long legs, high breasts, thick hair. She'd be a force of nature in bed, a typhoon of sexuality, demanding he offer more than just a good time. He preferred soft, adoring women. Women who bought into his hero image. He didn't like the smart-ass expression on Maggie's face. Her eyes didn't miss a trick. He had the feeling Maggie Savannah thought of him as a joke, a fraud.

She saw through him.

After the seatbelt lights went off, Jack opened the door leading into the galley. Laughter from the main cabin's inhabitants pealed his way. Maggie's throaty, sexy laugh mingled with the male chuckles. He didn't know what the joke had been, but he was pretty sure he'd been the butt of it.

"So, tell the truth, fellas," he heard Maggie say, "who's the real brains behind this dog and pony show?"

Jack froze in the galley, wanting to hear the direction of this interrogation.

Edith's spry voice answered the question. "If it weren't for Jack, none of us would have a job. Jack is center of our universe and we all spin off his energy."

"You're biased. He's your nephew," Maggie scoffed. "How about you, Mulligan? Do you think the earth revolves around Jack Campbell? Isn't he all action and just one banana short of a bunch? Don't you wonder about someone who likes to wrestle pythons and grizzly bears?"

Jack ground his teeth. What the hell did she know about him? And where did she get off undermining him to the crew? He'd see about shutting up her smart mouth.

Closing his eyes, he allowed his mental door to crack open. Connection with his red-haired quarry came quickly. He probed.

He chuckled softly and murmured, "Sometimes it's just too easy."

Jack flung back the curtain to the cabin and made his entrance, all smiles. "Ah, everybody comfortable? Auntie have you introduced Maggie around?"

Everyone nodded and affirmed. Seats were arranged in a square, a regular flying living room. The six crew members sat surrounded by magazines, books and drinks. Edith's nimble fingers knitted another sweater for Mr. Jiggs, who lay curled asleep in her lap. His darling Lorelei dozed, perched on Auntie's shoulder.

Maggie crossed her arms with subtle defiant body language. "They all know where their bread is buttered. I couldn't get them to utter one disparaging word against you."

"'Course not. I'm a very loveable bloke."

Jack reached up into the overhead and pulled down a small video camera, handing it to Mulligan. "Here, mate. No time like the present to start some footage for the next show. Let's introduce my new assistant to the television audience." He slid into the empty seat beside Maggie and wrapped his arm around her. He flashed the famous Jaguar Jack dimples.

Mulligan held up the camera. "We're rolling Jack."

Jack turned on the television persona, sending energy waves pulsing through his hands and eyes. "We're here at thirty-thousand feet aboard the Lu-Lu Bird heading off for another great adventure on Paradisio Island. And I'm happy to introduce me new assistant, a fearless sheila who'll give those crocs a thrill when she jumps on top of them, I can tell you. Meet Magnolia Savannah. Say hello to thirty million friends, Maggie."

Maggie gulped and said, "Hello."

Jack jostled her in his grip. "Say, I've got a great idea. I think you need to meet Harry."

"Who's Harry?"

"Why he's Mulligan's little pet. I have Lorelei, Auntie has Mr. Jiggs and Pete Mulligan won't go anywhere without his Harry. Isn't that right, Pete?"

Mulligan chuckled. "You got it, Jack. He's under my seat."

Jack reached down and lifted a rectangular plastic box with a blue lid and placed it in her lap. "Harry is a world traveler, he is. And he just loves making new friends."

Maggie leaned over curiously. "What is it? A frog? A hamster?"

Jack popped opened the lid to reveal Harry in all his fuzzy tarantula glory. Maggie yelped and shot back into her seat as far as she could go. "Sonofabitch, sonofabitch, sonofabitch," she muttered.

"No swearing, darlin'. We'll have to edit that out." Jack reached in and pulled Harry from his comfortable leaf and twig nest.

"Harry is a genuine tarantula. He and his cousins can be found all over the world." Jack placed Harry on the palm of his hand directly under Maggie's nose. "Isn't he a beauty?" Maggie began breathing in short pants, looking cross-eyed at the hairy, leggy creature. "What's the matter, darlin', don't you like spiders?"

Maggie squinted her eyes and spoke through gritted teeth. "I love 'em. They taste just like chicken."

Jack grinned. Damn, the girl had balls. He grabbed her hand and engaged in a minor tug-of-war until he won and dropped Harry in her palm. The spider crawled a tickling journey up her forearm.

He said, "Fear of spiders is a very common phobia. Nothing to be ashamed of. Lots of people share your fears. And the best way to overcome fear is to face it head on."

Maggie called on every lesson in mental toughness to keep from screaming at the top of her lungs and flinging Harry at the ceiling. Unfortunately, her restraint didn't keep the famous Maggie-mouth from spouting off. "Did they teach you that in the loony bin?"

A collective gasp rippled through the crew. Aunt Edith put down her knitting. Mulligan stopped the camera.

Maggie dumped Harry back into the box and slammed the lid.

Jack dropped his jovial facade. Why was he surprised she knew about his stint in the psych ward? Of course she knew. Big Brother knows everything.

Jack and Maggie faced each other, nose to nose, ready to do battle.

Realizing all eyes and ears of the crew riveted rapt in attention on the exchange with his new "assistant," he grabbed her hand and pulled her up.

"Come with me, Magnolia. I want to have a word with you in private." He yanked her hard toward his private cabin.

"Don't call me Magnolia," she hissed. "Only my mother can call me that!"

He took long strides as she tripped behind him. They both ducked as they passed through the hatch into the next compartment. He pulled her into the leopard decor room and slammed the door shut.

"You're a bloody brat, Major Savannah. I don't appreciate you undermining me before me crew."

"And I don't appreciate your attempt to humiliate me. If you have it in that Aussie head of yours that you can scare me off with spiders and snakes, you've got another thing coming."

"I don't like bossy, brash women."

"Tough." Maggie looked around her surroundings. A double bed in a jungle love nest. A booze cabinet displayed a wide array of alcoholic aphrodisiacs; soft lights cast a romantic glow. "Say, what is this, the Tarzan version of the Mile High Club?"

Jack strode over to the bar, opened the Plexiglas case and poured himself a scotch. "Don't worry, sweetheart, I like compliant women with genteel manners. That tongue of yours is a lethal weapon."

Ouch. Maggie turned away not wanting to give this yahoo a glimpse of the hit he'd just made. Maggie the Mouth strikes again. Oh, hell, maybe she did have the charm of a Mack truck. "So, what does a girl have to do to get a drink around here?"

Jack's blue eyes gave her a measuring look. "Just ask. What'll you have?"

***

Two stout shots of bourbon took off some of Maggie's edge. In fact, she stretched out on the fake-fur bedspread as Jack sat in a comfortable easy chair. They talked some shop; discussed a plan for covering the island to track down Hannah Smith. Maggie had to admit a grudging respect for Jack's clear grasp of the difficulties ahead, though his eyes held a brooding darkness when he spoke of Paradisio. Maybe he wasn't such an airhead after all. As the alcohol at thirty-thousand feet hit her brain, she dropped her military bearing.

The fuzzy cover felt fabulous under her fingers. She kicked off her shoes and dug her toes into the downy fabric. She propped up on one elbow, her feathery hair falling over her shoulder. She gazed across the room to find Jack staring at her in a predatory manner. An unexpected spark of heat spiked down low. Man, she better lay off the sauce. "So, Jack, why do you wrestle pythons and grizzly bears?"

He dropped the deep, probing stare and shrugged. "Oh, I guess everybody's good at something. I love animals, but after growing up in jungles, I couldn't see myself as a zoo keeper. I do better away from people. Not everybody fits into civilization."

"Is that why you spent six months in a psych ward?"

Jack's mouth thinned. "That isn't any of your business, Major Savannah. It's over. Nowadays I travel the world, film my television show and work for causes I think are important. This whole Jaguar Jack phenomenon suits me just fine."

"You get to play King of the Jungle, and then come to civilization and pick up any chick you want." Maggie lifted one leg as she lay prone on the bed and wiggled her toes.

"Something like that." He sipped his scotch. "You make me sound damned shallow. I guess my life doesn't compare with fighting battles from the halls of Montezuma to the shores of Tripoli." He leaned toward her, eyebrows narrowing. "But tell me something. Isn't it awfully futile? There's always another war, always another threat to Western Civilization. How much of the world can you save, Maggie? Don't you get flippin' lonely?"

Maggie dropped her leg and lay flat on her back, taking in his meaning. God, had he gotten coaching lessons from her mother? Or was she just beginning to notice that she didn't have a life? She only had one assignment after another. A hollow existence.

She shook her head. The bourbon was making her brain go soft. Something about this assignment, this Outback TV star had shot her concentration all to hell.

She sat up and swung her long legs to the floor. "So when do we get to Paradisio? I need to check in with Derby."

"We're not on our way to Paradisio."

"What?"

"No, next stop is Honolulu. You can check in with your Derby there. Then I have a special treat for you. The Lu-Lu Bird will continue on to Paradisio. You and I are picking up my new flying machine. A lovely helicopter that I'll fly the rest of the way to the island. We'll really feel the wind beneath our wings in that baby."

Maggie lifted an auburn eyebrow. "I hope Hannah is still in one piece by the time we finish with your pleasure cruise."

"Don't worry. I've done business with Moktar; he's not such bad sort unless he decides to chop your head off."

"Swell."

"I'm sure he's taking very good care of his valuable hostage."

Maggie frowned. "You don't give a damn about Hannah Smith, do you?"

Jack shrugged. "I'm sure she's a fine young lady, but right now I consider her to be a major inconvenience. And tell the truth Miss Magnolia, is your heart bleeding for this missionary or is she merely another assignment for you? Perhaps a chance for you to make up for your foul ups in Yemen?"

Maggie jutted her chin defensively. "All the hostages got out safely in Yemen."

"Yeah, but your partner bit the dust. That doesn't bode well for *me*, now does it?"

Chapter Eight

Hannah felt bleary-eyed, beaten down and disconnected. Ahmed Saeed had been verbally pounding her with a diatribe of anti-American propaganda for nearly twenty-four hours. Held captive on a fallen tree that served as a bumpy bench, Hannah caught winks of sleep during the five brief Muslim calls to prayer. Other than those moments of respite, she'd endured unrelenting lectures and interrogation by Saeed or his underlings.

"How long have you been an American spy?...How do you send back your intelligence to your superiors?"

"I'm not a spy. I'm a missionary. I work for the Bethel Bible Translation Foundation. I'm working on an Acaban Bible."

"Your father is an American Senator. Admit that you work for the CIA. Tell us who your CIA contact is."

"I don't know anyone with the CIA."

"Ah, so you know about the CIA!"

"Everyone knows about the CIA. They're in every spy movie made in the last fifty years."

"What is the real reason why you have come to Paradisio?"

"I told you; I'm working on an Acaban Bible."

"Why waste your time with a handful of natives? That makes no sense. Do you think I am stupid? Admit you are a spy."

Round and round they went. The monotony only broken up by a harangue of complaints against the West—for which Hannah was held accountable. She could almost repeat their accusations verbatim: the plight of the Palestinians... the death of thousands of innocent Iraqis... the decadence of Western television...American women being nothing more than immodest whores...a barrage of Israeli crimes...America as the great Satan.

On and on it went, hour after hour. As she got hungry, as she got thirsty, as she had to go to the bathroom. She tried thinking of other things—her mother's face, her pet cat, the man she'd left behind for the missionary field. She clung to Scriptures, Psalms, the words of the Savior.

I am with you always, Jesus had promised, but she felt very much alone.

When they showed her the pictures, she broke down.

"You see, Hannah Smith, this is what your American government has done to innocent Arab women and children by supporting the Jews. Their blood is on your hands. The crusaders have not begun to pay for the injustices done to my people."

Hannah's eyes roamed over the faces staring at her from the photographs. Grotesque death masks, grieving mothers, severed limbs, burned out homes. She tried to look away but her head was forced down. Her tears rained on the glossy paper.

"I'm sorry...I'm so sorry," she said, gulping between shaky breaths. "I'm sorry for the children, for your lost sons, your lost homeland. But I don't know how to help you. America has made some mistakes. What do you want me to say?"

"Apologize for America. Tell me you are ashamed of being an American, ashamed of being a woman from the West. Tell me that you hate America."

Hannah wiped her cheeks with her hands and took a steady look into the seething face of the accuser hovering over her. How could someone be alive and have such dead eyes? He wanted hatred. He wanted fear. He wanted her to be like him, filled with an all-consuming vengeance, a whirlwind of malice devoted to the Jihad.

But Hannah Smith had long ago been filled with a quieter power, a deeper strength. Even in her extreme physical weakness, a spiritual hand held her like a raft bobbing in a turbulent sea. An image came to her of clinging to that lifesaver in the midst of the political typhoon that had swept her into an unfriendly ocean.

Hannah blinked her eyes and spoke softly. "I can't hate America. I can't hate you. My heart weeps for your people and mine. Looking in your troubled eyes, my heart weeps for you."

Ahmed stood straight and gazed down at her with an unreadable expression. "Stop the camera. Take her to her tent. Give her something to eat. Be sure to erase her last response and then send the tape for editing to our good friends at Al Jazeera."

***

The creature waited, resting on the volcanic mountain, tail swishing. Thinking, conniving. The Saint would soon be completely in his power. When he'd first realized the little missionary was indeed the Saint, he'd been angry. He'd come so far, gained strength, increased his influence over vast portions of the earth. Millions now resided in his spiritual domain.

The Saint could strip him of all he'd achieved. But only if she joined forces with the Warrior.

He laughed. The Warrior still lived in ignorance of his spiritual potential.

The plan was clear. Turn the Saint to his side before she could join the Warrior.

Chapter Nine

Maggie raced to keep up with Jack down the crowded Honolulu terminal. Cripes, she usually left everyone else in the dust. But Jack, with his boundless energy and legs even longer than hers, presented a challenge. She hitched the leather strap holding Derby's precious equipment on her shoulder. The Lu-Lu Bird would carry her clothes and personal items to Paradisio, but she couldn't let the military's pricey gear out of sight.

Jack wore sunglasses and a slouchy hat in an attempt to travel incognito. He'd gotten about fifteen feet ahead of her when he realized she'd fallen behind. He turned and made the mistake of opening his Aussie mouth.

"Get a move on, Magnolia. I thought you were in better shape than this."

She was about to issue a wiseacre reply when Jack was recognized by one of his adoring public.

A middle aged woman, who probably hailed from Nebraska, wearing a lei and camera around her neck chortled with delight. "It's Jaguar Jack! The girls back home are never going to believe this!" She tugged on Jack's sleeve. "Oh, please, Jack, can I have my picture taken with you?"

Jack sighed, but smiled. "Sure, darlin'. I always have time for my fans."

He wrapped his arm around the dumpy woman as her bald husband in the Hawaiian shirt snapped their picture. Soon a whole group of admirers gathered around, including several children. Jack knelt to accommodate his young fans, charming, teasing and signing autographs. Maggie was impressed with his patience. Her preconceived image of him as a vain, pretty-boy television star kept crumbling.

Maggie tapped her foot as she waited, and stepped out of the thoroughfare into a seating area. The hourly CNN report music jingle floated over the murmuring crowd.

"Al Jazeera released footage today of Hannah Smith, daughter of Senator Gerald Smith, who is being held hostage by Muslim militants on the island of Paradisio."

Maggie's attention whipped to the television hanging above her head. Her focus zoomed in on the headlines flashing by. Jeez, this thing had just switched from a covert operation to a major media event.

Senator Smith and his wife, Rita, had granted an exclusive interview to Miles Huxley. The secret kidnapping of Hannah Smith had burst out into the open. As her hands twisted a tissue, Rita Smith tried valiantly to keep tears at bay. The Senator stoically answered questions. The bottom line--the U.S. doesn't negotiate with terrorists. Then Miles turned to the camera and announced the first film of Hannah Smith since her kidnapping.

A thinner Hannah appeared on the screen, blond hair covered with a scarf. She listened, nodded, shook her head at the comments of the accented voice accusing her of all the crimes of the West. Maggie recognized that voice. Ahmed Saeed. She wanted to leap through the monitor and choke his damned terrorist neck. This attention-grabbing propaganda-fest made her sick. CNN played right into his murdering hands. Clips of Hannah showed her growing more tired, less alert.

Then tears rolled down her pretty face, a face too fragile to be on a wild jungle island. "I'm sorry for the children, for your lost sons, your lost homeland. But I don't know how to help you. America has made some mistakes." Hannah's strangled sobs came through loud and clear.

Maggie blinked away tears of her own. A hand rested on her shoulder and squeezed reassurance. Maggie turned her head and gazed up into Jack's serious face. Time stood still; the noise of the airport faded into the background.

Jack's flinty eyes bored into her. "We've been a couple of bloody idiots."

She nodded, somehow understanding his meaning without needing a long explanation. They'd been at odds, each irritated at being stuck with the other through circumstances beyond their control. Hannah Smith had been only a vague black and white picture. A target. An assignment. Now she was flesh and bones, a real person whose best chance of survival was them, two bickering opponents.

Maggie said, "It's time to bury the hatchet and become a team, Jack. Hannah Smith's life depends on it."

His voice vibrated with conviction. "We're going to get that sheila out of the hands of those madmen. You can count on me, Major Savannah."

Staring into his midnight blue eyes, she decided to make the leap and trust the guy. "I think I've underestimated you, Jack. Let's go to Paradisio and whip some terrorist ass."

They marched down the shining tile floor, shoulder to shoulder, two soldiers about to go into battle.

The creature paced the volcanic floor of his mountain lair. So close to freedom. His believers grew in numbers every day. Ahmed Saeed served him well. The man spread the call across the world with human communication resources while the feline ruler released spiritual influences to devoted followers. Human minds twisted under his control; human hearts shriveled. Each one made him a little stronger. And when the Saint joined him, he would break the bonds of his captivity once and for all.

Chapter Ten

Ra-ta-tat-ra-ta-tat!
Ra-ta-tat-ra-ta-tat!

Hannah startled out of her exhausted slumber. Automatic repeat gunfire ripped through the air. Self-preservation kicked in as she rolled off her sweat-soaked cot and flattened on the ground. *Oh God, another gun battle.* She'd never get used to it. She waited for bullets to strafe the canvas, but soon realized boy soldiers were playing with their all-too-grown-up toys.

She eased off the ground and slumped on her cot. Hair now past her shoulders dangled alongside her downcast face. She wanted to fold into a ball. *Suck it up, Hannah.* A precious strip of denim material lay under her pillow. She dug for it and tied her hair up, then poured a small amount of water into a bent metal bowl that served as a washbasin. She cleaned herself with shaky hands. Each blast of gunfire made her jump.

Her life had changed since the arrival of Ahmed Saeed and his guards to the camp. These guys were more than mercenaries cloaked in a guise of Jihad. They were the true believers, stony-eyed and mirthless. They wore robes or long one-piece garments, even in the jungle where jeans and fatigues made a lot more sense. While Hannah could converse freely with Felipe and most of Moktar's native men, she felt intimidated by the Taliban-trained cadre of Saeed. Hannah learned to avoid their eyes. Their piercing hatred of all that she represented—America, Western women, Judeo-Christianity—made her feel wounded. They seemed to shoot her with poison spiritual darts and she wished she were some sort of Super Christian, a Joan of Arc of the Jungle. But, she was only Hannah Smith, who at best was plucky.

High in the mountainous terrain, they'd stopped mobiling. No IMA had been spotted for some time. Saeed's men began organizing and training Moktar's men, turning them from rabble to soldiers. A darker spirit fell over the camp.

As Hannah pulled on her baggy cotton pants and loose over-blouse, The Voice came to her, reminding her of Scripture from Ephesians: *For we are not contending against flesh and blood, but against the principalities, against the powers, against the world rulers of this present darkness, against the spiritual hosts of wickedness in heavenly places.*

Hannah stood frozen in place, shivering, *Oh Lord, I'm in way over my head.*

***

On the other side of the island, settling in her tent, Maggie reorganized her backpack on the cot. Sweat trickled between her breasts. She unconsciously slapped a mosquito. The patter of a light tropical rain hitting the canvas walls mingled with sounds of the crew setting up base camp on the outskirts of Acaban territory. She and Jack would set off at daybreak in search of Little Miss Muffet.

Jack unfolded a squeaky card table in the center of the tent. He unfurled the map of Paradisio, a hand-drawn affair that appeared more folk art than topography. Maggie moved in for a closer look. Its distances were obviously imprecise.

She frowned in doubt. "This thing isn't exactly Army issue."

"It's the best we've got. Acabans carry their maps in their minds, not on paper."

Maggie ran her fingers over the aged parchment. "Where did you get this?"

"Found it in a tree knot when I was a kid. Fascinating, isn't it? Must have been drawn by a stranded sailor decades ago."

Maggie looked over Jack's shoulder as he set rocks on the edges of the curled paper. Kerosene lamps lit the interior as Maggie and Jack studied the crude map.

A lock of dark hair fell over Jack's forehead. "I think our best bet for finding these blokes will be in the hills above this little cove. From what the Acaban leader, Ysway, tells me he believes the guerilla camps are in this area. Near the smoking mountain. Makes sense, too. That cove would be the best access by boat onto the island."

Maggie pointed her finger on the map. "There's one big mountain and a series of smaller ones here. What are these squiggles?"

"Lava, darlin'. This island has a real live volcano. 'Course it hasn't erupted in a hundred years, but every once in a while, it belches. The Acabans get nervous and send a party to throw a few sacrifices into the crater."

"Human sacrifices?"

"Just kids mostly."

"Kids! They throw their children into the volcano?"

"Goats, sweetheart, goats." Jack grinned his million dollar smile.

"Oh." Maggie turned to the map again, trying to ignore a prick of attraction. "Okay, we're here. We'll travel across this valley and get to these mountains. Right?"

Jack scratched his chin. "That does look like the most direct route, but staying on the ridge of hills might be the safest way to go."

The circuitous route that Jack described looked like a tremendous time-waster to her. "I don't understand. It'll take days and days to traipse over these hills. Why can't we just cut through this valley? Looks like there's a river. We can boat most of the way."

"Yah, that's true in theory. But do you see these little decorations on the map in the valley?"

Maggie leaned in to get a better look. Camouflaged in the greenery were monster faces—voodoo-like skulls from the Day of the Dead. For a moment they sprang to life with horrible grimaces.

Maggie jumped back. "What kind of weird-ass map is this?"

"Let's just say it's picked up some of the flavor of the island."

"So the boogey man lives in the valley?"

Jack sighed and stared intently at the map. "I'm not sure what's in the valley. I just know the Acabans won't set foot there. The few hunters that have returned from forays have come back terrorized."

Maggie tapped her foot impatiently. "Look, if we stay on the river and mind our own business, how long will it take to get to the volcano side of the island?"

"Probably two days."

"And if we walk across these hills?"

"A week."

Maggie placed her hands on her hips. "You saw Hannah Smith on television. How much longer do you think she can last in the hands of those fanatics?"

Jack continued studying the map, running his fingers over the river and valley. The intensity of his concentration fascinated Maggie. He appeared in a trance, caught between two worlds. The atmosphere around him changed almost glowing gold, charged by the machinations of his mind.

Minutes ticked by.

She edged closer. "Jack?...Jack?"

A shiver visibly ran through his body and he shook his head, blinking his eyes. He turned his gaze on her; the blue of his irises sparked a sapphire gleam. His expression stopped Maggie's breath as his hand reached up and cupped the back of her head. His warm fingers shot flicks of fire into her skull.

"We'll go through the valley, Red." His voice was low, husky. "But it's going to be dangerous, *real* dangerous. You're going to need every bit of the macho Marine balls you pretend to have."

His eyes caught hers in their laser beam, boring into her as if trying to measure her strength.

Hypnosis. The man was a damned hypnotist, but she couldn't break the spell. Didn't want to. She moved into him, drawn like a magnet.

She whispered, "Try me, Jack, I'm up to the challenge."

Trapped in his energy force field, the air hummed. He gazed down at her lips, then her breasts, making them pearl. Sexual energy ricocheted between. One minute the mysterious valley seemed the topic of discussion and the next, the valley on her chest. She pulled back slightly, but his free hand shot out around her waist as the fingers in her hair drew her closer. She could taste his breath on her tongue. A tangy scent rose like an invisible fog around them.

His mouth quirked slightly. "I've never kissed a Marine before."

Oh, God, her armor began melting, her hard-assed persona dissolving into a puddle at her feet, revealing the real, skittish Magnolia.

"Don't Jack…"

"You've got lovely emerald eyes. Remind me of the Caribbean, they do."

Her eyes widened. Cripes, wasn't that the kind of line she'd wanted from the honey lips of Chris Matthews? But this guy was overpowering her with his Aussie will.

"I'm not one of your kewpie-doll bimbos."

"No, you remind me of a lioness. Or a beautiful mare with a wild red mane flying in the air."

She should have shoved him away, but now curiosity and hormones had the better of her.

God, would the man not just shut up and kiss her? One kiss and she'd know what the fuss over Jaguar Jack was all about.

She lifted her mouth in invitation and he smiled. A nice, languid, I-won-this-round, smile. And then he kissed her. A wonderful, warm exploration, as if he had all the time in the world, as if she was a fine wine to savor and appreciate. Tasting, teasing, titillating.

For a moment, she remained passive, arms dangling at her sides. Then desire kicked in big time. She wrapped her arms around his waist. *What the hell*. She returned the kiss with unbridled enthusiasm. It had been a long, long time. *God, Jack, you feel so damn good.*

 She could get used to such kisses.

He released his hold, leaving her slightly mesmerized. His eyes glittered down on her.

His thumb ran over her lips. "I'll never think of Marines in the same old way after knowing you, Red."

She turned away, not wanting him see how he'd rattled her. She glanced over her shoulder at him with a saucy smile. "Well, you know how we are in the Corps—just looking for a few good men."

Chapter Eleven

Jack stood on a ridge overlooking the valley. Taunting words tormented his mind. *You're a coward...You're no match for me.*

His hand held an ancient sword, pitted and bent from eons of battles and centuries of earthly exposure. The metal had become so brittle, a light blow would probably shatter it into shards. He collected them in his journeys--relic swords, helmets, and shields. Some unfathomable search kept him on the hunt for the right ones. The ones that molded to his hand, fit his body like a second skin. Where the obsession began, he didn't know. He simply went with the urge. Like learning the martial arts to go with the weapons.

Standing alone on the precipice where grass fought for life among the volcanic rocks, he wielded the sword high, slashing and turning. He parried an invisible opponent and became one with the weapon. Sweat ran in rivets down his chest as he engaged in a fierce battle against an unseen enemy.

Fear tightened his chest. The words echoed in his head.

You're a coward...you're no match for me.

Always in the past, he'd let the fear drive him away. Up to the edge of the valley and no farther. But not this time. Too much was at stake to allow a muddle of childhood memories to keep him away. Hannah Smith might not live if he couldn't overcome his balmy personal demons.

He projected thoughts back to whatever taunted him. *Rack off, bugger. This time I'm coming through.*

***

Maggie hauled out her bag of transmitting equipment and tried to raise Derby. Jack had left the tent to talk with the crew. She only had a few minutes of daily opportunity when satellites were positioned over the island to receive her signal. Sitting on her cot, she punched the buttons as she'd been instructed.

"This is Mag-Pie. Do you read me, Big Brother?"

"We read you, Mag-Pie. How's the weather up there?"

Good old Derby.

"It's raining. At least the volcano isn't erupting."

"Ah, a little volcano eruption wouldn't be any big deal to you," answered his nasal reply. "Say, I've got someone here who wants to talk to you."

The Deep South velvety voice of Chris Matthews danced over the airwaves. "How soon until you anticipate making contact with Little Miss Muffet?"

"We're hoping for fifty-two hours from now." *If we can avoid the Creature from the Black Lagoon as we cross through the Smoking Slithering Swamps, or some such superstitious crap as that.*

Chris' voice crackled with static. "The assailants have issued more demands and they've threatened to start sending Little Miss Muffet's fingers and toes as tokens of their sincerity."

"Shit," she muttered. "What's the time frame?"

"You've got seventy-two hours before they've threatened to start sending body parts. We're trying to stall them. Time is of the essence."

Cold fury swirled in Maggie's gut, the kind that kept her focused and surged her forward. She mustn't let the TV show nonsense, animal psychics or hypnotic cobalt-blue eyes distract her. Ahmed Saeed was too evil to live, too evil to win. Maggie possessed the great American belief that good guys always win in the end.

Maggie gripped the microphone. "Don't worry. Miss Muffet will keep all her fingers and toes."

"Execute the plan as soon as possible." All languid Southern warmth had dissolved from Matthews' voice, replaced by cold urgency.

"I'm on it, Big Brother." Just then she noticed Auntie Edith peek her nose in the tent. "Over and out."

She smiled at her visitor. "Just testing some new walkie-talkies," she said, stowing away the equipment.

Edith marched in, a burst of floral cotton and bushy gray hair, with Lorelei perched on her shoulder and Mr. Jiggs following in his jaunty monkey manner. He headed for a fruit bowl that graced a small table.

"Well, ducky, all cozy in your new digs?"

Maggie looked about the tent interior noting the quick work that had been made of setting up cots, folding chairs and camp tables. Jack's crew obviously knew this routine well.

"It's a regular home away from home."

Edith crossed to examine the map still open on the table. "Good heavens, I didn't know this thing still existed. Haven't seen it in years.

Jack was fairly obsessed with it at one time. As a matter of fact, I thought we burned it."

"Jack showed me the layout of the island. We'll be heading for the other side in the morning, going through this valley."

Edith's chin shot up. "You're going through the valley? That's a terrible idea. The valley is…very unhealthy. Bad spirits, as the natives say."

"Oh, come on. You can drop the melodrama with me." Maggie walked to the table. "The camera isn't rolling. I think you and Jack are just pulling my leg."

"Why, what did Jack say?"

"Not much, really. He just got all spooky and then used his famous 'it's going to be dangerous, *real* dangerous' line."

Edith nodded her head and stroked Lorelei's satiny feathers. "I don't think Jack really remembers much, at least consciously."

"Remembers what?"

"How his mother died. She was killed in the valley, you know."

"I didn't know." Maggie sat in a folding chair. "Tell me what happened."

Edith gazed at her, uncertain. "We don't ever discuss it."

"It may be important to Jack's safety that I know everything I can about what's ahead of us."

Edith hesitated, nodded, and crossed to sit on the cot. "Jack was a young tyke. Eight years old. Phillip and Miranda had set up camp in the valley. No natives would go with them for fear of the evil spirits. Phillip, of course, didn't believe in such things. He was intent on finding a new species of beetle or some such insect. Anyway, he went off on a bug search, leaving Jack and Miranda at the campsite."

She petted Lorelei for comfort as Mr. Jiggs explored the room. "When he returned, the place was a shambles. The tent and their clothing had been torn and shredded. Much of the area smoldered as if darts of flames had struck like bolts of lightning. Miranda's body had been trampled, chewed and singed, bones broken many times over." Tears welled in her eyes. "Phillip searched everywhere for Jack. Finally found him huddled in an underground animal burrow. Miranda must have shoved the boy in there and then led whatever it was away from him."

"Good God," Maggie muttered.

"Jack didn't say a word for many months after that. Phillip brought me in from England to help care for the boy and eventually he came around. Still, I know he has occasional nightmares, even to this day. But, on the whole, I don't think he remembers his mother's death. Some things should just be left buried."

Good grief, what was really going on here? No wonder Jack appeared spooked out at times. How much did he recall? How had the experience affected him? Would he be able to carry out the mission?

Maggie returned to the map, running fingers through her hair. "Cripes. And I was hoping this would be a stroll across Gilligan's Island."

Mr. Jiggs' monkey squawk caught their attention as he dumped the contents of Maggie equipment bag on the floor. Auntie Edith bent over and retrieved a Marine issue revolver. "What's all this about?"

Seeing the gun in Edith's hand, Maggie reached over and shoved it back in the bag, along with the transmission device. "Didn't your mother tell you not to play with guns?"

Edith squinted her eyes. "Who are you, really? And what's so important on the other side of the island?"

Maggie tapped her foot, wondering what to say. "Oh hell, if you're being dragged into this mission, you probably need to know what's coming down. Sit down, Auntie, while I tell you a story about a little missionary taken hostage by a bunch of bad guys."

Edith listened to the Hannah Smith saga, sensing the threads of destiny weaving their tapestry. Maggie laid out the plan and the added need for haste if Hannah was to be delivered back home in one piece.

Edith shook her head. "The poor dear. Well, I understand now why you must cross the valley. Time is of the essence, isn't it?" She peered into space, thinking. "I've always hated this place and yet Jack has felt compelled to return again and again. Maybe his time has come also. Time to face the ghosts of his past. This may be a bit of synchronicity."

"Synchronicity?"

"When circumstance and coincidence collide to determine destiny."

Maggie scoffed. "I think we all determine our own destinies."

Edith gave a wise little smile. "Do you, dear? Well, this might be an enlightening journey for you."

Chapter Twelve

A heavy hand shoved Hannah into her tent. Grainy, greenish light surrounded her in the airless enclosure. Saeed's harsh voice still rang in her ears. What did he want from her? She'd offered apologies and asked forgiveness for every transgression of America, real or imagined. But that wasn't enough.

He launched a systematic attack on her beliefs, naming them false and foolish. He confused her with some of his questions, planted seeds of doubt. Had she heard the call of the Lord? Was it all in her head? Did she follow a powerful, loving God, or a delusion?

He tried to get her to denounce her Christian faith, call Jesus a false prophet. She couldn't. But she wasn't sure of the truth anymore.

Heart pounding, stomach clenched, she gave up control, let her defense fall to fear and desolation.

My god, my god, why hast thou forsaken me?

No Scriptures of comfort skimmed her mind. Hot tears rolled down the corners of her eyes into her hair as she lay on the cot allowing all the roiling pain to swamp her senses. She gave into depression and wallowed in hopelessness, beaten and pummeled.

Where is your God now?

Her chest contracted as high-pitched mewling noises emitted from her throat. Salty tears bathed her face. As she lay heedless of her runny nose, her crying jag developed full-blown, noisy, painfully satisfying. Hannah Smith never used to cry. The old Hannah Smith pondered the goodness of the Lord. She entered His gates with Thanksgiving and Praise. But the gates appeared locked, the praise strangled in her throat.

She pulled herself up to a sitting position and prayed aloud. With all the camp sounds, who was going to hear her? Who was going to care?

"I'm scared, Lord. I've never felt so alone. Where are you? Why did you do this to me?"

She wiped her face. "I'm mad, Lord. Do you hear me? I'm very angry with you for putting me in this situation! I'm really not the right person for this job. Please, let me go home. I want to go home. I want to see my mother. I want to see my father. I want to see…"

The images of the faces she longed to see caused a stab in her heart greater than she could stand and she moaned like a wounded animal, panted like a hunted dog until her emotional blood-letting dissipated.

She lumbered to her feet, crossed to a tin of water and splashed her face. She took a shuddering breath. Well, one good thing, she didn't have a mirror to see how rotten she looked.

The flap of her tent flipped open and two dark-haired women were shoved in. They landed in a heap, screamed with fright and huddled together on the ground. A swarthy soldier barked Eastern-sounding words. He shot the three women an expression of contempt before his quick exit that shut out the glimpse of daylight. The two Asian women, one probably near Hannah's age, the other barely a teenager, whispered to each other in yet another dialect she couldn't understand. Truly the camp was a modern Tower of Babel.

Hannah approached them cautiously and knelt beside them. They wept with fright and despair. She placed her hands on them. Their olive-black eyes registered terror she recognized, but refused to revisit. Giving into fear gave the terrorists victory.

How to begin communication? And then she knew. She pulled the cross that always rested on her chest from the folds of her shirt and dangled it before their eyes.

"Cristos," she said.

The women took ragged breaths and sat back. Each dipped into the tangled clothing that covered their chests, pulling out their crosses.

"Cristos," one whispered.

"Cristos," murmured the other.

Hannah sat back on her haunches and smiled at the girls, eliciting timid smiles in return.

"Okay, God," she said. "I get it. I'm here for a reason. I'll try not to let you down."

***

Auntie Edith and Jack waited for Maggie along the river's edge in the early morning light. Heavy humus odors arose from the mucky bank. Algae-thick water slapped the motorboat's faded sides. Lorelei explored the wooden rimmed edges of the hull, waiting for the next adventure to begin. Funny that a bird claimed part of his soul, but he'd come to accept it.

Edith's round purple-clad backside bobbed prominently as she bent over Jack's pack, making sure he had the necessary supplies.

"I'll rest easier when you return from this little errand, Jack. Sounds terribly dangerous. I want you to use every talent you possess to protect yourself. You know what I'm talking about."

Jack caught her meaning, but he didn't want to discuss it. He checked the petrol for the skiff. "No worries, Auntie. You know I'm half-cat. Nine lives and all that. I'll be back before you know it. I'm strictly working as a scout on this expedition. No rough stuff."

"Oh bosh," she said standing up and stretching her back. "At the first sign of trouble, you'll be into the fray. Just keep all your channels open and listen, Jack. Your gift is there to help you."

Jack gave her a kiss on the cheek. "You're the only one with a gift. I'm just an ordinary bloke who sometimes has an overactive imagination."

Edith clutched his arms, wrinkle-lined blue eyes stared up at him. "You've got to face it someday. I could help you."

"If you really want to help me, just make sure everything is taken care of here while I'm away. Shoot as much footage as you can of your segments. I want to have something to show for this detour." Jack stowed his duffel bag. "Where is that flame-haired Amazon?"

As if conjured up, Maggie appeared through the foliage, dressed in a khaki shirt and trousers, ready to take on trouble. Carrying her duffel and equipment bag, she marched toward them, power in every long-legged step, a sexy swivel in her hips. Sunlight reflected off her russet mane in shimmering waves. *Lordy, what a bonzer woman.*

"Morning, Jack. Hope you had your Wheaties for breakfast," Maggie said as she stepped into the skiff.

"Nothing so ordinary as that. Started out m'day with termite griddle cakes."

Maggie lifted an eyebrow. "Yum."

She waved at Edith as Jack started the motor.

Auntie wrung her pudgy fingers. "Take care of yourselves. Use your talents, Jack!"

Jack intended to use his five good senses and ignore any sixth sense hogwash.

***

Sweat trickled down Jack's back, making his shirt damp and clingy as he guided the small motorboat. The whirr of the engine echoed along the bank of the river. Scents of the jungle drifted in the air—plant decay, animal droppings, sweet vine flowers all mixed in a pungent bouquet. He lifted his nose to test the wind like the creature of the wild that he was. He absent-mindedly fed Lorelei a few nuts from his pocket as she rested on his shoulder. Then she flew off into the surrounding trees.

Maggie glanced back at him from the front of the boat. "I can't believe you're bringing that cockatoo with us. This is a military operation, Jack."

"I don't go anywhere without me Lorelei."

"Aren't you afraid she'll get lost or eaten or something?"

"Nah, Lorelei can take care of herself. Better than you, I expect."

Maggie sighed, shook her head and muttered something Marine-like. She turned away from him.

His gaze scanned the dense growth along the water's edge. Verdant greens, dashes of brown, splashes of red and yellow blossoms rolled by through seemingly placid hunter-green water. Parasitic vines hung from branches over the river; drooping green leafy fingers slapped his face if he didn't duck.

Maggie occupied the seat directly before him. Her auburn hair glinted when rays of sunlight dappled through spotty shade. He studied her profile and liked what he saw—the high cheekbones, strong brows, wide mouth. Her strength challenged him. Okay, he admitted it. It turned him on. But now was neither the time nor place for such thoughts.

Menace lurked out there, just out of sight, just out of scent. Something out of his dreams, dark and loud. It stomped and howled as he cowered.

The black dream enveloped him now in the daylight. Dirt seemed to fill his nose and mouth as fear rose hot in his belly. *Smothering... scared...he was so scared...*

Screaming...a woman's scream echoed in his mind.

"Cripes!" Maggie's irritation jarred his daydream.

She joggled the boat as she grappled with a large green striped snake that had fallen off a branch onto her head and chest. He enjoyed watching her deal with the non-poisonous interloper. Most sheilas would squawk and fuss. Not so, Miss Magnolia. She managed a firm hold under the serpent's head and subdued it.

As she reached for her knife, he stayed her hand. "What's the matter, darlin'? Not a snake lover?"

"Only when they're made into boots."

He took the snake from her grasp and examined it. Lovely patterns of green and black. "Ah, he didn't mean any harm, did you?" Jack released the snake into the water. It slithered and disappeared into the depths. "Good thing you're not as scared of snakes as you are of spiders. You might have overturned the boat in a panic."

She dug her fingers into the cushions of her seat as she steadied her breath. "How do you know that I'm more afraid of spiders than snakes? How could you possibly know that?"

Jack sputtered for a reply. "Well, just a law of averages. I'd seen your fear of spiders. Didn't think a dinkum Marine like you would have two phobias."

Maggie squinted skeptically. "Mmm…whatever."

"Oh, look." He snagged a flower dangling from a vine. "An orchid. Look at those colors—violet and yellow." He tucked the flower behind her ear and admired. "Lovely against all that gorgeous red hair."

She blinked at his unexpected compliment and touched the flower. "Uh, thanks." Ms. Marine appeared uncomfortable with the simple gift and quickly changed the subject. "I've been in jungles before, but this is very different from the Amazon or central Africa. It feels like 2000 BC or something. And it's so quiet. Where are all the birds? The monkeys?"

Jack sensed a malevolent force. "Maybe they're just watching, waiting."

"What exactly are we talking about here, Jack?"

He shook his head as if to clear it. "Don't mind me. I'm in a bumfuzzled mood."

She waffled the front of her shirt to pump some cool air on her hot body. Her hand dipped into the water and dripped moisture down her neck. He watched the drops run a path toward her breasts. Damned distracting breasts they were, too. Made him wonder about the woman under the Marine. "So, Major Savannah, have you got a man waiting for you in the States?"

Maggie answered a little too casually. "Sure. Several."

"But have you got your cap set on one?"

Much to his surprise, the hard-assed Marine's eyes softened. "Well, there is a certain Colonel…of course, he thinks I'm just one of the guys."

"Aw, I don't believe it. I need to apologize for that crack about your femininity in the hotel. I was just trying to get back at you." He scanned the skies as gray clouds shrouded the sun. "The truth is you're a striking woman. Haven't you fluttered those green eyes and wiggled that fine, firm arse at him?"

She shrugged in self-deprecation. "I'm not so hot at fluttering and wiggling. But thanks for the compliment on my ass. In my experience men don't fall at the feet of a woman who can out-run and out-shoot them. And I seem to have a problem with girly-talk."

"You've got to learn how to send the right signals." Jack's hand maneuvered the rudder past a tangle of floating roots. Grateful to get his mind off the shadows of his subconscious, he launched into a Jaguar Jack teaching time. "Typically the male of the species likes to make a show of strength to impress the female. Gorillas beat their chests. Rams knock themselves senseless during mating season."

Maggie smiled, responding to his charm, despite of herself. "And what do the females do?"

"They just give off the scent of sex. They go into heat."

She laughed. "I don't think I'm up for that."

"Women display many of the same sexual attraction tactics as their animal counter parts. I talked about wiggling your arse earlier. Ever seen a chimpanzee during mating season? Her rear end swells bright pink. Jane Goodall called them her 'pink ladies.' All the male chimps fight over those blooming pink ladies. Men aren't much different. You could learn a lot from the mating rituals of animals."

"So instead of reading *Cosmo*, I should read *National Geographic* to improve my love life?" She leaned back against the wooden hull, pulling the shirt tight across her breasts.

Under other circumstances he'd have simply relished her beautiful female form, but something urged him to speed the boat beyond this part of the river. He strove to keep the conversation light while pressing forward. "Well, you could, but I'd be happy to give you some pointers."

Maggie lifted an eyebrow and crossed her arms. "Thanks, but no thanks. If I was just looking for sex, I know where I can find it. I work in a highly male-oriented world. I get hit on all the time. I don't like giving control of my body over to some horny guy. Meaningless sex leaves an empty feeling in the pit of my stomach. But, you're one to talk. I'll bet you keep a little book of all the rich and famous babes you've boffed. Do you have a rating system?"

"Don't be crass." He scanned the bank for signs of disturbances—flocks of birds taking to the air. A heavy quiet persisted, sunlight blocked by cloud cover. "I appreciate beautiful women. When I make love to a woman, it's an act of admiration."

Maggie rolled her eyes. "You are so full of it."

A roll of thunder cut short their discussion; gusts of wind whipped up the water. A strange, putrid scent rode the breeze. Branches groaned; shushing, creaking sounds of leaves quivered. Limbs waved overhead from the approaching storm.

Jack surveyed the sky. Tropical storms came swiftly, nothing unusual in that. But these black clouds swirled with rare speed, as if pushed by an unseen hand. Calm water quickly turned into a boiling cauldron. A curtain of fog fell, dark and thick. Along the bank, just behind the first screen of trees, Jack thought he saw a figure pass.

Trees shook in great disturbance.

A lightning bolt split a tree, sending it up in instant flame. The sudden illumination flashed on a long, dark body. A feline shape with a huge head. It reared up on hind legs and revealed front feet with extended bear-like claws. A savage howl tore over the storm's din; the smell of death permeated the air.

Darkness shrouded the creature in shadow once again.

"Holy shit! What was that?" Maggie yelled. Her exclamation faded in the storm cacophony.

Jack struggled to keep the boat on an even course. Hard rain let loose from the skies. He threw a bucket to Maggie and shouted, "Start bailing."

Water pelted from every direction. Drenching…sloshing…soaking. Deafening crashes of thunder rumbled overhead, followed by jagged spears of lightning striking the ground.

The little boat bobbed and twirled like a toy in a tempest. Waves slapped his face and chest with stinging force. He fought to keep the rudder steady until his arms quivered with fatigue. Maggie's soaked figure worked furiously before him against the onslaught of water into their small vessel. At one point a flash of lightning illuminated the magnificent defiance on her face.

Almost as quickly as it came, the rain slackened…

The darkness faded…

The river settled…

Jack righted their course down the middle of the rushing river. Plant debris floated past in the currents.

Maggie pushed a clump of hair from her face and slowed her bailing to catch her breath. "What kind of animal was that back there?"

He didn't know what to tell her. It was nothing ever mentioned in any zoology books, that's for sure. It might have been his overactive imagination, if she hadn't seen it, too.

He'd just glimpsed the stuff dreams were made of—*his* dreams, *his* nightmares. Crikey, could such an animal be possible? Surely those tales of mythology were exaggerations.

"I've only seen it called one thing. In the Book of Revelation it's known as The Beast."

Chapter Thirteen

Thunder rolled. Ahmed Saeed shoved aside the fern fronds that grew in the volcanic dirt. His robes caught on the jagged outcropping of solidified lava. He'd given up his normal cloth shoes in favor of American boots. In some things he had to give the enemy credit and sturdy boots was one of them. There was no shame in taking advantage of what the enemy had to offer, especially if you used it against him. Like taking American airplanes and turning them into weapons of mass destruction.

He drew closer to the localized storm. The odor grew stronger; the smell of charred human flesh, so familiar after suicide bombings. Ahmed wound through the dangerous terrain, moving up hill. A lightning strike guided his way. He pushed through razor sharp fronds that tore his clothes. He retracted his hands into his sleeves to protect them, tucked his chin down to his chest. One spear-like branch whipped across his face. He pushed clear, but knew the sting on his cheek meant blood had been drawn.

A plateau of lava rock protruded on the side of the mountain, forming a natural bowl. A ring of ferns circled the area, giving the sense of a protected fortress. Overhead, turbulent clouds, thunder, and lightning rotated, modest in size at the moment, but capable of turning into a wild tempest at the Master's whim. Small flashes of light illuminated the ground from the storm above.

Ahmed's heart raced in his chest, excited, terrified. The Master waited before him, resting in cat-like repose, back legs tucked, massive front paws stretched forward. Oh yes, Ahmed knew where inspiration for the Sphinx had come. Which heads would he see tonight? Lion? Man? Woman? Ram? The Master's visage changed to suit his mood.

The Lion face stayed enigmatically in place as Ahmed approached. The long cat tail whipped in agitation, contradicting the calm attitude of the rest of the creature's body. Ahmed trembled, as he always did in the Master's presence. He fell on his knees and prostrated himself on the ground before his god.

Ahmed chanted words of praise before the Master, words that would be considered blasphemy to Christians and Muslims alike. But the prayers poured over the Master like warm honey. His tail calmed; his growl turned to a purr.

"Rise, Ahmed. You have done well. I can feel my power growing stronger day by day. As you spread my gospel throughout the world, the day is soon coming when I will be able to break loose from the boundaries of this cursed island and be able to walk the earth again."

Ahmed struggled to his feet and backed away from the overwhelming power that emanated from the Master. A mere mortal could only stay a short while in his presence. "Yes, Lord, more and more believers join our ranks every day. You were wise to send us to the poor children. We feed them, clothe them, train them what to think and worship."

"As each one gives their soul to me, my strength increases."

Ahmed saw it was true. Twenty years ago the Master's coat had been mottled and scraggly. Ribs had outlined his emaciated body; scabs marked his hide. Losing World War II had been a big setback. Most of his followers had been destroyed. He'd had to wait and search for new worshipers, lost souls; angry souls; souls that sought revenge and power. The Master found them in the poverty-stricken avenues of the Third World.

Ahmed first learned about the Master in the hieroglyphics of the Pyramids. As a young scholar in Egypt, he became obsessed with the Beast, as the Master was called by unbelievers. The ancient words had opened his soul. He repeated the forgotten prayers and traveled in his spirit body to Paradisio. As his connection to the Master grew, he eventually found his way in the flesh to the island.

He sat at the Master's knee and learned. Taking the teachings of Muhammad and twisting them, bending them into an adulterated form had been an inspiration. Pockets of believers were springing up everywhere, like bursts of wildfire. They were young, full of energy and zeal. Their prayers fed the Master's spiritual power. Their deeds brought in more followers and destroyed the unbelievers.

Fear and revenge fueled the Master, made his coat sleek and fattened his loins. Oh yes, the Master looked better and better.

"How goes it with the Saint? Have you turned her spirit yet?" the Master asked.

Ahmed didn't want to discuss Hannah Smith. He wanted to kill her, but that would only admit defeat. Turning the missionary was worth the spiritual power of a thousand children from the streets of Kabul. Hannah and her kind kept the Master trapped, his power leashed. But, if she and others of equal spiritual strength would worship the Master, he would finally gain complete dominion of the earth. But, so far, the Saint remained behind her spiritual shield.

"I am making progress, Master. She is weakening."

"She is the key. She must renounce the Other, and turn to me of her own free will."

"Her confusion grows. I'm enlightening her about the myths of her beliefs. Perhaps, Master, I should just bring her to you now. When she sees you in your glory, surely she will worship as I do."

The Beast knew that would not happen. Until the Saint renounced the Other, she would be able to see through the veil of lies that enchanted ones like Saeed. She must not see him with clear eyes.

"Push her harder. Use drugs to bend her mind, if you must. Make her see a mere man could never be a god, a ruler of all nations. Show her the folly of faith, hope and charity. Meekness begets weakness. Only a powerful Master will put an end to war and hunger. When I am in control there will be no need for war."

Saeed bowed. "Ah, and what a glorious day that will be when every knee bows before the Master."

A glorious day, indeed. Liberated from his island prison. Worshipped and feared by all.

Only the Saint must never meet the Warrior.

***

"Lizard on a stick," Maggie said. "You could start a new trend at county fairs."

Maggie watched chubby green reptiles turning a charred brown as they sizzled in the center of the campfire. Night fell suddenly, bringing out the nocturnal creepies and creatures. Squawking, chirping, and whirring filled the black air. She imagined millions of winged, bugged-eyed insects rubbing their legs together creating an electric buzz in the high branches. Stars pulsed through the gaps between the tree canopy way, way above.

Mossy ground beneath her boots felt springy, like a padded carpet, still filled with moisture from the afternoon soaking. She and Jack had stayed on the river until nearly sunset. Dodging debris from the storm required their full attention. Roots tangled in their motor blades slowed them down. Even though Jack claimed to have the night vision of a cat, he admitted that continuing on the river in pitch darkness was foolhardy, and selected a clearing on the bank to anchor the boat. Then he disappeared in search of "tucker" as she built a tent from a poncho in an attempt to secure dry shelter should another storm pass through. She checked her communication equipment for water damage. It appeared in working order.

Now they sat by the fire munching wild berries, waiting for the reptilian main course to finish cooking. Lorelei perched on a nearby limb. Jack fed the white and yellow creature berries, and petted her while murmuring Aussie endearments. The way the bird preened her head and chattered back, you'd think she knew what Jack was saying to her.

"Gosh, Jack, who are you, Dr. Doolittle?"

Jack looked startled. "What's that?"

"Do you talk to the animals like your aunt or something?"

"Nah. I think one psychic in the family is enough, don't you? I don't have any bent toward that hocus-pocus."

"Because if some boa constrictor is thinking of having a little snack on me, I want you to speak up."

"Can it, Red. I have no psychic powers whatsoever."

Maggie wanted to bring up the subject of "The Beast," but remembering Edith's tale of his mother's death made her leery. Dark undercurrents seemed to flow beneath the jocular façade Jack kept up. Now, alone in the jungle with a guy growing more mysterious by the minute, Maggie the Mouth bit back the blunt questions she longed to ask.

He turned the lizards one more time. "If Auntie Edith were here she'd whip us up some kind of jungle dipping sauce, but these appear to be fat little fellows that should have a nice flavor on their own. Open up that pouch, luv, and get out the salt."

Maggie did as instructed and sprinkled salt on her Paradisio kabob. "I think this will be easier to eat if I cut off his head. I don't like swallowing food that stares back at me."

She hacked off the head and feet, zipped off the crispy, scaly skin and pretended it was chicken. She took a nibble. Not bad. What the hell. She sunk her teeth in for a real bite.

Her eye caught Jack's sparky grin in the reflecting light. "You are the gutsiest sheila I've ever met, Red."

She shrugged. "No gutsier than you, willing to cross this valley when you knew that horrible creature might still be here—the one that killed your mother."

He froze, his hand in mid-air about to take a bite of lizard-kabob. His eyes glowed over the campfire like his jaguar namesake.

It wasn't in Maggie's nature to back down in a search for the truth. She really wanted to know what was going here. And what had happened to Jack.

She spoke in a whisper. "Edith told me. We should talk about it, Jack. Pretending it never happened won't make it so."

Jack set his dinner aside. "You did see it, didn't you, Red? It wasn't just in my imagination."

"Definitely not your imagination. It was a real, live humongous animal. A cross between a cat and a grizzly bear."

He ran fingers through his straight hair. "In some ways, it's almost a relief to know it exists—that I'm not totally balmy."

"Well, that remains to be seen. I'm afraid I can't buy into your remark about that thing coming out of the Book of Revelation. It's just a freak of nature, a crazy anomaly. Not some supernatural creature."

Jack stood, too twitchy to sit still. "You're probably right. I've always been cursed with an overactive imagination." He glanced at his watch. "You'd better call up your commando friends before you lose your window of opportunity."

Despite setting the timer on her watch, it hadn't gone off. All that bailing in the storm probably knocked it out of commission. "Damn! You're right."

As she scrambled for her equipment, Jack crossed into the shadows, grateful she'd been easily distracted. *Not some supernatural creature,* she'd said.

Oh, Lord, how he wished she was right. Jack gripped a tree branch, trembling. Fearless Jaguar Jack fought the urge to turn tail and run. Whatever it was, the bloody Beast created a supernatural fear in Jack like nothing else.

Jack could stare down lions, join a stampede of angry bulls, drive the freeways of L.A., but the Beast turned him into a sniveling wuss. Jack slammed his fist into the tree trunk. Pain jolted up his arm.

Rubbing his knuckles the real pain grounded him. *Got to learn the difference between fantasy and reality, Jack.*

The difference between truth and lies.

Chapter Fourteen

"Rroww!"

Maggie lay dead asleep when a bone-jarring yowl jerked her to semi-consciousness. Tucked in her sleeping bag next to Jack under the poncho tent, her eyes cracked open.

Cave-like darkness engulfed the campsite. Warm, damp air carried earthy aromas of dying embers and a decidedly male scent. Jack's hair tickled her nose. In the uninhibited state of sleep, she'd curled as close to his body as the two sleeping bags allowed. *I'll walk hot coals before I admit how affected I am by America's Hottest Hero.*

Coming to full awareness, she realized a sniffing creature had invaded the campsite, pawing their cooling fire ashes, presumably for scraps of food. Maggie moved slightly and felt Jack's hand clamp her shoulder.

"What is it?" she whispered.

"Rroww!"

She tensed at the cat howl.

Jack's hand squeezed harder as if to say "be quiet." She slapped at him, wanting to be free from the confines of the bag. The best she could do was lift her head a bit and peer over Jack's body in the direction of the open camp, trying to get a glimpse of their intruder. As if on cue, a shaft of moonlight escaped from behind cloud cover and allowed her to see a dark figure a few feet away.

Pewter light from hovering trees cast ghostly shadows on the midnight visitor. A cat for sure. But not the Beast. Not nearly big enough. Probably a jag. She could make out a tail whipping the air and the feline head held high. A slight scraping sound registered in her mind--the zipper of Jack's sleeping bag slowly being undone. Maggie's breath hitched as the tension rose.

Her mind searched for survival manual instructions. Play dead or scare the creature away? What did it say about basic jaguar behavior? Surely Jack knew which way to go.

Without warning, the jaguar leapt. A black body flew toward them, claws bared. At the same time, Jack burst out of his bag and met the attacker in mid-air, hollering a blood-curdling Aussie outback yell. His broad shoulders silhouetted in the moon light.

Two powerful creatures collided in primeval confrontation. Maggie vaulted from her resting place and grabbed the sidearm she always kept close at hand. In the inky atmosphere she couldn't tell where the man ended and the cat began. Cripes, she couldn't get a clear shot.

She pointed the revolver to the sky and discharged, hoping the cat would run off. *Blamm!*

Jack and the cat rolled on the ground. Maggie ran in the direction of wrestling bodies, circled the combatants, trying to figure out the best way to help.

Somehow Jack had ended up on his stomach with the cat perched on his back. *Oh, shit.* The jag swiped a long scratch down his back before Maggie managed to give the feline a good hard kick in the ribs with her military boot. Always sleep with your boots on in the wild. Thank God she hadn't broken her rule. The creature stumbled off Jack's body. He leaped up and let loose with another yell while wildly waving his arms.

"Ya-raaw!" Jack howled.

Still concerned Jack might get in the way of a bullet, Maggie found a stone and used her fast pitch to pelt the attacker. "Get lost, kitty-cat!"

The cat growled low and galloped off into the underbrush. The crunching of leaves and branches grew fainter as it disappeared into the dark.

Jack leaned over hands on thighs, panting.

Maggie threw down her stones and ran to his side. "How badly hurt are you?"

He straightened up. "Not too bad. She got my back and arms. Stings like a son-of-gun. Get the first aid kit. I'll build up the fire."

He'd raised a small glow from the flames by the time she returned with the kit. He settled on the ground, sitting Indian style.

Maggie ripped off what was left of his shirt. She examined the long scratches that cut into Jack's flesh and winced. Her hands trembled, knowing he could have been shredded to ribbons. She forced a calm to her voice she didn't feel. "This could be worse. At least it didn't get your throat." She dabbed the dripping blood. "Isn't it unusual for a jaguar to attack people like that?"

"I think she was settling a score." He glanced over his shoulder, a grin tugging his lips. "She's kind of an old girlfriend."

"Jeez, Jack, do you bring out these reactions in all your ex-girlfriends?"

She poured hydrogen peroxide on his back, eliciting a yelp. "Crikey! You're a lousy nurse."

Working quietly for a moment, she cleaned the open cuts. The sinewy muscles of his upper arms rippled under her touch. *Don't go there, girl.* She forced her attention to the business at hand. "You thought it was the Beast at first, didn't you?"

Profiled in the amber light, his jaw tightened. "Yah, at first. But then I realized there were too many elements missing. The jag's howl is a kitten meow compared to the roar of the Beast." She watched him slip into another dimension, a transformation before her eyes. His voice deepened. "And the scent was wrong. The Beast smells like death and decay. And fear. Fear has a heavy scent. The air was too still. The Beast brings a storm in his wake. Remember the lightning strikes hitting the ground today?"

The small hairs on the back of Maggie's neck rose. *Don't fall for Jack's mumbo-jumbo.* "That was just a tropical storm. Coincidence."

"I'm not sure. All this time I've thought the dreams were figments of my imagination and bad indigestion. The body of a leopard, the feet of a bear and the mouth of a lion." Jack rose and paced the camp area. Turbulent energy shimmered in his wake. All TV celebrity persona dropped away. This was Jack in his natural habitat. A creature of the jungle. "It killed my mother. Most animals only kill for food. It's part of the natural order. But the Beast kills for the pleasure of killing. Just like some men. Evil exists—in man and in the Beast."

Maggie shivered. "Come on, Jack, you don't believe all that superstitious stuff, do you?"

Jack turned and stared at her with sorcerer's eyes. "You believe it yourself."

"I do not."

"No, then why are you a Marine?"

"I was born to be a Marine."

"But, why, Red?" He kneeled beside her. His bare, well-defined broad shoulders so close. Utterly primal. "Ask yourself why."

She fought to keep her breath steady. "To protect my country."

"From what?" His eyes hypnotized her soul.

"The bad guys, the whackos, the crazies." She shook her head to break his spell.

He grabbed her jaw and forced her to look into his face. "From evil."

Maggie trembled at the power emanating from Jack's touch; the pools of mystery in his eyes. *Oh, cripes, what have I gotten myself into?*

Chapter Fifteen

A sharp prod awakened Hannah from a blessed, deep sleep, her only time of escape. One of Ahmed's men nudged her with the butt of his rifle. Forcing her eyes open, Hannah focused on a pool of light pouring from a lantern held in Saeed's hand. His long nose and heavy features appeared even more menacing in the flickering lamplight.

Guards roused the Filipino women, Corazon and Amelia, who slept huddled on a pallet. English, Farsi and Spanish words mixed in the air. Female cries and male barks.

Obviously it was time to get up. Hannah groaned. "All right already. I'm up, I'm up." She pulled a scarf over her head and stood.

"Good evening, Miss Smith," Ahmed Saeed said. "We shall continue your education."

Hannah sighed. *What now?*

A panicked yelp caught Hannah's attention. The women resisted a turbaned guard. Hannah rushed over and put herself in the middle, wrapping her arms around Corazon and Amelia. A stern frown and defiant stance put off the guard.

"You're scaring them, Saeed. Just tell us what you want. We obviously don't have much choice."

She whispered a few words of comfort to the women in Spanish.

Looking annoyed, Saeed said, "We wish them no harm. We merely are taking you to evening prayers. It is time you learned about the Master."

Herded into the pitch night, Hannah held hands with the girls as they marched between Saeed's guards. The white of their tunics appeared ghostly against the dense jungle. Hannah noted empty hammocks hanging where Moktar's men usually slept. Moktar's burly frame came briefly into view. He leaned against a tree as they walked past. He radiated seething anger.

Leaving the camp clearing, they trudged single file up a small trail, fighting branches and dangling vines. Hannah struggled not to stumble. Earthy night odors hung heavy in the air. A flickering of light in the distance grew bigger and brighter. Torches burned around a mossy grotto. Emerging from the jungle, the party entered an open, rockier area. Volcanic layers of solidified lava formed a rocky wall, a makeshift altar.

Hannah's gaze lit on a strange idol resting on a boulder. It reminded her of a Sphinx. Saeed's guards mingled with Moktar's men, bowing and praying before the dog-size statue. Murmurs of prayers echoed off the jagged stone.

Ahmed glided to the altar while Hannah and the women were forced to their knees in an area separated from the men. Seeing their high priest arrive, the worshipers increased their chanting fervor. High-pitched, staccato chants pierced the air, pulsing with energy. Hannah covered her ears against the assault to her brain.

Ahmed lifted robed arms above his head. Torch light cast ghoulish shadows. His hands gripped a jeweled chalice. He recited a prayer in a foreign tongue. Without understanding his throbbing words, Hannah realized a bastardized communion ceremony must be taking place. Ahmed dripped the cup's contents over the Sphinx's body. Red liquid sluiced over the metallic statue. Wine? Blood?

The crowd's chanting rose to a frenzied pitch.

Hannah shivered. *Oh, Lord, protect me.*

On the heels of her inward prayer, a boom of thunder crashed.

A cup was thrust into her hands. Similar cups now passed between the worshipers. They drank in great gulps before passing onto the next person.

Hannah stared down at the suspicious ruby liquid. "I think I'll pass."

She tried to hand the cup back. Instead, two guards forced her to drink, one holding back her head, the other pouring the substance down her throat.

She swallowed and choked. A fermented berry wine mixed with unknown ingredients hit her stomach with fire.

A quick glance at her female companions showed them docilely drinking as ordered.

Her sense of danger increased with each passing moment. *Oh God, oh God, oh God* echoed around and around in her mind.

As drugs hit her blood stream, reality distorted. She dropped in a helpless heap, semi-conscious. Men twirled in ecstasy around her. Dizzy…she was so dizzy. Objects blurred. The wavering torch light swirled in fingers of flame. Hallucinogenic images revolved and formed. The altar transformed into a fighting arena.

A winged white horse descended from the heavens. On its back rode a warrior. They landed in the arena, kicking up dust. The horse's tail whipped around as the man pulled the reins. The warrior dismounted the horse, patting its neck before sending it back up into the sky.

Crowned with a head of dark hair, the warrior stood dressed in the fashion of Roman gladiators before donning their armor. His face appeared chiseled in stone with deep blue eyes surveying the crowd. Ropes of muscles delineated his arms.

Two attendants dressed in white gowns approached him, a man and a woman. The red-haired woman buckled a gleaming silver belt around his waist. The fair-haired man fitted a breast-plate in place and secured a helmet on his head. Finally, the woman handed him a magnificent jewel-encrusted sword and shield. The two attendants bowed and left the warrior alone.

Now, fully battle-ready, the warrior circled the arena, wary and alert.

From the shadows, his opponent stepped forward—the idol come to life—a great shaggy beast, part bear, part lion. Terrible, but fascinating in its power.

Man vs. Beast.

They circled…They charged.

They struggled. The warrior slashed his gleaming sword at hairy limbs. The beast attacked with vicious teeth and claws. Round and round they went—grunting, tearing, bleeding.

A battle for control of the world.

From outside her mind, Hannah heard the chanting. "Master… Master…Master!"

Voices of reality mixed with the drama of her drug-induced dream. Sweat beaded her forehead. She swayed on crumpled limbs, barely able to keep her head up. Yet the battle before her eyes appeared so real. So important. She must know the outcome.

Master…Master…Master! A cacophony of ranting drummed her ears.

Her perception changed. It wasn't Man vs. Beast.

It was Man vs. Master. The Master Ahmed insisted she must follow.

Master…Master…Master!

The battle raged. The Man and the Master locked in mortal combat.

And in her confusion…she didn't know who she wanted to win.

Chapter Sixteen

The next day, Jack and Maggie made good time down the river. She was relieved to see the sun shining in tropical brilliance, not a storm in sight. Yesterday's hocus-pocus had definitely creeped her out.

Birds called from the shoreline, spider monkeys swung across tree limbs, blue fish jumped out of the water. Lorelei disappeared into the jungle. Maybe she was looking for some action on the wild side. The ominous mood of the river had lifted—for the moment. Maggie sat on a cushioned bench as she guided the rudder. She thought back and wondered if she'd had a momentary mental lapse, falling for all that Beast malarkey. Jack's overactive imagination must be contagious.

He stood facing forward at the prow of the boat. A khaki shirt loosely covered his broad shoulders. Those scratches on his back probably still hurt like hell. The shirt billowed over his black shorts. A few white scars streaked his tanned legs covered with a light dusting of dark hair. He'd have a new set of scars to show for this adventure.

Maggie had a few scars of her own. The kind that showed, and the kind that didn't. Jack ran his hand over the back of his neck. The movement fascinated her; his masculine fingers kneaded a knot near his shoulder. His fingers mesmerized her. She could almost feel them massaging her neck. A wave of yearning washed over her, engulfing and unexpected.

The engine started sputtering, cutting in and out. Jack turned around, alarmed. "What did you do?"

"Nothing… Not a damn thing. Maybe there's some water in the engine."

At that point the engine died all together. Jack wobbled toward the back of the boat. "We shouldn't be out of petrol yet."

He dropped anchor, checked the engine and came up with a punctured gas line. "Must have nicked it in the storm. I'll have to repair it."

He didn't have a new line, but used some kind of adhesive and clamp. Maggie watched those clever fingers go about their business. At one point, he looked up at her and seemed to read something in her expression. He gave her a smug little wink. She blinked and looked way.

Get a grip, Maggie.

He stood and peeled off his shirt. "Good time for a swim."

She gulped at the sight of his naked chest. "This isn't a pleasure cruise, Mr. Campbell."

"I'm aware of that, Major Savannah. But we have to wait about half an hour for the adhesive to set up. I don't know about you, but I'd like to get some of the jungle stink off me back."

She tore her gaze off him and glanced at the water. "Is it safe? What about piranhas?"

"This isn't a Tarzan movie, Red."

Clad only in his shorts, Jack dove over the side. Poetry in motion.

His dark crown broke the surface. He shook his head like a dog to whip glistening hair out of his face. Did he have to be so frigging good looking? Flipping on his back, he did a leisurely backstroke. "Come on, have a little faith in good old Jaguar Jack. I swear there isn't anything with venom or razor sharp teeth for at least fifty feet."

The shimmering water looked awfully inviting, promising relief in the steamy heat. God knew she felt downright twitchy. Maybe a swim would relieve her increasing tension. She'd obviously been in dry dock too long. Noticing every nuance of Mr. Celebrity was getting damned annoying.

What the hell. She kicked off her boots, stripped off her shirt and dove in the water, dressed in her bra and shorts. The cool rippled down her skin. *Heaven.* Her arms pushed through the liquid and she rocketed to the surface. After being cramped on a tiny boat for two days, the freedom of movement felt wonderful. Her legs and arms picked up a steady rhythm, and she pounded away.

Jack floated and watched this fit female churn the river like an Olympic contender. She constantly surprised him. Her gorgeous long legs kicked with precision. If she'd been a cat, she'd have been a cheetah, able to reach astonishing speeds with power and grace.

And he wondered if she would also purr like a cat given sufficient stroking. He'd like to find out. Having Maggie wrapped around him would chase away all thoughts of ghosts and goblins, at least for a little while. *Maggie, Maggie, swim my way.*

He frowned at the intensity she displayed, pounding the water like a military exercise. The woman didn't know how to relax. How to enjoy life.

Maggie needed to play. All animals possessed a natural sense of play. He saw it every day, in cubs, in kits, in birds and beasts. Maggie the Marine needed to regain the innate joy of play. And Jack was just the man to help her.

He pushed off and joined her as she circled back toward him. They swam in tandem. He found her rhythm and matched it. She slowed; he slowed. She increased; he surged ahead. She somersaulted under to change direction, and he was right with her.

Breathing heavily, she treaded water and faced him. "Cute, Jack. So we know you can keep up with me. But can you beat me?"

They were some distance from the boat.

"Let's give it a go. Should I give you a five second lead?"

"Only if you want to be staring at my ass the whole way."

"I can think of worse things."

Maggie was raring to go. She loved a race. "Okay, on your mark…"

"Wait a second. What do I get if I win?"

"What do you mean? The satisfaction of winning. But you won't."

"I need more incentive than that."

"Okay, what?"

"You take off your clothes for five minutes and let me look at you."

"Oh, right. Are you some kind of perverted peeping Tom or something, Jack?"

"I assure you it's nothing sexual, though you do have stunning breasts and legs. You're a beautiful female of the Homo-sapien species and I want to study you."

"Man, does that line work with other chicks?"

"I swear it's not a line."

"I'm a fit, athletic woman. I'm not beautiful. Beautiful is small and delicate. I'm not any of those things. Do you want to race or not? I'm getting tired of treading water here."

"Red, you don't know yourself at all. If I win, I get a look."

She rolled her eyes. "Fine. You don't stand a chance anyway. On your mark, get set, go."

They took off in a dead heat, splashing with their long bodies. Maggie didn't waste energy looking at him. She felt him at her side. Her competitive nature lurched to the forefront. She wanted to win; she had to win. Harder and harder, faster and faster she thrust her limbs into the water. *More Maggie, give it more.* Her heart and lungs were fair to bursting as she closed in on the boat, one long arm ready to touch the wood. Finally, the end. Her glance shot over her shoulder to see how far behind he was.

His arm leaned against the hull, a cat-who-ate-the-canary grin on his face. "Better luck next time, Red."

Don't be a sore loser, Maggie, she told herself. *Damn,* she hated to lose. Oh cripes, the stupid bet. She'd rather face a firing squad than Jack studying her birthday suit. "I suppose you want to collect your prize."

"Later, we'd better be getting a move on. I want to savor my five minutes." His eyes twinkled.

***

Pacing his lair, The Beast sensed his race against time. The Warrior drew closer to the Saint every day. The thought waves of fear and lies no longer worked. The Beast knew better than to get too close to the Warrior. If he realized his potential, even without unity with the Saint, the Beast could be severely set back. Better to keep his distance.

His best hope rested on turning the Saint. Soon, she would be his.

Chapter Seventeen

The river narrowed as they continued on. Jack took footage of any interesting wildlife that came into view. Maggie listened to his running commentary into his microphone. He really was an amazing mass of knowledge regarding animals, recognizing them, naming them both in English and Latin, reciting their unique characteristics. He even knew his bugs. And he certainly seemed preoccupied with mating habits.

"Look down there on the surface, Red. Those are damselflies having a bit of a cop."

"A 'cop'?"

"Short for 'copulation.'"

She rolled her eyes. "I should have known."

"The bright blue males have injected their sperm in the females, and they are staying in place to make sure no other horny male comes along and swaps theirs out."

Maggie gazed across the algae green water. Dozens of aqua blue dragonflies hovered above the surface attached with needle-like bodies to their lady-loves. "How long do they stay connected like that?"

"Those blokes have real staying power—about an hour to make sure the deed is done."

"That's a lot better than most men, if memory serves me correctly."

"Ah, Red, you just haven't known a man who understands the secrets of the female anatomy."

"I suppose you'd be willing to show me, in the name of science."

His devilish grin ignited a surge of heat in her blood. The thought of paying off her racing debt made her squirmy. Oh, she'd been buck-naked before with mixed company. But that had mostly been in the context of field operations under hurried conditions. In those settings her body was a well-trained instrument used for athletics or military assignments.

The idea of Jack just staring at her, like he did his animals, was a whole other kettle of fish. She remembered the way he'd stroked some mousy creature and crooned, "Isn't she a beauty?" If he ran his finger down her back like he did the mouse, she'd be a mass of goose bumps and probably blush the same shade as her hair. Oh man, she really didn't need to borrow this kind of trouble. She turned her attention to the changing terrain.

The volcano with its bowl-shaped peak stood at the west, the beginning of a line of mountains that blocked off the sea. Maggie sniffed the air, trying to sort the scents. Sulfur, probably drifting down from the slumbering fire mountain, along with decaying greenery. As the river narrowed, the air grew closer and dense. Gnats swarmed in irritating clouds. She grabbed a can of insect repellant and doused herself.

Reeds and water plants ultimately choked the passageway. Jack killed the engine. "I think this is the end of the line, Red. The pleasure cruise is over."

Maggie smacked a biting bug on her neck. "Some pleasure cruise," she muttered.

They managed the logistics of backpacking their gear and communication equipment. Jack secured the boat. They worked well as a team, and slogged out of the swampy area for higher ground. When they reached a clearing, they stood and surveyed the mountainous terrain before them.

"What do you think, Jack? Is our missionary behind door number one, the volcano; door number two, the hill before us; or door number three, that really treacherous mountain to our right?"

Jack roved the landscape, standing very still. He seemed to go into some otherworldly mode, spaced out, listening to a signal sent from the Twilight Zone. Maggie was getting familiar with the look. Jack lifted his arm and from nowhere Lorelei appeared, a splash of yellow and white against the curtain of green jungle. Somehow he'd called her without uttering a word or whistle.

Lorelei landed on his arm and did a little cockatoo two step on his forearm. He stared at his pet, nodded his head and fed her a couple nuts from his pocket.

He kissed her beak and said, "Good girl." He stroked his bird's downy feathers as he spoke to Maggie. "We need to head up that direction on the tallest mountain. There's a cove the pirates use on the other side."

Maggie knit her brows and looked back and forth between Jack and his bird. "Oh...my...God. The bird told you. You *are* psychic like your aunt. You sent Lorelei on reconnaissance."

He looked at her with scorn. "Don't be ridiculous. I'm just taking an educated guess. I'm no bloody crazy freak. Let's get a move on."

He made long strides toward the mountain.

Maggie ran to catch up. "Wait a minute, buster. How come it's okay for your aunt to be the animal psychic, but you don't want to be a crazy psychic freak?"

He pushed through low limbs. "Auntie Edith has a gentle gift. I'm nothing like her."

Jack's expression shuttered down. Did he even know when he went into that Transylvania trance routine, she wondered? Was there a connection to the months he spent in the psych ward?

Cripes, they've sent me on assignment with a lunatic.

Maybe he had petit mal seizures or something. Great, that's just what she needed on this mission. One thing was for sure, the fearless adventurer held a secret inside, and she'd ferret out the truth before their mission ended.

***

Dusk settled on the mountain, as night bugs emerged and birds set up a racket grabbing their final meal of the day. Moktar didn't like the way this was coming down. He chomped on a soggy cigar and sat on a log, staring at the tent that enclosed Hannah Smith and Ahmed Saeed. Saeed's bloodless guards stood sentinel, more like robots than men.

Since letting Saeed in on the operation, everything was getting more complicated. Moktar knew the kidnapping business. Grab a few tourists, kill a couple poor ones to make a point, get a nice ransom. Release them, maybe go home or take a vacation. Now politics, religion and fanaticism got in the way. What did Moktar care about all that? He wanted the money.

His representatives on the mainland were holding secret negotiations with the Smith family. Perhaps the United States didn't deal with terrorists, but wealthy parents did. He was really close to a cool million dollars for Hannah Smith—the biggest ransom to date. When he'd told Saeed of the progress, the fucking Egyptian looked down his crooked nose with an expression of disgust. Then he'd entered the woman's tent again.

The murmurs of the deep male voice and the female replies were barely audible; a calm discussion punctuated by an occasional strangled cry on the part of the woman.

Moktar cared nothing for the mind games Saeed carried out on the woman. But now he worried that this wasn't about the money at all. They'd stayed in one place long enough. Negotiations were nearly complete. Time to stash the woman on the mainland for the delivery. If he didn't deliver, his credibility would be completely ruined. Ransoms were paid, hostages released; that's the way the business worked.

Saeed had approached him at a gambling resort months before. Combining resources, he'd said, could only be good for both of them. Believers of the Jihad should be united against the infidel. Moktar had been raised by his mother, a whore, in Bangkok. Everyone had been Muslim. That's the way it was. Moktar claimed no burning spiritual fire. Moktar believed only in Moktar, but he'd found spouting the rhetoric of the Islamic fanatics brought in young recruits, thinking they were fighting for a mighty cause.

Saeed told him the blond missionary would be worth the biggest ransom of his career. Moktar did his part and kidnapped her from the village. Saeed was supposed to bring worldwide attention to drive the stakes higher. Once the anxious parents paid, the daughter would be happily reunited with her family. Everybody wins.

But something strange was going on. Saeed's men had swept into camp and created a new order. A rigid order of harsh regimen and regular prayers. They chanted, too. Hidden ceremonies in the jungle made him uneasy. One by one his men had been sucked into the Arab's control. Moktar remained the only one not attending the nightly gatherings. Even the women were included. Last night, the captives-turned-wives had been carried out afterwards, unconscious and naked. Obviously well-used. Hannah and the two Filipino women had emerged fully-clothed, but catatonic. If Moktar believed in souls, he'd have said theirs had been stolen. A chill ran down his spine, despite the heavy heat of the tropics.

Saeed kept brushing Moktar aside, intent on his meetings with the missionary. Moktar would take no more. Only the forbidding guards kept him from storming into the tent and getting into Saeed's swarthy face. Nobody ignored Moktar. He wasn't squeamish about thrusting a knife straight into the Arab's belly, or lopping off his head. Yes, he might find that most rewarding.

Saeed opened the tent flap, ending his session of intimidation. For a moment Hannah Smith was visible, slumped on her cot. The canvas fell back into place. Moktar stood, fingering the weapons strapped around his waist for security.

Saeed managed to look cool and clean in his robes and flowing headpiece, towering several inches over Moktar. The kidnapper felt like a stinking turd in his torn shirt and pants.

He planted himself in Saeed's path. "We must talk. It's time to take the girl to the mainland. I'll need to make the exchange quickly when it comes."

Saeed gazed down with hooded eyes. "It's time for evening prayers."

Rage simmered in Moktar's belly. "Screw your prayers. We are talking *now*. I will wait no longer."

Saeed's hand shot out and gripped Moktar's throat. Two Arab guards flanked the kidnapper. The tips of deadly knives pulled from the folds of their robes stung a sharp impression in Moktar's back. A quick thrust would bring certain death.

Moktar's panicked eyes looked for one of his own men. They all carried assault rifles. Yet, the boys in ragged clothes might as well have been holding toy guns. They now looked to Saeed for leadership, not Moktar. He read their faces. They would do nothing in his defense.

He gasped for air as Saeed squeezed a little harder and spoke. "When I want to talk to you, I will call for you."

Saeed dropped his hand and looked at it with revulsion, as if he'd touched something unclean. The lean Arab disappeared into the jungle with his guards, off to perform their nightly rituals.

Moktar stood panting in the clearing. His men averted their eyes and went about their business.

Thunder rumbled across a clear sky, followed by a gust of wind carrying the scent of rotting carrion.

Chapter Eighteen

The next afternoon Maggie trudged up the mountainside, the forty-pound backpack felt more like a hundred pounds strapped to her shoulders. Sweat trickled down the valley between her breasts. A piña colada would be great about now.

Jack trekked ahead of her, still carrying that Aussie bounce in his step, the damn bird catching a free ride on his shoulder. Sometimes he couldn't resist pointing out a unique animal or plant, whispering with great enthusiasm.

Pausing at a frog perched on a fern frond he said, "Look, luv, it's a *Dendrobates auratus!* Oh, it's a beauty."

Maggie stared down at a weird-looking turquoise and black amphibian and rolled her eyes. "Listen, Jack, if we stop for every freak of nature that catches your eye, we'll never get off this friggin' island."

Frowning at her lack of appreciation, he moved on. "I keep forgetting that I'm with the female Terminator. I'll start calling you Arnold."

In truth, she was having a hard time keeping up with him, but his constant awe and wonder at dangling fuchsia orchids, ruby-throated hummingbirds and even huge shiny beetles irritated her. The dark cloud over his personality had moved on for the moment, and the jocular Jack remained her companion. Nobody should be so cheerful in this heat and humidity.

Jack waited for her in the shade of a palm tree, drinking from his canteen. "My throat's as dry as a dead dingo's donger. What do you fancy for supper, Red?"

Maggie caught her breath, grateful for the moment's rest. "Oh, I don't know. How about a T-bone steak, rare, with mushroom sauce? Can you whip that out of your Jaguar Jack bag of tricks?"

Jack stripped a flower stalk off the palm, took out his knife and used the instrument to force nectar out of the tip of the flower. "Open up, darlin', you could use some sweetening up."

He held the flower to Maggie's mouth. Her lips remained sealed tight; her mind suspicious. His free hand reached out and tickled her tummy, catching her completely by surprise and causing her mouth to fall open. He took the opportunity to spritz her tongue with flower juice.

MMmm…her mouth filled with a tangy, sweet refreshing flavor.

Jack's eyes sparkled. "Good, isn't it?"

Maggie nodded and couldn't help smiling. "What is it?"

"Sugar palm. They're grown commercially all over these islands. The seed for this one must have drifted by on a trade wind." He cocked an eyebrow. "Ticklish, aren't you?"

"Not ordinarily. You surprised me."

"If you say so. I may have to conduct a ticklish test on you later."

Oh, he'd better not. She was ticklish as all get out.

She changed the subject. "Show me how to get the juice out of these flowers."

They took a break, and drank the wonderful nectar from the life-restoring tree on the mountain. It dripped down her chin, but she didn't care. Okay, maybe Jack wasn't all that irritating.

After she made another contact with the Special Op team, they pushed on, wanting to make use of the daylight available. As the sun began to sink, Jack told her to keep moving upward, he would catch some supper and find her. He disappeared into the undergrowth.

Oh, swell, she wondered what kind of creature would be staring at her from the skewer tonight.

She marched on in monotony, stepping over roots, pushing through wide leaves and dangling vines. If the sun hadn't been fading, if the slanting light hadn't made it invisible, she'd have been fine.

She simply didn't see the biggest damned spider web in the history of the world, and walked smack dab into the center of it. A sticky curtain of spider spit enfolded her entire body. Her arms flailed. She fought the gunk on her face and in her hair. Oh, cripes, how she hated that cloying feeling on her skin.

But, she kept her cool, fought for control. She wasn't close to losing it until she freed her vision and looked down at countless fist-size spiders, black and hairy with tan stripes, clinging to her on the shroud of their webs.

Oh my God. Though her military training kept her from emitting a sound, inside her head, she yelled bloody murder. Her life-long arachnophobia exploded in full hysteria. Silently, she screamed like a banshee.

Jack had just filled his pouch with a nice morsel for dinner when he sensed the silent screams. He wasted no time analyzing whether they were real or unreal. Inside his head, her screams jarred his brain.

Maggie's distress reached him like a homing device, high-pitched and furious. Lorelei took to the air and Jack nearly flew also, jumping and racing back down the slope.

He rounded a huge kapok tree and saw her, shaking and panting as she yanked at arachnids dotting her body.

He trotted up to her. "Hold still, Red, and I'll take care of it."

She hissed in barely contained fury. "Get them off, get them off, get them off!"

Lorelei circled around them cawing, "Crikey, mate!"

He plucked them away, tearing the sticky silk. "They're more afraid of you than you are of them."

"I doubt that," she said, gritting her teeth and clenching her eyes.

The critters scurried into the underbrush as he cast them aside. "I'm not sure I've seen this kind of spider before. Red, you may have stumbled upon an undiscovered species."

"Who the hell cares? Are there any in my hair? Get them out of my hair." Her voice ended in a squashed squeal.

She stood trembling, barely keeping it together. He cleared her hair of interlopers, then dropped her backpack and weapon to the ground, searching for any hitchhikers caught in the crevasses of her clothing. He stretched out her arms and patted his hands over her body. With long sleeves and pants tucked into her boots, she'd been fairly well protected.

"I think that about does it," he said.

She sighed with relief, offered him a chagrined half-smile and lowered her arms. Then she gasped, her eyes opened wide with alarm and she started tugging at her shirt. "Oh, cripes! There's one on my chest."

Jack grabbed the front of her shirt and tore it open, sending buttons flying. Sure enough, nestled on the pillow of her left breast, partly resting on the lacy edge of her C-cup, a startled spider was biting her skin. *Cricky.* He hoped the venom wasn't too poisonous. He flipped it off and tore the rest of her shirt off, inspecting her torso and back.

"You're clear."

She threw herself into his arms and buried her head on his shoulder, giving into a shuddering little cry. His arms wrapped around her. A scent of sugar palm and woman hit his senses. Her round breasts surged a rhythm against his chest that matched her choked-back sobs. His hands ran soothingly up and down her bare back, covered only by the lines of bra straps. In another setting, it would have only taken a flip of his thumb and index finger to set her breasts free.

Rather than a randy response, Jack felt surprised and touched by this display of hidden feminine vulnerability in the tough-talking Marine.

"There, there it's all right." He continued to coo Australian-accented solace until she calmed down.

Maggie pushed away, wiping her eyes with her fingers. Her red nose and cheeks matched the shade of her messy hair. He let his gaze travel to the flesh-colored undergarment that supported her fine bosom. Twin mounds puffed nicely over the cups and he imagined a delightful handful of woman responding to his touch.

She turned, more embarrassed by her outburst than her state of undress. She bent down and dug another shirt out of her backpack. "I'm sorry. I don't usually lose my cool like that."

Maggie hadn't lost it in a long time. Even when Al bled to death in her arms, she'd held on, held it in. What was happening to her?

She'd thought her childhood fear of spiders a thing of the past. *Okay, cut yourself some slack. An army of huge spiders would scare anyone.*

Still, she'd dissolved into a complete puddle on Jack's shoulder. When had she done anything like that since she was five years old and run to the General with a skinned knee?

Jack's arms felt good, his shoulder just the right height, his crooning accent fell over her like a wave of warm sea water.

She couldn't look at him. He'd seen her weakness. Worse, if he looked her in the eye he might see it there still. Something about Jack made her want to spill her guts and confess her secret fears. She wanted to tell him, *I'm not who I'm pretending to be.*

But if she wasn't who she was pretending to be, then who was she?

Chapter Nineteen

Dusky half-light filtered into Hannah's tent. She lay on the filthy cot that had become a refuge. Sleep was her only escape from heat, humiliation, and hunger. Her mind was always fuzzy nowadays. Her Bible had been confiscated, but she searched her memory for Scripture. Confusion befuddled her thoughts because the Word now mixed with a new Gospel. Daily lessons from Saeed seeped into her mind like a drop of dye in a glass of water—coloring everything.

He told her about the lie of Calvary, scoffed at her believing a man could be dead three days and walk out of a tomb. He explained crucifixion in great detail. No one could live after hanging on a cross and then be stabbed in the gut. Her religion was a pack of fairy tales. He was leading her to a new understanding, but she couldn't grasp all the implications of it.

Her head had barely cleared from the bizarre hallucination of the night before. Every time she closed her eyes, the fighting between the gladiator and the strange beast raged on.

Corazon and Amelia had been gone all day, no doubt involved in some indoctrination of their own. Since they'd arrived, she'd felt driven to protect them in any way she could. Amelia, especially, brought out some fierce maternal instinct. Hannah doubted the girl could be more than fifteen. A pretty, penniless girl like that would soon be claimed by one of the men. Even care-worn Corazon would be a prize in the woman-hungry camp.

Using what little mental focus she possessed, Hannah sent up a prayer of protection for her tent mates. If they were the reason she was here, she'd better do her part. But even as she tried to pray, her sleep-deprived, nutritionally depleted body dozed off.

Hours later, a crash of thunder and a flash of lightning jolted Hannah awake. Night had fallen. Wind buffeted the canvas walls. Eerie blue light diffused the air, punctuated by white strobes. A terrible stench almost made her retch. When did a storm carry such an odor? Had dead bodies been unearthed from the deluge?

Hannah glanced to check if Corazon and Amelia had returned. They clung to each other in the center of the tent, gasping at each clap of thunder. Amelia whimpered in her older sister's arms. Corazon whispered soothing words in Spanish. Amelia murmured her fears. Corazon answered them. Hannah struggled to translate. Often fatigue kept her from having the mental energy to comprehend the foreign languages that swirled around the camp.

Don't want to go…Afraid…Honor…Master calls…No, no

At the height of the storm with rain pounding the tent, and wind threatening to blow its meager protection away, the flap opened. Saeed stood silhouetted against the flailing trees and downpour of water.

Hannah sat up and hugged her knees.

He stepped in and gazed at Amelia. "It is time."

He put one hand out, a long arm extending from his damp robes.

"No!" she cried and buried her face in Corazon's shoulder.

Saeed looked disgusted. He spoke harsh Spanish words. Corazon hissed urgent words to her sister, the tone of her voice growing more strident.

Amelia kept shaking her head. "No, no, no."

Saeed's patience snapped. He bent down, grabbed Amelia by the shoulders and yanked her up. She screamed and tore away from him in a panic, scrambling to Hannah's cot. Hannah protectively wrapped her arms around the girl. She didn't know what was going on, but a well of defiant courage rose in her chest.

She jutted her chin at Saeed. "Leave her alone."

Corazon stood and approached Saeed, speaking rapidly. Hannah caught a few words. She seemed to be begging Saeed to take her somewhere.

Please…me…I want…honor.

Saeed roved Corazon's begging figure and pursed his lips in irritation. "You are a poor offering for the Master."

Offering? A deep chill traveled through Hannah. Images of human sacrifice flashed in her mind. Amelia was by far the prettier sister. Corazon had small eyes, a large nose, an over-worked bony body. Saeed gazed at Amelia and Hannah on the cot. His eyes burned at Hannah, pure hatred exposed, usually disguised with a civilized veneer.

He shrugged at Corazon in apparent resignation. "Come. The Master requires a willing heart." He said the words to Corazon, but stared at Hannah.

Saeed turned, his robes sweeping behind him as he departed the tent. Corazon followed. She never gave her sister a second glance.

***

On another part of the island, away from the localized storm, Maggie enjoyed the spray of a waterfall hitting her head and sluicing down her body. Her toes gripped smooth rock to keep her from sliding into a tropical lagoon. A bar of non-army issue unscented soap worked as shampoo and body wash to cleanse away any spidery residue.

Maggie not only took orders from the General, but from the General's wife. *If you must be out in the sun all day, always wear protection on your skin.*

Maggie took guilty pleasure in fine soaps, body lotions and secretly ex-foliated on a regular basis. On this assignment, she steered away from insect-attracting scents, but she still went for top quality.

Jack had pointed her in the direction of the waterfall, and gone about the business of setting up camp. He promised her a gourmet meal when she returned. His attitude after her spider fit was solicitous, which threw her for a loop. It took the wind out of her sails, set her to mumbling and feeling out of whack.

The shower revived her, though the spider bite on her chest hurt like a son-of-a-bitch. She dressed, but had to leave off a bra because the cup rubbed painfully on her chest.

Jack had a nice little fire going when she reached camp. This would be their last cooked meal. Tomorrow they would reach the summit, and head into enemy territory.

He squatted before the fire, poking at something obscured in smoke. Darkness had fallen like a veil. Flickers of amber light played across his face.

He smiled up at her. "You're a sight for sore eyes, Red. Lucky for you to have that naturally wavy hair."

Her hand traveled self-consciously to her hair. "I should have had it hacked off before we left. It's a pain to deal with in the jungle."

"A sheila with such pretty hair should never hack it off."

For some reason his compliment made her furious. "Cut it out, Jack. Stop being so nice, it's really pissing me off."

He lifted an eyebrow. "Excuse me. I'll try to be more rude and crude like you military blokes." He spoke gruffly. "Sit your arse down, Major Savannah, while I rustle up some grub…Is that better?"

She had to bite her lip to keep from chuckling. She sank beside the fire and sat cross-legged. "What's on the menu? Sautéed salamanders?"

"Actually, I came across these before your little run-in with the spider village. They have a wonderful flavor, a lot like crab. I hope you can get past their appearance."

He pulled a smoked tarantula the size of a dinner plate out of the fire.

Maggie gasped, closed her eyes and whispered, "Oh, cripes."

Jack placed it on a banana leaf and began to crack its outer body. He crooned a sound of delight as the charred skin opened up to reveal light tender meat. The more he worked, the less it looked like the spider from hell.

Okay, she was a tough Marine who'd had a momentary phobic lapse. She could handle this. She took the offered food and eyed it suspiciously. "Got any Tabasco to go with this, Jack?"

***

Ignoring the deluge, Ahmed Saeed pushed the ugly Filipino woman into the prayer grotto. He swallowed his bitterness and fear. Would the Master accept such an offering or would he strike Ahmed down in anger?

The Master waited, pacing in impatience. Water coursed down his tawny fur. Lightning forks struck the ground around him. Ahmed had never seen the storm so intense.

The Master stared at the woman. "She is not the one."

"The sister didn't have a willing heart."

The Master's eyes flashed. "You have not done your job well."

Ahmed wanted to scream in frustration. He couldn't change everyone's hearts and minds! It was one thing to intimidate and kill. Capturing people's souls was a different matter.

Corazon ran forward and fell at the Master's bear-like feet. At least with this one, Ahmed had been successful, even if her soul was no bigger than a kumquat.

Corazon chanted the phrases she had been taught. *Praise to the Master...obliteration to the Other and all His followers.*

The strength of the storm lessened. The Master gazed down at the prostrate woman, drenched from the storm. She cared nothing for her comfort, intent only on worshiping him. His tail whipped once.

"This one will do for a sacrifice, but I need the missionary and her spiritual strength to join me. Together we can break the cords of bondage and be freed to roam the earth. Make her come to me of her own free will." The Master's eyes reflected the lightning.

Ahmed looked down; the power of the Master's gaze was too powerful to bear. "She is close."

"The Lake of Eternal Fire is full of others who have failed me. I would hate to see you join them."

Ahmed quaked. "Soon, Master, soon."

The Master issued a roar that shook the trees and reverberated along the hillside. Ahmed fell to his knees; pounding rain beat upon his head. The Master grabbed the woman with a huge paw. A clap of thunder forced Ahmed to shut his eyes. A bolt of lightning struck.

The ground sizzled where the Master had stood. Nothing remained but a gouge in the jungle floor.

The Master had taken his sacrifice back to his lair.

Chapter Twenty

Maggie set out their bedrolls while Jack took off for the waterfall. Maybe he was part cat, able to see in the jungle night. She would check his eyes to see if they actually glowed when he came back. Noisy evening creatures surrounded her, going about their nocturnal business, finding mates and food. Eating, sleeping and screwing—that pretty much described the animal kingdom as far as she was concerned. Why did humans have minds and emotions to complicate their lives?

She sighed and wondered at her growing discontent. Something had been out of whack with her since Al's death. Maybe before then, but she'd been too busy to notice. Her month in the Bahamas hadn't been restful, healing or fun. Long jogs on the idyllic beaches ran off some restless energy, but had given her no mental clarity.

His death had only magnified her growing sense of futility. No matter how hard she worked, how many hours she put in, the bad guys would always be out there. Seeing the cruelties people inflicted on others wore her down. Jaded her.

And she was lonely, but didn't know what to do about it. Being Maggie the Marine meant she did her job, and went back to her solitary quarters. There had to be more in life, but damned if she could figure out how to get it.

A flashlight beam caught her eye as Jack returned from his nocturnal bathing. So much for the cat vision theory.

"Here, catch. It's a lovely sweetsop for breakfast," he said.

Quick reflexes moved her hands to capture the object flying her way. A round, lumpy fruit thudded her chest. A perfect hit to the inflamed spider bite that was running its painful course. She winced and emitted a little moan.

Jack must have seen her expression in his light beam. "What the devil? What's wrong?"

"Nothing. It's just that damned spider bite."

"Why didn't you say something? Let me see."

He bore down on her. She backed up.

"I'll be fine by morning."

"Don't be a bloody fool."

He stuffed the flashlight in his waistband, light shining up, grabbed her shoulder with one hand and began unbuttoning her blouse with the other. She dropped the sweetsop and slapped at his hand.

"Don't, Jack."

A man used to handling poisonous snakes and dodging crocodile teeth, had no trouble finishing the task at hand despite a fussy sheila. He pulled open her shirt; her breasts spilled out.

He held the flashlight above the troubled area and gently ran a finger over the wound. "It's flaming, it is." He glared at her. "Think you'll get a medal for enduring a venomous bite, Red? Is that why you didn't mention this?"

"What was the point?"

"The point is I could help you, if I knew you were hurting. It's not a crime to admit you need a little help or you've got a wound that hurts like bloody hell. You don't have to be the bravest woman on the planet every minute."

Tears stung her eyes as her chest tightened. She didn't have a snappy reply to his reprimand. She pulled away and spun around. God, she must be overly tired.

He sighed. "Sit by the fire. I'll fix a poultice to take down some of the swelling and pull out the poison."

She settled on her bedroll. "What are you going to put on me? Eye of newt?"

"Yeah, and a little kangaroo dung for good measure."

He worked from his first aid kit as she buttoned her blouse to be half covered. Being a topless dancer had never been one of her ambitions.

He mixed this and that and actually spit into the pasty mess. He turned to her and applied a clay-like substance to her upper chest. It felt amazingly cool and began to tingle a minute later.

In the shadowy light his face held stern concentration as he worked. His hair was still damp from his shower. A lock dangled over his forehead. She wanted to smooth it back. His breath puffed over her throat and exposed skin in gentle whiffs as he tended her. He adhered some kind of leaf over the clay mixture with a little tape.

His eyes never wavered as he doctored her. She imagined him fixing broken bird wings, cradling orphaned joeys, studying baby panda bears. Such a strange, complex man—gentle, but demanding. He possessed a powerful body, but kept his might restrained. He clowned for the camera and then fell perfectly still, listening to his inner voice. She didn't know what to make of him.

He finished his job and laid his right hand over her poulticed wound. She imagined a healing force radiating through his palm.

His mouth, inches from hers, murmured low. "I think you're going to live, Red."

"Glad to hear it," she whispered back.

"Do I get a reward?"

"What did you have in mind?"

"This…" His lips caught hers. Before she had time to protest, his left hand traveled into her hair, leaving his thumb at her cheek, stroking a sweet circle on her skin. His mouth worked a gentle magic on her, coaxing, giving. This was nothing like the crude face sucking of her last lover. Jack made the kiss a gift, a tumble into a sparkling whirlpool.

Maggie traveled to a new place, unchartered territory of the heart. His mouth brushed over hers, back and forth. Soft, oh so soft, exploring the texture of her lips; his tongue flitted across and flicked inside. Without conscious acquiescence, she tipped backward, falling onto the length of her sleeping bag, the open flannel cushioning the jungle floor. He followed her, like a dancer glides with his partner on a rhythmic twirl.

He didn't jump her bones. In fact, he seemed intent on reaching her with only his mouth. He hovered above, pulling on her lips, gently tugging and licking, but never plundering. She fought the urge to wrap her arms around him and pull him close.

I should stop this.

Her hands formed fists at her side, not clinging to him, but not shoving him away, either.

His lips tortured her. She tried to play it cool, offer small kisses, for small kisses. Waves of desire steadily grew. Soon, small kisses weren't enough. Oh God, she wanted him deep inside her mouth, wanted the taste and fulfillment. Her lips dropped open in full invitation.

Please, Jack, please.

He accepted, penetrating and passionate. A moan rose from her throat, mixing with the animal sounds that surrounded them. Once again his hand caressed her cheek, seducing her with gentleness. Feather light fingers fluttered over her eyelids and cheekbones, trailed down her throat, moving in tandem with his ever-exploring mouth.

Maggie knew how to fight an opponent, how to match wits and go for the jugular. Her previous sexual experiences had been fast, furious and unfulfilling. This slow, tender assault caught her unawares, turned her bones to jelly and stripped off the protective barrier to her emotions.

The buttons of her shirt gave way again to his deft fingers. He sat up on his knees, spread open the cotton material like a quiet breeze. Dying embers of fire cast a dream sequence glow on his handsome features. A slight smile lifted the corners of his mouth.

Terror struck Maggie's heart. This man had made love to screen stars and models, small pampered women.

Don't look at me, don't look at me. I know I'm not pretty.

But Jack took his time looking, appreciating. His hands covered her breasts, thumbs drawing across the responding tips. "Lovely, lovely. Just like I thought they'd be."

A well of tears rose in Maggie's chest and filled her eyes. She couldn't explain her emotions, as jangled and as exposed as her breasts, open to Jack's watchful eyes and tender touch. He bent and kissed a trail down her waiting left breast, as his hand held the other, careful not to hurt the inflamed area. She had no sensation of pain now, only the longing for Jack to take her in his mouth, taste her, suckle her, heal her.

Again, he took his time. Kissing and whispering accented terms of appreciation, as if she were giving him the greatest gift in the world. But she knew she was the one receiving tonight. He made her feel beautiful. Her athletic body wasn't something to be ashamed of.

She lay supine and languid, not reciprocating caresses, too overwhelmed by sensation and emotion. Hot tears rolled down the side of her face into her hair. She wasn't supposed to cry; she never cried.

His hands and mouth took control of her now, washing her with longing, hot and pulsing. His hand circled her stomach, moving lower and lower as his mouth laved her heavy breasts. The drawstring of her pants gave way, giving his fingers access to her urgent wet core, ready, so ready for his touch.

He cupped her, covering with his warm hand as his mouth trailed up her smooth breast and throat again.

Inside, Jack, inside. That's where I want you.

No rush, no hurry. His hand went round and round, pushing on the rise of bone, curls and soft flesh, hidden folds waiting to be touched by him as no man had ever touched her before. His tongue teased the lips of her mouth the same moment his fingers teased the lips of her womanhood. Tongue and fingers worked in perfect rhythm together on the most vulnerable, silky parts of her body.

Now her arms couldn't resist reaching up to his shoulders as he stretched out beside her. With only her chest exposed and a fully clothed lover beside her, it was the most erotic moment of her life. He smelled tangy, essence of the lagoon and subtle male scent. His fingers opened her, found her, delved into her softness as his mouth made love to hers.

This shouldn't be happening. This can't be happening. I can't let this happen.

"Don't be scared, Red," he whispered. "I've got you."

With a sob, she came. Crying and climaxing at the same time. Her body and emotions let go. She shook and shimmered and sobbed. Jack held her all the way through it. She wept for Al, pictures of his last moments flashed through her mind, moments she'd worked to suppress. She cried for Hannah and all the lost souls in the world she couldn't rescue. Oh hell, she cried just for the pleasure of finally being able to cry. Because in Jack's arms it was okay to be weak--okay to be herself, Magnolia Savannah, a tough Marine concealing the heart of a Southern Belle.

Chapter Twenty-One

Maggie's rhythmic breathing told Jack she'd fallen asleep. Her hand rested on his chest like a trusting child. He pulled back to gaze at her face in the dim light. Strong cheekbones under lush lashes couldn't hide the vulnerable woman beneath the hard veneer. Her legs tangled with his; her wild mane shrouded his fingers. While she'd been sated by their encounter, Jack decidedly had not. Not that he really minded. Maggie needed a special touch tonight.

He slid away, fastened her blouse and zipped her light sleeping bag. His fingers gently smoothed her hair. The mystery of Maggie continued to unravel. He followed his instincts with her, like he did in everything. Tonight she'd needed some kind of healing, a chance to let her defenses down.

Jack knew about defenses.

He sat crossed legged by the fire, watching fingers of yellow flame claw away the bark of the branches. A gust of wind disturbed the canopy above; flickers of stars blinked through the open spaces of the foliage. A distant howl. His female jag. She sounded sassy tonight.

Maybe it was being back on the island, but somewhere during his encounter with Maggie, his mind shields slipped. The mental gate swung open.

Images flashed. Tonight he'd shared Maggie's grief for the lost partner, Al-Jabbar. He'd seen the cruel face of Ahmed Saeed shooting the undercover agent from the departing helo. Hatred burned in Arab eyes like ignited coals. Jack felt Maggie's heart ripping when Al-Jabbar died in her arms.

He'd glimpsed Maggie's insecurities. A beautiful woman who had no knowledge of her beauty. Maggie saw the truth about everyone, except herself.

And that made him nervous. How soon before she glimpsed the truth about him? She'd already noted some of his "fey" moments with Lorelei. But, hang it all, a lot of people had special connections with their pets.

Quit kidding yourself, Jack. You've got a lot more than a "special connection." You've got a bloody "gift" that almost drove you mad.

Now the "gift" ran strong, colliding in his brain. He hated catching Maggie staring at him.

She'd lift one eyebrow, and he easily read her mind, *Oh, cripes, they've sent me on assignment with a lunatic.*

He thought she'd spoken out loud, so clear was the phrase heard in his mind. But her lips hadn't moved.

As he sat before the fire, the wavering flames held his gaze, hypnotizing him before he realized what was happening. His breathing slowed, a strange buzzing filled his ears. The sound came from within his mind, pulsing louder and louder like a siren heading toward him in busy traffic. And suddenly he floated, hovering over the sleeping figure of Maggie and--good God, his *own* still body, sitting before the fire.

He jerked, then zipped through the air like a ghost, which he guessed he was. Had he been bitten by a deadly snake? Had the spider meat dinner been hallucinogenic? His spirit body rushed over the canopy of trees toward some unknown destination. Above him, the stars sped by in a glittery silver blur. He glanced over his shoulder. A long shimmering cord appeared tethered to his back. A spiritual bungee cord of some kind?

The island moved swiftly below. He passed over the peaks of the island mountains. He started to descend, like a skydiver landing on a tarp in a stadium, toward an open area on the side of the mountain. He knew that was his destination. His feet landed on the stony ground of the open expanse. A localized thunder storm swirled in the air. He couldn't feel the ground beneath his feet; his body appeared opaque.

What a ruddy, peculiar dream, if indeed a dream this be.

An animal yawn caught Jack's attention. Lounging in the center of the grotto was the object of Jack's childhood horrific dreams, at least it resembled the feline creature. At the moment it displayed a passivity unlike his nightmare monster. The Beast licked his massive paw; his tail wagged indolently; red eyes studied Jack with hooded interest. Resting on an expanse of smooth rock, he looked almost like a real over-sized lion with bear-like feet.

Jack glanced about. Flashes of light from a hovering storm illuminated the area. He stood in a grotto, surrounded by dense palms. The Beast's face appeared serene, a fine king of the jungle in his throne room.

"So, you have found me, Warrior." The Beast spoke in a low growl.

Warrior? What the bloody hell did he mean by that?

"It has begun. Why don't you just surrender now and save us a lot of trouble?"

Jack didn't know if he was having the damned weirdest dream of his life or if he'd slipped into another reality. But he knew one thing, he'd never surrender to this creature in any universe.

"Not bloody likely, Beast."

The Beast's eyes sparked like exploding coals. "Do not call me by that name. Call me Master."

"Never."

The Beast's face transformed from benevolent feline to a fierce, jagged-toothed tyrannosaurus rex. "You will worship me. I shall have dominion over all."

Scenes flashed in Jack's mind. Teenagers carrying assault rifles into schools...Men throwing acid on Eastern young women...African men hacking their neighbors with machetes.

The horror of it brought Jack to his knees.

Spiked teeth shone in the mouth of the beastly dinosaur face. "Yes, that's it. Fall at my feet."

An aura of pure evil enveloped Jack like a deadly fog, choking him. Fear simmered in his belly.

"Feel the power of fear," the Beast said. "It's raw and strong, and will rule the world."

Suddenly, Jack was eight years old again, filled with the worst terror he had ever known. The Beast created the fear that stalked the world. Fear that drove people to do terrible deeds of destruction and murder. Fear that turned tribe against tribe, neighbor against neighbor.

A woman's voice whispered, "Come to me, Jack."

Jack's head snapped up. The Beast's face had transformed into Jack's mother.

His mother's voice, so long missed, called to him. "You don't have to be afraid. Only those who don't follow the Master must live in fear. When you give your soul to him, he takes away all fear."

The seductive, gentle voice of his mother, promised living without fear. No more nightmares, no more battling the unknown demon of his mind.

The face of the kindly lion returned. "You've been running away from me for a long time, but I am your destiny. Once I cleanse the world of unbelievers, we will all live in peace. Join us, Jack. I can give you dominion over towns, cities and countries. Think of it. You can halt violence, destruction of the environment, man's inhumanity to man. Through me, you can bring unity to the world."

Instinctively, Jack knew promises of peace and unity were a lie.

Still on his knees, he bent forward; his hands supported him. The overpowering presence of the creature drained his strength. He fought to hang onto his soul.

Jack crumbled.

In the mist of his mind, he managed a prayer. *Help Me.*

A crack of thunder jolted the air, followed immediately by a spear of lightning. The Beast laughed. "Dare you reach out to the Other in my presence? There's no help for you here."

Faintly, Jack heard Maggie's voice. "Jack! Jack! Wake up!"

The cord attached to Jack's back pulled taut. He made a high-speed trip back to his body; the island trees zipped past him, a green-black blur. Like a spirit yo-yo, he was yanked through the cosmos to his comatose body, now collapsed beside the fire.

"Jack, damn you! Snap out of it!"

Maggie rolled him over on his back, and shook his shoulder for all she was worth. "Come on, you lousy Aussie, open your bloody eyes."

Jack struggled to do just that. Blimey, he had the mother of all headaches. Maggie's hair dangled over him. He reached up to touch its silkiness. His arm felt like it weighed a thousand pounds.

"Hello, Red," he mumbled.

Maggie sat back on her knees, and pushed her hair back. "Thank God. What happened? I heard you call 'help me' and I woke up."

Jack turned his head toward her, still too weak to raise his body. "I just had a bad dream."

"Bull. You were nearly dead. I could barely find a pulse. I don't know how I heard you."

He closed his eyes. Oh lordy, she'd heard his mental cry for help inside her head. His balminess was contagious. He and this sheila had forged some kind of psychic bond, and now she had a window to the crazy mind of Jaguar Jack Campbell.

Wonder how she was going to like that bit of news?

Chapter Twenty-Two

Thunder rumbled in the distance, a storm on the other side of the mountain. Maggie shifted in her sleeping bag, vaguely aware of something missing. She reached behind her for the warm reassuring presence against her backside. The empty space felt wrong as she reached consciousness. Jack was gone.

As she sat up, a clacking sound captured her attention. In the grey pre-dawn light, Jack wielded two bare branches as make-shift weapons. Executing a series of martial-arts maneuvers, he reminded her of a deadly ballet dancer, full of grace and danger.

"What are you doing?" she croaked, morning still caught in her throat.

He ignored her, concentrating on an invisible opponent. He spun and lunged, deep in a discipline of ancient warfare. She rose from their resting place, fully dressed as always in the field.

When she approached Jack's training ground, he tossed her one of the staffs. "Morning, Red. How are you at hand to hand combat?"

She balanced the pole between her arms and assumed a fighting stance. "I may not be a black belt, but I might show you a move or two."

He grinned, but a lethal sparked gleamed in his eye. "You are a bonzer woman."

And then he attacked. She parried his weapon and turned away. The soldier in her awakened, and she went on the offensive. The clash of their staffs woke the birds and scattered the reptiles.

Maggie held her ground against this intense Jack, this warrior Jack —the one she'd only glimpsed beneath the TV hero surface. Something in the night had called him forth. Her concentration broke as she remembered his lifeless form beside the fire, a body without a soul. What had happened?

Her momentary lapse cost her. With a series of fast attacks, he cornered her against a massive tree trunk. Their crossed weapons pinned her in place. His eyes possessed a predator's intent.

A shiver ran down her spine. "What's up with you this morning, Jack?"

He had that Twilight Zone look in his eyes again. "We have to be ready. Have to stay in shape. The time is approaching."

His cryptic response brought more questions than answers. "Are we talking about Hannah's rescue or something else? What happened to you last night?"

"You wouldn't believe it if I told you." He stepped back and released her.

Her sharp reply froze on her tongue when she glimpsed armed militia emerging from the shadows. "Oh, cripes, we've got company."

Four AK-47's in the arms of native IMA forces stared them down.

Jack pivoted slowly and offered a full-wattage celebrity grin. "G'day, mates. May I interest you in a cup of java?"

***

After being stripped of her knife and side arm, Maggie managed to boil water and offer instant coffee to the men who traveled with their own rudimentary eating utensils, including cups. She wasn't exactly set up to hostess a tea party. As she hustled around the camp, she worried that the troops might interfere with their mission. Maggie and Jack didn't need to be detained, or worse, taken back to some IMA camp for questioning. And, Lord knew she didn't want to be forced to kill any IMA soldiers. She could just imagine the kind of international incident that would blow up if word got out an American Marine purposely took out friendly forces to perform a covert operation.

Jack's famous face worked to their advantage, not to mention his charm. When they started asking questions, Jack turned up his television persona full blast. He pulled out his video camera. "How would you blokes like to be on television? Come on now, General, hold this anole lizard for the camera."

Maggie relaxed a bit as she watched Jack perform his charismatic magic on the four young IMA grunts. They sat in a semi-circle around the fire, sipping coffee and posing for Jack's camera. One toyed with the knife Maggie generally kept strapped to her hip. She'd have to figure out a way to get that back, along with her weapon. She felt naked without them.

Jack turned TV director, and cajoled any hostility out of the undisciplined recruits. While he held their undivided attention, she loaded her backpack. She was about to stow the special audio equipment, when an older IMA soldier emerged from the foliage.

He barked orders to the men, who sprang to their feet and pulled their weapons once again.

"Crikey," Jack muttered. He sauntered toward the new arrival. "Hello, mate, you must be the head honcho. Jack Campbell is the name. Maybe you've heard of me, Jaguar Jack Campbell? The missus and I were just taking a little jungle honeymoon, and filming a new segment for me show."

Maggie barely kept her eyes from rolling. Holy cats, Jack had them married. Well, considering she might be up for grabs and be forced to whip some IMA ass if these guys had been away from the mainland for too long, she thought Jack's improvisation a smart move. The IMA commander stood stony faced. The stocky Asian obviously didn't buy their honeymoon story. His gaze roved suspiciously around the campsite.

Maggie stood still, holding a backpack and the green audio equipment bag. The commander's stare zeroed in on it.

He barked an order for one of the soldiers to get it.

She couldn't give up the equipment. The success of the mission hinged on Maggie sending the location coordinates to Derby and Chris. The underling started to bear down on her across the campsite.

She sent Jack a wordless message: *Sorry, Jack, gotta run.*

He nodded and, swear to God, she thought she heard him say, *Go, Red. I'll take care of these blokes.*

But his lips never moved.

She flung the backpack at the approaching soldier and knocked him in the stomach, catching him off-guard. Then clutching the precious equipment bag, she dashed for cover in the jungle.

Gunfire erupted. She ran, jumped, zigzagged through an endless green leafy sea. Face slapped by vines and branches, she charged ahead, listening for the noise of armed pursuers. Blasts of bullets, the howls of angry monkeys gave her a pretty good idea where they were. No wonder the Sons of Allah always managed to get away. These guys moved through the jungle like a herd of elephants.

Maggie charged uphill into changing terrain. Bare rock jutted from the earth. The soggy jungle floor gave way to stonier ground, cutting down the density of plants. Monster ferns towered twenty feet in the air while scrubby bushes grew in the cracks of the rocky terrain. Early morning sun raised a fog as the night dew evaporated. Maggie slowed down. Heavy mist provided an excellent cover.

The fog also muffled sounds, but she sensed the troops turning away from her. A stand of blue-gray boulders offered protection. She sat her butt down on the pebbly ground and caught her breath. She gulped in air that tasted of metallic rock and earth. Thick air limited visibility to a few yards. Rough trunks of scrawny trees, and the outlined mounds of rocks in the mist, lent an otherworldly atmosphere to the surrounding.

She leaned her head back on the jagged boulder. Well, the good news was it appeared she'd lost the soldiers; the bad news was she'd also lost Jack. She imagined him, even now, walking before an IMA recruit with a rifle pointed at his back. Of course, Marvel Man might have gotten away. For an instant she really thought she heard him in her mind and made her move. *How weird was that?*

And now she was on the assignment alone, without weapons, a compass or any real idea where Hannah Smith might be. Still, she wasn't being held prisoner. Things could be worse.

"Rroww!"

Things got worse. Maggie startled at the cat howl directly behind her. She looked over her shoulder and saw the black tail of a large jaguar whipping in agitation, pacing on the rocks above her.

She froze. Maybe it hadn't seen her.

The cat screeched again, sprang off the ledge and landed directly in front of her. Its sleek, long body paced the ground, trapping her against the rocks. She drew her legs up and hunched down as much as possible, peeking at the feline between the V of her clenched kneecaps.

The jag revealed long, carnivore teeth as she hissed and uttered a low growl.

Think fast, think fast. Can't run...Should I fight?

Maggie didn't think she was a match for six feet of brawny cat, complete with lethal teeth and claws.

She couldn't be sure, but this might be the same animal that attacked their campsite—the old girlfriend of Jack's. Its yellow eyes glowed in the black face, boring into Maggie's soul.

That cat wants to scratch your eyes out. The thought came out of the blue, sure and strong.

Maggie raised her head, and engaged the animal in a staring contest of wills. She felt compelled to speak out loud. "Forget it, sweetheart. I'll kick your furry ass clear to the next island. Scram."

"Rroww!"

Maggie began to inch her back up the rough support at her spine. She might have a chance if she kicked her feet. The jag appeared ready to pounce at any moment.

Just as it crouched, a blur of white feathers swooped from the jungle, squawking, "Crikey, mate!"

Maggie stood up. Lorelei. She couldn't believe it.

Next, the famous Aussie Abo battle cry and a rattle of leaves heralded Jack's entrance. He charged the jag like a madman. A gorgeous, stubble-chinned action hero.

Startled by all this lunacy, the jag backed up, whipped her tail in irritation, and loped off. Her big paws barely made a sound as she disappeared into the fog.

Jack stood in the clearing, surrounded by mist, the sort of special effects usually produced by dry-ice machines. But this was real, and Jack had thrown himself into harm's way for her.

He gave her a lopsided smile. "You all right, Red?"

Maggie's knees felt a bit shaky. Was it the chase, the jag, or Jack's sapphire eyes? She took a deep breath. "Yeah, I'm fine."

He walked over and gripped her upper arms. "You're sure?"

The protective concern in his eyes unnerved her—made her feel distinctly female. "How did you know where I was?"

Jack frowned. Should he tell her? Should he say, *I'm attached to you now. I'll always know where you are.*

He shrugged. "Lucky guess."

He wrapped his arm around her shoulders as they started to walk up the hill. She turned her head toward him. "Jack, I had the strangest experience. When I was looking at that cat, I swear I knew what she was thinking."

Jack winked at her. "I wouldn't share that with too many people, Red. They'll think you're balmy."

Chapter Twenty-Three

Hannah held Amelia's hand as they headed for the swollen stream to bathe. Felipe followed as their guard, casually dangling his rifle. The sunny, steamy morning offered relief after the tumultuous storm of the night before.

Thanks to a batik wraparound skirt called a malong, the women could maintain a modicum of modesty by washing and dressing inside the confines of the malong. That simple garment also served as a pouch for carrying items, or a flimsy makeshift pillow. Hannah handled her malong with care.

She clutched a precious bottle of shampoo. A new shipment of supplies had arrived with a few of the things on her list. Earlier this morning, she shared her cheese crackers and peanut butter with Amelia. Small items from the outside world became rare treasures. She forced down her desire to horde. The fear of deprivation brought out the worst in people, including herself. She constantly fought selfishness, resentment, and anger. Some days she lost the battle.

But, not today. Today the sun sparkled and Amelia had turned to her. Today she wasn't alone.

This morning she enjoyed respite from the constant sessions with Saeed. He sent word that they wouldn't be meeting. He and his guards remained cloistered in their part of the compound, deep in some sort of session. That was a real *praise-the-lord* as far as Hannah was concerned. Moktar's men cleared away fallen branches and limbs that littered the camp after the storm.

For Hannah, it felt almost like a holiday. After bathing, she, Amelia, and Felipe sat under a tree and talked. Actually, Amelia and Felipe talked. Hannah listened to them share their stories of living in poor villages. How could she compare her life of luxury as the daughter of a Washington politician? Contrasts in their lives seemed planets apart.

Threads of attraction began to weave between Felipe and Amelia. He'd watched her from afar, smiling shyly when he brought them a meal. A pretty girl in a camp of almost all men was under constant scrutiny. Hannah didn't know why Amelia hadn't been sexually assaulted, but it probably had something to do with Ahmed's plans. Last night's scene in the tent made Hannah think of human sacrifice, especially since Corazon had not returned. Hannah knew some cults didn't confine themselves to the sacrifice of chickens. And she wouldn't put anything past Ahmed Saeed. She shivered, even in the humid warmth.

Laughter between Felipe and Amelia brought back her attention. Felipe gazed at Amelia with cow eyes, even as she blushed at his attention. Hannah couldn't help but smile. Even in the midst of terrorists and fanatics, a couple could fall in love. And with that, Hannah felt a ray of hope.

***

Jack and Maggie moved faster without the burdensome packs of equipment. Once Maggie had made a run for it at the camp, Lorelei had swooped at the IMA's heads, causing enough of a distraction to make the shots go wild and allow Jack to escape. All their possessions, except the audio equipment and Jack's pocketknife, had been left behind. Maggie felt disgruntled without her weapons.

They made the summit of the mountain by early afternoon. Lying on their bellies to avoid detection, they had a panoramic view of the east side of the island clear to the ocean. Trees formed an interesting canopy, growing tall, but avoiding touching each other, leaving an airy outline in the sky. Sunlight and shadow created a mosaic effect under the leafy umbrella.

The coastline appeared to be a series of sharp cliff drop-offs. Maggie couldn't see an access to the shore. She scanned the area for signs of human life, but it all looked like virgin wilderness from their vantage point.

"What do you think, Jack?"

He seemed to be tuning into his alternate universe channel, getting that glassy look in his eye. Funny, it used to give her the creeps and now she found it sort of comforting, like a secret weapon.

He pointed toward the north. "I think there's a cove right over there for them to get on and off the island by boat. Makes sense that their camp would be in that direction. Think I'll send Lorelei to scope it out."

"Oh, so now you're admitting you can communicate with her."

Jack shrugged. "You've found me out, Red." He sent her a knowing glance. "Besides, there's getting to be fewer and fewer secrets between us all the time."

She flushed, remembering the episode of the night before when she'd fallen apart in his arms. How deep did Jack's psychic powers go? Was he a Peeping Tom of the mind?

Lorelei proved to be a damn good scout. She led Maggie and Jack right to the terrorist camp. Night was falling. Smoke from several small cook fires hazed the air. Maggie's stomach growled. She and Jack subsisted on edible plants and fruits throughout the day, but a greasy hamburger dripping in mustard and ketchup washed down by a cold beer would really hit the spot.

The two huddled flat on their bellies, surveying the lay of the land. Jack nudged her, and silently pointed at a bored guard who paced the clearing perimeter. She'd also assessed the slack security.

Two tents, one appreciably larger than the other, were set up at opposite ends of the compound. The smaller of the tents looked like it had seen better days, with noticeable rips and tears. There appeared to be some sort of segregation. Asian men dressed in assorted rag-tag clothes milled in one area. Hammocks hung suspended between trees. The other men, congregated near the large tent, wore the long one-piece garments of Arabs, which Maggie thought must have been inconvenient in the jungle setting.

The flap of the larger tent opened. Maggie tensed when she recognized Ahmed Saeed dressed like the Sheik of Araby in the middle of the friggin' jungle. She wanted to spring forward, and attack the son of a bitch. Her powerlessness to do anything but lie on the fetid jungle floor and watch the scene unfold sent her blood pounding in frustration.

Jack placed a calming hand on her shoulder. She turned her head and looked into his Aussie eyes. *Don't get your knickers in a knot, Red. We'll get the bloke.* His lips never moved, but she could have sworn she heard him speak. Oh man, she must have eaten some hallucinogenic berries or something.

Turning her attention to the camp, there was no sign of Hannah Smith. Was she in one of the tents? Maggie would have to find out to give Chris and his team good intel for a successful mission.

A boyish guard spooned something out of a cooking pot onto two banana leaves and carried it into the smaller tent. Maggie would have bet her Aunt Fanny that Hannah was in that tent. When night fell she just might have to take a closer look to know for sure.

***

Jack and Maggie retreated far enough away from their observation point that they could talk without fear of discovery. They found a small stream and thankfully drank from the running water as they sat and discussed how to proceed.

Maggie said, "I need to be sure Hannah is there. We can't risk an international incident by attacking on foreign soil without positive identification."

"If we bide our time watching the camp, we're bound to see who they've got stashed in the smaller tent." Jack leaned back on the bank against the exposed roots mingled in the earth.

"We've run out of time. If their threats hold true, they are going to start sending body parts out as incentive for their ransom demands."

Jack sighed. His midnight blue eyes brooded. "I know what you want to do, Red, and it's too dangerous."

"What are you, a mind reader?" She leaned over her crossed-legs. "Okay, you're so smart. What do I want to do?"

"You want to go back under the cover of darkness, crawl on your belly like a snake and sneak into the tent right under the nose of the bloody terrorists."

Maggie blinked. "That's right." She frowned. Jack really creeped her out sometimes. "Okay, well, lucky guess. But don't you see, that's the best way to verify the hostage?"

"I see it's the best way for you get your arse in a sling." He sat up. "If you get caught, I don't have a small army behind me to get you out. A lone television star and a cockatoo isn't very good back up, Red."

She crossed her arms. "I'm sure as heck not going to let you go. You have no training for this kind of maneuver."

Jack nervously tapped a hand on his thigh, as he stared off, thinking. "Let's send in Lorelei. I've seen her open and close her cage door. She'll be able to slip into the flap of a tent. She'll see who's in there, and send me a mental picture when she gets back."

"You have got to be kidding me, right? You expect me to send in the forces of the United States Marine Corps, based on the impressions you think you pick up from the mind of a cockatoo?"

"She's gotten us this far, hasn't she?"

Maggie rolled her eyes. "I'll admit we've made good time getting here based on what you think she's told you. But it also makes logical sense that they'd be camped in this vicinity for access to the ocean. So,

I'm not putting a hundred percent faith in what very well may be simply delusions on your part."

An expression of dark steel transformed Jack's face. The teasing TV star had been replaced by a man of danger, a man with a secret.

He gripped her arms. "You think I'm delusional, Red? Well, believe me, I wish it were only delusions when I see the pain or tragedy that has passed through someone's life. Like the way Ahmed Saeed laughed at you when he took off in a helicopter after he had gunned down Al-Jabbar."

Maggie gasped. "How?—"

Jack continued, relentlessly. "You blame yourself for being just a minute too late to prevent those needless deaths. You let the bad guys win that day because you hadn't driven the jeep across the desert fast enough. You hadn't run those long legs hard enough to get your weapon within firing range. Saeed mowed down your friend as he shielded a hysterical woman he was rescuing from the bombed out building where the hostages had been kept. You held him in your arms as he bled to death, and you wanted to scream, rage and cry. But you wouldn't let yourself, not Maggie Savannah, toughest lady Marine in the whole bloody Corps."

Maggie trembled. Her body felt icy cold despite the humid air that surrounded her. Jack slowly released his grip, but continued staring into her soul. His recitation was far more than a lucky guess. He knew her guilt, the emotions she worked hard at hiding from the world.

Her eyes pooled with unshed tears. "You're a mind fucker, Jack."

"So do we send Lorelei to find Hannah Smith?"

Maggie took a deep breath, and struggled to stop the quaking in her gut. "Fine. We'll play it your way. Just promise me you won't tell Chris Matthews that I got my intel from a damn bird."

Chapter Twenty-Four

They made their way back to the camp under the veil of darkness. Lorelei rode on Jack's shoulder. His claim to have the night vision of a cat proved to be true. Either that or he was half bat. At this point, Maggie wouldn't have been surprised by anything.

Most of the inhabitants were asleep. Dozing forms dangled in hammocks. A group of three Asian fighters sat around a small campfire, playing some sort of game of chance they'd fashioned with pebbles. A solitary guard stood leaning half-asleep against a tree, his weapon slung over his shoulder.

Surrounded by greenery, Jack knelt next to Maggie in the shadows. Lorelei side stepped along his forearm. Man and bird stared at each other in silent communion. Then the bird took to the air, the sound of her wings making a *thwat, thwat, thwat* noise that quickly faded. Maggie felt absurdly anxious for the creature. Since when did she worry about a cockatoo?

Peeking through palm fronds, Maggie and Jack crouched shoulder to shoulder as the bird made her flight. The white feathers were easy to spot. Too bad they couldn't have darkened her for the mission. She circled above the camp, as if chasing darting insects, then landed on the tent canvas.

Maggie held her breath, watching the bird cling to the canvas with sharp talons attempting to nose her way inside. Finding the opening proved difficult.

"Come on, baby, come on," Maggie silently mouthed.

She felt Jack's tension beside her. He seemed tight as a bow about to shoot an arrow.

"Mira!" One of the three fighters playing with pebbles pointed at Lorelei. The trio talked a string of Spanish and then began pelting poor Lorelei with their rocks. Evidently using the bird as target practice seemed like a fun way to break their boredom.

"Squawk!" Lorelei slipped her grip.

The soldiers laughed. Fortunately most of the rocks missed their mark, but a couple smacked her hard.

"Crikey, mate!" Lorelei abandoned the tent, and flapped toward the assailants. Now they'd made her mad. Lorelei attacked. She wasn't exactly lethal, but her swoops toward the men sent them diving for cover, and laughing even harder. Maggie wondered if they'd been sharing a pint of jungle juice.

The guard left his post to see what the commotion was all about.

Maggie saw her opportunity and seized it. Before Jack could stop her, she slithered into the undergrowth and moved with reptilian speed toward the back of the tent. The crazy antics of the cockatoo provided enough distraction for the Marine to enter hostile territory undetected.

As Lorelei circled around the camp, Maggie pulled out Jack's pocketknife, enlarged a tear in the canvas and dove into the interior.

Dim lantern light illuminated the space. Maggie held the knife defensively as she stood to assess the situation.

Seated on the cot, Hannah Smith blinked, wide-eyed with surprise. Beside her in his long flowing robe, staring down his hawk-nose, stood the unforgettable figure of Ahmed Saeed.

Ahmed lifted one eyebrow. "Hannah, you appear to have a visitor. If memory serves me, this is Major Maggie Savannah of the United States Marine Corps. If you've come to rescue Miss Smith, you are not only clumsy, you are late. Tell her, Hannah."

The initial surprise faded from Hannah's face, replaced by a dull, slack jaw droop. Her shoulders slumped.

Hannah's voice held no emotion, and her eyes appeared unfocused. "I don't want to go home. I must serve the Master."

Chapter Twenty-Five

Jack was steamed. Feeling impotent and immobile, he cast about in his mind for a plan. What in blue blazes should he do now? He'd lost sight of both Maggie and Lorelei. The thought of Maggie getting captured by these bastards made his blood boil. Not to mention, his precious bird might at this very moment be nothing but a heap of lifeless feathers on the jungle floor. All was quiet in the tent, so he could only pray that Maggie would soon exit the way she entered and crawl undetected back to him.

No such luck. Maggie exited the tent through the main flap, hands bound, followed by none other than Ahmed Saeed himself. Wasn't that bloody loverly?

Saeed barked orders to his minions, mobilizing them into action. Where one Marine existed, others must follow. The camp sprang to life.

Maggie's hands might be bound, but that didn't stop her mouth from working. "How do you sleep at night, Saeed? Don't the faces of all the people you've butchered come and haunt your dreams?"

Jack's gut cramped. Maggie's mouth would be her downfall. He had to get her out of there before she got herself beaten to a pulp, or worse. The thought of her lovely skin covered in bruises made him want to dash in and fight off the Al-Qaeda alone.

Think, Jack, think.

He needed assistance. He decided to retreat, and see if he could raise the Marines on Maggie's magical audio equipment. He bent down, picked up the pack and turned to edge away.

A familiar *thwat, thwat, thwat* reached his ears. Lorelei!

Sure enough, white wings glided toward him. She landed on his shoulder, rubbed her beak against his chin and cooed. He petted her thinking, *darlin, darlin' cockie.*

Then he froze as leaves and branches rustled, advancing toward him. The foliage parted, revealing the unmistakable stocky figure of Moktar, pointing a rifle at television's hottest hero. For a moment, the two simply stared at each other.

A band of rebels searching for Maggie's cohorts beat through the perimeter, approaching. *My arse is in a sling now.* Moktar lifted a finger to his lips, indicating silence. The kidnapper yelled at the unseen troops in Spanish, sending them in another direction. Then, amazingly, he lowered his weapon and smiled, white teeth visible in the moonlight.

Motioning Jack to follow, they wound their way through the jungle, away from the patrols. When they had gotten out of harm's way, Moktar leaned against a banana tree, pulled out a cigarette and lit it. He offered one to Jack. Though he didn't smoke, Jack thought the gesture of camaraderie promising. He grabbed the cig and tried not to choke.

Appearing nonchalant and confident, he blew smoke. "Long time no see, Moktar. How's the kidnapping business? Taken in some new partners, haven't you? The fucking Jihadists."

"You are looking good, Jack. I recognized your bird from our last visit. Only one cockatoo in the world yells 'Crikey, mate.' What you doing here, Jack?"

Jack considered lying, but couldn't come up with anything plausible. The old I'm-filming-my-TV-show wouldn't work, as he'd lost his camera. And, Maggie was obviously known to Saeed as a Marine. The fact that Jack wasn't bound and gagged next to Maggie right now stirred his curiosity.

"I'm acting as a reluctant guide. Seems you kidnapped the daughter of a very important person, and the US government is none too happy about it."

Moktar threw down his cigarette butt and cursed in his native tongue. "How long before the troops arrive?"

Ah, now here was a good spot for a lie. "They're on their way. I phoned in the coordinates."

Moktar scratched his stubbly chin. "You want to live, Jack? You want the long-legged redhead to live?"

"Seems like a good idea. What have you got in mind?"

***

Maggie sat on the spongy jungle floor, hands tied behind her back and tethered to a scratchy palm. Dawn was still a while off. Dying fires, old cigarettes and jungle rot permeated the air. She studied her gray-green surroundings.

Anticipating an imminent military invasion, the camp hustled with the efficiency of rebels familiar with sudden departure. She noted the

Asians appeared faster on their feet than the Arabs. Saeed issued terse orders, sending his men into action.

He turned and strode across the compound to her. "We've not located your companions, Major. But we will. You are putting us to great inconvenience. Still, I look forward to the instructional video we will make of your final moments for Internet viewing. The Crusaders will see what happens to harlots of the West."

Details of reports filed on Saeed's previous handling of prisoners sent a lump to her stomach. He used electric prods with diabolical imagination. Still, she sucked up some bravado. "The American military is going to be all over your ass like a nest of angry wasps. Hey, I think I hear the Black Hawks now."

Ahmed glanced toward the sky. Yeah, he wasn't as cool as he put on. He darted his gaze back to her like a lethal spear. "I look forward to personally supervising your purging."

He left her to complete his moving preparations. She knew she was living on borrowed time. Her last transmission to Matthews had been some distance from the camp. She prayed Jack managed to send off another one when the satellites were in position.

She'd been assigned one guard whose gaze roved the perimeter as the camp hustled behind him.

She wiggled, ropes cutting into her wrists, but couldn't get them to give. Damn, she hated feeling helpless. But at least she had hope. Okay, the fact her hope lay in the form of a cocky TV star and a cockatoo was a little loony. But Jack, with his cat vision and otherworldly insights might just save her bacon. At least he hadn't gotten caught. Way to go, Jack.

Of course, to her knowledge, he had no weapons. Not even the pocketknife she had purloined from him. So, how he would carry out a rescue was anybody's guess. Maybe he could do the Tarzan thing, yodel like Carol Burnett, and send a herd of elephants through the camp. But she doubted Paradisio had any elephants.

A swaggering, long-haired Asian she recognized from intel photos as Moktar emerged from the jungle and approached her guard. He engaged the underling in conversation, pointed across the camp, and ordered him away. Moktar pulled a long dagger from his belt and bent over Maggie. She winced, flashing gruesome thoughts of Moktar the Beheader. But he whacked the ropes at her wrists, and yanked her up. He tugged her into the jungle interior, leaving behind the camp confusion. Freedom felt much better than being hogtied, so she followed along without hesitation, waiting for a moment to break loose from his grip.

They rounded a massive trunk and suddenly Jack's face was close enough to kiss. She gasped in surprise as Moktar released her arm, and Jack grabbed her shoulders.

She said, "Ja--"

He squelched her word with a quick, fierce kiss, and a million-dollar grin.

Moktar thrust a rifle into each of their hands and beckoned them to follow. Holy shit, this was an interesting turn of events.

Jack's laser eyes beamed into her. *Stay close, Red.*

Damn, it happened again. That weird mind-read thing. Plus, she could also sense his concern, and a trace of anger. She didn't have time to analyze these strange happenings at the moment. But later, she and Jungle Man would have a heart-to-heart.

They made their way around the back of Hannah's tent. The slit Maggie had cut earlier gaped open. Hannah's subjugation appeared so complete, Saeed had no fear of her escape. Moktar gestured Jack and Maggie inside the tent, while he approached a nearby tree to relieve himself and keep casual watch.

Maggie followed Jack into the tent. While there were two cots in the space, only one was occupied. Jack approached Hannah's sleeping form. Her blond hair fanned out over the cot, visible in the emerging light. Despite the outside clamor, her soft, rhythmic breathing marked what appeared to be contented sleep, or perhaps exhaustion or even drugs. Hannah's words rang in Maggie's ears, *I must serve the Master.*

What the hell did that mean?

Jack placed a hand over Hannah's mouth, and gently shook her shoulder with his other hand. Her eyes flew open. Fear and confusion filled their blue depths.

Jack whispered, "It's all right, darlin'. We're getting you out of here."

Instead of taking this as good news, Hannah stiffened and struggled against Jack's restraint. He pulled his hand away.

Hannah whispered with urgency. "No, I can't leave. I must serve the Master."

"Bloody hell," Jack murmured.

Cripes, he actually seemed to know what she was talking about. Maggie had clearly been left out of some loop. But there wasn't time to talk about it now. She tugged at Hannah's hand.

Escape now, talk later.

Hauled to her feet, Hannah tried to disengage her hand from Maggie. "No! Please I don't want to be responsible for you, too. Please go away."

She's going to have the whole friggin' camp converge on us, Maggie thought. The five foot two American missionary struggled against her rescuers. *Okay Hannah, I hate to do this, but it's for your own good.* Maggie formed a fist and popped Hannah in the jaw.

She moaned and would have collapsed, but Jack caught her. "Nice right jab, Red. Let's go."

Ducking down, he carried Hannah's limp body out the back of the tent as Maggie retrieved the rifles and the audio equipment. Just as she was hauling ass behind Jack, the front flap of the tent opened, revealing a young Asian girl. The two women stared at each other for a moment. Maggie thought she was in the clear.

But then, whether the girl meant to do it or not, her surprise overcame her silence and she screamed.

Maggie pushed out of the tent into the open. Jack had flung Hannah over his shoulder.

Moktar nodded his head. "Go!"

Jack, carrying Hannah, ran with Maggie close on his heels. She held one rifle ready to fire, the other kept in reserve. Moktar covered their backs. Soon shouts and shots echoed from the camp.

Zing! Ping! Crack!

Running with greyhound speed, Jack seemed to know where he was going. Thank God for his muscle-bound upper body strength. Hannah's weight didn't faze him a bit. Rifle fire exploded the audio equipment bag dangling at Maggie's hip. She zigzagged and dove for the densest cover possible, keeping Jack in her sights. Returning fire would only slow them down, and she might hit Moktar in the process.

Had Moktar suddenly turned into one of the good guys? Yeah, right. But, he appeared to be their ticket out of here.

More rifle fire sounded from behind them. Moktar must have engaged their pursuers, buying them time. Maggie had no chance to assess their position. Morning mist hovered over the jungle floor, making the air heavy, dense to the lungs. They dashed through a green blur obstacle course-- shadows, roots, slapping branches.

Jack moved like a stealthy jungle animal, even with his missionary burden. Hannah's head flapped over his back like a rag doll. Jeez, hopefully Miss Moffett was still alive. Maggie made sure she'd pulled her punch.

Maggie huffed as they climbed. The air hinted of a change of scenery. A salty scent of sea clued her to their direction. They were heading for the cove. The ground grew rockier, the plants less dense. The gunfire more distant.

Jack rounded a protruding hunk of lava and disappeared from view. She pushed her aching calves to complete the sharp ascent. Her hands reached out for the black rock. She raised herself to its level, and stepped around it.

Jack stood, panting, leaning one shoulder against it, Hannah still secure and unconscious over the other shoulder. The strong sea breeze hit Maggie's skin as she edged next to Jack, and looked out over the panorama.

They stood at the edge of the island. A rising sun revealed jungle behind them, churning sea before them. White caps slapped the volcanic walls of the island, slowly wearing it away through the eons of time. Brilliant blue sky met an emerald sea at the horizon. Jagged cliffs curved as far as the eye could see.

Maggie caught her breath and said, "So what do we do now, Jack? Jump?"

Looking down at the turbulent ocean smacking into the rocks far below, Maggie thought of Butch Cassidy and the Sundance Kid leaping into a roaring river gorge.

Jack gave her the hero's grin. "You might even do it, wouldn't you, Red? You are really something. But, we're walking. Come on."

He edged his way along the ridge, and spotted the beginning of a tiny trail Maggie would never have seen. They descended a series of switchbacks down the side of the cliff.

Loose rocks skittered under their feet as they took the trail too fast, running for their lives. Distant shots sounded closer, but none blasted around them. Curves in the rocky wall obscured their view of the shoreline. Maggie wasn't sure there was any kind of beach. Only violent waves churned below. Down and down they went. She concentrated on keeping her feet on the narrow path. God love Jack, he kept his balance while carrying Hannah's dead weight.

Jack felt every bit of that dead weight in his back and legs. He hoped memory and instincts were leading them in the right direction. They rounded a curve, now only about ten feet above the water, and saw the small cove before them. A good sized cruiser floated over its anchor smack dab in the middle of it. Gleaming blue, white, and chrome sparkled in the morning light.

All they had to do was get down the rest of the way, cross a sandy little beach and swim to salvation. He wondered if Hannah could rouse enough to help swim the distance.

Ping! A bullet ricocheted off the wall. Moktar was running full tilt toward them from the other side of the cove, followed by the rebels. He managed to find cover from various rock formations, and get off a few shots. Answering fire went wild and exploded near Jack and Maggie. While Jack struggled to manage the last few feet to the ground without dropping Hannah, Maggie jumped down and ran over the rocky terrain to a small rise of boulders. She raised a rifle in position, and proceeded to pick off some of Moktar's pursuers, forcing the others to scatter and run for cover.

Sensing his chance, Moktar sped toward the slapping waves on the beach. He yelled at the boat. A small launch soon headed toward the shore.

Jack grunted as he negotiated uneven ground to get Hannah into the small boat.

Behind him, Maggie still lay shooting at the rebels, drawing their fire.

"Red!" he yelled. "Get your arse in the boat!"

Moktar had climbed in and told his man to go.

"Wait, you bastard!" Jack said.

"Go!" Moktar ordered.

Jack grabbed the pistol strapped to Moktar's belt, and pointed it at the swarthy sailor.

"Wait!" He leveled the pistol.

Maggie rose and ran for the launch, shooting as she went. Her boots hit the water. The boat wobbled as she flopped in and stayed low.

She looked up at Jack, seated upright, and yanked his arm. "Get down, you dumb Aussie." She yelled at the boat operator. "What the hell are you waiting for? Go!"

Jack hovered next to Maggie, his pistol useless in his hand as Maggie aimed her rifle and continued to shoot at the terrorists now running towards them into the water. He might be good at handling a boa constrictor, but actually shooting a gun at men was not in his experience. She, on the other hand, had gone into soldier mode and efficiently went about her business. Crimson spurts hit white sand as men collapsed.

The boat lurched off, sending an arc of spray over the passengers, taking them out of firing range. Frustrated shouting of the rebels carried across the water.

Jack vaulted onto the cruiser, carried Hannah below, and placed her on a padded bench. He checked her eyes. Drugged. She slept on. He needed to make sure Maggie was safely aboard. He wouldn't put it past Moktar to leave her behind.

He found her standing aft staring at the group of terrorists gathered on the beach, tending their wounded and dead. Ahmed Saeed stood facing the boat, water lapping his feet, locked in visual contact with Maggie.

What was it between these two? Maggie's cold, iron expression reflected the icy thoughts he picked up from her mind. She was a seething statue.

More disconcerting, he could see the kind of death Saeed would impose on her--slow, tortuous in a dank, hot room. The image shook him to his core. He had to break the contact.

He grabbed Maggie and spun her toward him. "Don't go down that road, Red. Revenge only turns back on you." Her hollow eyes alarmed him; he shook her. "Let it go. Be grateful we escaped with Hannah, and got out in one piece."

She blinked. Warmth replaced the ice in her eyes; a smile lifted her lips as she emerged from her daze. Her arms wrapped around him. "We did it, Jack!"

The engine roared to life, and the boat took off. Jack and Maggie huddled closer in each other's embrace.

"Crikey,mate!" A familiar, sharp set of talons landed on Jack's shoulder.

He released Maggie and looked Lorelei in the eye. "Glad you could make it, darlin'. That was quite a show, wasn't it?"

He snagged an arm around Maggie, and watched Paradisio shrink as they sped away. Good riddance, he hoped he never had to go back.

Suddenly, an explosion rocked the air. Maggie reflexively clutched his chest. Together they turned their heads toward the source of the blast —the highest peak on the island. The volcano. A billow of steam and ash rose from its hellish core.

Maggie shuddered. "Jeez, it's like a sign or something."

Jack's eyes narrowed. A wave of psychic anger nearly knocked him off his feet. As a gray plume ate up the blue sky, he knew--

The Beast is not pleased.

Chapter Twenty-Six

The cruiser sped over open sea. Maggie planted her feet in the cabin, determined to get her sea legs. Hannah continued to slumber on the bunk. Maggie loosened the young woman's clothing. She appeared flushed and feverish. Maggie wiped a wet cloth over the missionary's face and exposed upper chest, then her hands and arms.

Was Hannah merely drugged, or had she slipped into a comfortable place of inaccessibility? Her cracked lips indicated dehydration. Maggie grabbed a bottle of water from the fridge and dribbled some liquid into her mouth. Hannah reflexively gulped and roused a bit, before drifting back into oblivion.

Maggie sighed. Time would tell if Hannah would wake up and be glad for the rescue, or continue with that I-must-serve-the-Master crap. Speaking of, she decided it was time to ferret out more information from Jack. Just what the heck was really going on here?

Leaving Hannah as comfortable as possible, Maggie climbed the steps back up deck, a rifle slung over her shoulder. Moktar and Jack sat on the aft deck sipping long necks, chummy as could be. Moktar's lackey manned the helm.

"Come join us, Major Savannah," Moktar said. "It is a great honor to entertain the United States Marine Corps."

Jack studied Maggie's face as she approached. Wary. Alert. Windblown. Her hair flew in wispy disarray. Irritated, she grabbed its unruly mass and contained it again in a thick black elastic band. She plunked her supple body next to Jack. The khaki material of her slacks and blouse showed stains and tears from their adventures. Still, she managed an almost aristocratic air of superiority as she gauged Moktar.

"Drink?" Moktar asked, indicating a cooler of assorted beverages. Maggie carefully removed a bottle of water, unscrewed the cap, and never took her gaze off the sweaty terrorist.

Maggie's assessment expanded to include Jack. "You two look like old buddies. Do you go way back? College roommates maybe?"

Jack and Moktar laughed. "What did I tell you, Moktar? The sheila has a bonzer sense of humor."

Moktar leaned back against the chrome railing. "A sense of humor is most necessary to get by in this world. Ahmed Saeed, for instance, is a humorless man. It will be his downfall."

"I saw him smile once," Maggie said.

Jack knew she remembered the cold smile on the bastard's face, after he'd killed Al-Jabbar and pulled away in the helo.

"He's a sick son of a whore, and untrustworthy business partner." Moktar spit over the side.

Maggie raised an eyebrow. "Birds of a feather, Moktar. Anyone care to enlighten me as to why we're here, and not chained to a tree in the jungle?"

Jack filled her in. "Seems Ahmed has a hidden agenda that doesn't include returning Hannah for ransom."

"Filthy mother-fucking goat!" Moktar exclaimed. "He used me to secure the most valuable hostage I've ever had. Even now, an American lawyer sits in a hotel ready to make the exchange, but Ahmed wouldn't let me take her out. He spends his days in her tent—talking, chanting, raving. At night, he and his followers disappear into the jungle to perform secret ceremonies. He turned my men against me—caught them under his power. They have weak minds. What can you expect?"

"So first *you* brainwashed them," Maggie said, "but later Saeed was a better spellbinder. That's why you needed Jack and me to get her out. So, what now? We've all got weapons. Do we start shooting, and see who the last man standing might be?"

Jack gave her arm a friendly pat. "Ah, Red, there's no need for military action. We're all reasonable people here. Moktar has to make a living."

Maggie pushed his hand off. "Kidnapping and killing is not making a living. The United States government does not negotiate with terrorists."

Jack glanced up to see Moktar's standover man aiming a pistol at Maggie's head. Her black-and-white American arrogance would get them both killed.

Jack assumed his most charismatic manner, put an arm around Maggie's shoulder and winked at Moktar. "Don't mind her, mate. She's a bit clucky, out-of-sorts. I'm sure we can work out an arrangement that will make all of us happy."

Moktar nodded his head. Wild black hair flew in the wind. "You have always kept your word, Jack. You are worthy fellow. I am worthy fellow."

Maggie snorted; Jack squeezed her in warning.

Moktar continued. "You keep your woman under control. When we arrive at mainland, we will exchange hostage for ransom. I let you live. Everyone will be happy." He stretched his arms. "I need to piss."

Moktar stood, and walked a distance away to relieve himself into the sea.

Maggie shook Jack off, and hissed. "I don't like this one bit. They are definitely the bad guys, Jack. We should be figuring out a way to neutralize them, not play patty cake with them."

"Take off the military mindset for a moment, Red, and use some common sense. Moktar is a professional kidnapper, not a religious fanatic. He'll only kill us if he has no choice. He knows I'm good for the protection money; I pay him to film segments of my show in his territories. If we try to take him or his man down, we're likely to get shot. He'll use Hannah against us, if he has the chance. Cooperation is the smart way to go here. He gets his money from Hannah's parents; Hannah goes home."

A dark shadow of doubt passed over Jack's mind. The Beast. How far did his influence go? Surely, the farther away from the island they went, the weaker the power.

Maggie chewed her lip. "This stinks. He shouldn't get a red cent. One condition. I don't leave Hannah's side until the exchange is made."

Jack sighed. He'd been looking forward to getting to shore, checking into a five star hotel and getting back to his TV star life. Guess his stint as a reluctant Marine wasn't over yet. "Make that *we* don't leave Hannah's side until the exchange is made. We started this together and we'll finish it together."

***

Below deck, Hannah tossed on her bunk, caught somewhere between darkness and light. Heaven and hell. Images floated in and out of her mind. Ahmed Saeed's face, the timbre of his voice, his coal-black relentless stare.

Amelia's expression, pleading and innocent.

A strange cat creature. Red glowing eyes.

A howl ripping the air.

Help me, Hannah…help me… Amelia's plea.
Return to me. Return to me.
The voice of the Master.

Chapter Twenty-Seven

Maggie lifted the window of a stifling, cheap Jakarta hotel room. Slightly cooler circulating air brought some relief, but, man, the street stench packed a wallop. As the afternoon sun beat on their third-floor cubicle of a room, she glanced over her shoulder at Hannah's feverish form lying on the double bed. Standing at the window, Maggie welcomed the sea breeze, even as she tried not to gag at the smell of fermenting fish heads, toasted dog-kabobs and human waste that wafted from the busy slum street below.

Moktar had stashed Hannah and Maggie in one of the few thousand ramshackle rooms rented by the hour in the city's dirtiest district. Clothes hung from bamboo poles stuck out of windows. A kaleidoscope of color met Maggie's eye when she gazed out the rectangular opening. Waving red, violet, blue, yellow shirts, skirts, and pants flapped over crumbling buildings. Garish signs on shops enticed customers to buy everything from dope to dungarees.

A tide of dark-haired humans crammed the avenue, walking, shopping, or riding bikes and scooters. Others squatted in clusters, talking, resting or arguing. Their chatter reached Maggie's ears in incomprehensible sing-song cacophony.

Though she hadn't liked being overtaken by Moktar's thugs upon arrival and kept prisoner, she begrudgingly admitted their treatment wasn't too bad. A shower in the communal bath down the hall and a fresh set of baggy cotton clothes, called pyjams, took the edge off her hostility.

Jack had been assigned the next room over, separated by a paper-thin wall. She could give them an adjoining suite with one swift kick. Whereas she'd been assigned two guards at her door, Jack had total freedom to come and go at will, which really ticked her off.

He'd sailed into her room with dinner, all chat and smiles, but answering very few of her questions. Certainly not heeding her demands to contact Chris Matthews, and let the Marines take over. Jack thought bringing in the military would only get them killed. She'd wanted to know what the plan was, how they were making the exchange.

"It's in the works, luv. It's in the works," was all he would say.

Maggie hated being in the dark. She'd been too tired to put the screws to Jack and throttle some answers out of him last night. But today was a different story. When he showed his famous face again, he wasn't charming his way out of telling her what the hell was going on.

To top it off, he'd left Lorelei in her care. Maggie had turned not only hostage-sitter, but *bird* sitter. And, darned, if she wasn't growing attached to the creature. Lorelei opened her beak for a grape while perched on the windowsill.

Maggie held her palm open for the bird to pick up the sweet fruits. "Your owner is going to have some 'splaining to do when he gets back."

Lorelei cooed.

Hannah stirred and moaned. Maggie walked across the room to her bedside. Eyelids fluttered open, cornflower blue coming into focus.

"It's about time, Sleeping Beauty," Maggie said.

Hannah gazed around the room, and finally settled on Maggie. "You're an American. Am I in an embassy?"

"Sorry, babe, this is the Rat and Roach Motel; complete with grimy walls and a picture of Jesus next to a topless movie star poster. We're working on getting you to improved quarters. Can you sit up and drink something?"

The missionary nodded and struggled to a sitting position as Maggie thrust some pillows behind her back. She slurped bottled water down her throat.

Hannah spoke from a groggy fog. "Where am I? What's going on? Where is Amelia?"

"Before we chat, how about you take a shower, put on fresh clothes and see about eating some solid food?"

Hannah's eyes lit up. "You know what I've been dreaming about for months?"

"What?"

"A Big Mac, fries and a coke."

Maggie smiled. "Spoken like a true American."

***

Maggie couldn't supply MacDonald's fare, but she was pleased to see Hannah chow down rice, vegetables and a mystery soup. Moktar's men understood her sign language enough to allow them the creature comforts they needed.

Hannah sat cross-legged on the bed in her clean cotton turquoise pyjams, eating rice with chopsticks like a native. Lorelei traversed the wrought iron headboard behind her, begging for bits of food. Maggie's body was wedged uncomfortably in the only chair in the room—a creaky wicker thing obviously made for small Asians, not tall Americans. Maggie explained the mission, and how they escaped the island. Hannah retained little memory of the past couple of days.

Maggie leaned forward. "You said something really strange when I entered your tent, and found you with Saeed. Do you remember?"

Hannah frowned and shook her head. "He must have been doping me up for some time. Seems like I've been in a dream."

"More like a nightmare. Do you remember saying, 'I have to serve the Master?'"

Hannah's hand froze in mid-air. Her face turned ashen. "The Master?"

"Am I ringing a bell here?"

"Saeed was always talking about the Master. He said so many things. It makes my head hurt to think about it." She pressed a palm to her temple.

Maggie didn't like the shaky way the girl looked. "Hey, forget it. That's all behind you. Whatever Saeed said, it was all lies."

Hannah's expression drifted far away. "The master of lies...or is it really the truth?" Tears suddenly welled in her eyes. "I'm very confused."

Maggie reached out and patted her knee. "You've had a helluva time. Saeed is a world-class brainwasher. You need to get some good counseling when you get back to the states."

"I suppose you're right." She smiled wanly and pushed her silky, straight blond hair over her shoulder. "I just don't feel like I'm supposed to go home yet. I haven't finished what I was meant to do."

"And what was that?"

"I'm not exactly sure. At first, I thought it was translating the Bible for the Acabans. But then after I got captured, I knew being a hostage was part of the plan. Maybe I was supposed to share my faith with some of the captors. But that never happened. Perhaps I've already completely failed."

"Look, you just got caught in the crossfire. Now you're out of it. Time to go home. The fate of the world does not rest on your shoulders." Wicker creaked as Maggie sought a comfortable position.

Hannah smiled. "I had a boyfriend who used to tell me that. When I talked about being a missionary, he'd say I was trying to save the world."

"Was he right?"

"Partially. I never thought I could save the world. But, I felt like I had a destiny to fulfill, a mission to accomplish." She frowned and seemed hesitant to speak her thoughts. "You'll probably think I'm crazy, but I thought I'd heard a voice telling me to go to Paradisio. It changed my whole life. Now, I'm not sure that it wasn't just a figment of my imagination."

"Honey, one thing this mission has taught me, is a lot of things that seem impossible or crazy are quite real." Her mind drifted to Jack's uncanny sixth sense, animal psychics, and weird mythical beasts. "Maybe you just don't have all the pieces of the puzzle yet. There's more happening on Paradisio than just a bunch of terrorists planning their next attack. From the hints Jack has been throwing at me, you'd think Paradisio is the gateway to hell or something."

Hannah frowned, repeating the phrase. "Gateway to hell…"

"Hey, eat. I can't deliver a malnourished missionary back to her VIP parents."

Hannah poked at her food, placed kernels of rice on her hand for Lorelei to peck. The bird seemed to be good therapy, rubbing her downy head against the young woman's cheek, bringing forth a gentle giggle.

Who would have thought that Hannah the Missionary would have something in common with Maggie the Marine? They'd both been giving their all to save the world. Hannah, because she felt some divine sense of destiny. Maggie, because she had been trained for it all her life. Maggie hadn't ever considered destiny, some grand plan. She'd just had a job to do.

Now, she and Hannah seemed to be suffering from a similar kind of burn out. Maggie had been fighting it, trying to maintain the fiery determination of the past, the confidence of her innate strength. She'd been so sure the world needed Maggie Savannah to protect it from the bad guys. But the bad guys were everywhere, and growing in numbers.

The excitement had worn thin, the sense of accomplishment fleeting, the purpose pointless.

Hannah laughed when Lorelei exclaimed her usual, "Crikey, mate!"

The effervescence of her pure spirit bubbled to the surface. For a moment, she nearly glowed. The tired, drugged, confused captive disappeared. "I never knew birds could be so smart, have so much personality."

"Yeah, she's growing on me, too," Maggie said.

Hannah smiled, a full-blown expression of joy. It took Maggie's breath away. She'd never experienced such joy, never sought it or seen the value in it. The blue-eyed delight reminded her of something. Of Jack when he saw a ruby-throated hummingbird, a rare flower, or even a shiny beetle. She'd thought he was some kind of nature nut.

But, now, she saw the rise in Hannah from despair to delight by the antics of a bird. Except, it wasn't really the bird. It was something else. Some secret Hannah knew. Jack knew it. Suddenly, with all her heart, Maggie wanted to know it, too.

Chapter Twenty-Eight

Jack thought his disguise quite ripping with his turban, fake beard, sunglasses, and typical white tunic worn by thousands of Muslims in the city. He blended right in, unless he opened his mouth and his Aussie accent gave him away.

Keep your bloomin' mouth shut, mate.

Moktar named him the Go-To Man to pick up the ransom money from the lawyer working for the Smiths. "You get money, Jack. If it's a trap, they catch you, not me or one of my men. You know nothing of my operation. They could interrogate you for days, and still get nowhere. Ha!"

Jack wanted to tell him to rack off, but Moktar threatened Maggie with nasty variations of bodily harm. Any hint of military or local police involvement, and Maggie's life wouldn't be worth a dead dingo. The thought of losing her bothered him more than he wanted to acknowledge. The threads of their bond spun stronger every day. When she walked out of his life, a chunk of him would go with her.

So that's how Jaguar Jack Campbell came to be walking down a seedy Jakarta alley. One of Moktar's men trailed him, none too discreetly. He hoped the bloke was an honorable thief, who wouldn't gut him for the payoff before Jack personally delivered it to the chief kidnapper.

He entered a combination coffee/cat house. The walls were decorated with red cloth that glinted with golden threads woven into intricate designs. Dim lanterns hung from the ceiling over small tables holding flickering votive candles and plastic ashtrays.

Sloe-eyed prostitutes congregated near a doorway adorned with a beaded curtain, concealing the staircase to the rooms where the girls earned their livings. Jack paused in the doorway surveying the area for a westerner sitting alone. Two dark-haired, ruby-lipped Oriental dolls clutched his arms.

"You come with us. Boom-boom, good time."

He shook them off. "Sorry girls. No boom-boom today."

The girls' faces transformed from enticing to hostile in the blink of an eye as they slunk back to their bored companions.

Jack recognized the bespectacled lawyer from a provided photograph. At the moment, the man appeared extremely uncomfortable seated at a corner table fending off his own boom-boom girl. The tart wasn't taking no for an answer. Jack crossed the room.

The lawyer squirmed under the unwelcome attention. "Really, miss, I'm just not interested."

She ran her blood-red nails down his pin-stripped suit. "Good fuckey-fuckey."

Jack threw her a coin. "Bug off, sweetheart. This is a private party."

With a flip of her hip, she sauntered away with a wink and a lick of her lips.

The pale lawyer wiped his brow with a handkerchief. "We couldn't have done this in the bar at the Hyatt-Regency?"

"Think of the story you can tell around the water cooler on the twenty-fifth floor of your Manhattan office building, mate." Jack settled into a chair.

The lawyer squinted at him. "You don't sound like any Arab I ever knew."

That's all he needed; some greedy, pasty-faced suit spilling his guts to the *National Enquirer* that Jaguar Jack worked for terrorists. His television show would be shot to hell.

He deepened his voice. "Just hand over the goods, pal, so we can get on with our lives. Where should we deliver the package?"

The lawyer pushed a wrapped parcel toward Jack with his foot. He gave Jack instructions to the hotel where Hannah's parents anxiously awaited the safe return of their daughter.

As Jack leaned over and grabbed the package, a large male customer jabbed him in the back while hurrying to a beckoning girl promising boom-boom. Jack's sunglasses flew from his face. He looked up at the lawyer.

Instant recognition registered behind the dark-rimmed lenses. "I'll be damned. Jaguar Jack Campbell. My wife makes me watch your stupid show every week. How in the world?..."

Jack's lips thinned in irritation. "Listen, mate, forget you ever saw me."

"You're a collaborator with terrorists?"

"It's not what you think."

The lawyer shook his head in disgust. "I've always thought you were a little crazy from watching you on television. But if you're aiding the Al-Qaeda, you're one sick bastard."

Oh great, Jack could see the headlines now: *Hottest Hero is a Terrorist*.

He leaned toward the lawyer with menace. "Don't go shooting your mouth off. If you Americans understood the cultures you deal with better, the world wouldn't be so mucked up. I was drafted into this situation against my will, and I'm doing my bloody best to return the package in one piece without starting another international incident."

Pale blue eyes widened behind the black rims. "Listen, I'm a lawyer. I know all about confidentiality."

Jack stood and took a step toward the door. "Glad to hear it."

The hairs on the back of Jack's neck rose. He sensed the danger just before it crashed into the room. Moktar's man and an Arab struggled in the throes of a life and death battle of knives and down-and-dirty street brawling. Chairs flew, girls screamed, daggers flashed.

The combatants dealt each other lethal wounds until they both staggered. Jack cast his lot with Moktar's man and bashed the Arab over the head with a table, bringing the blighter down. He rushed to the bleeding Asian and braced an arm around him.

The terrorist sank to his knees. "Saeed's men have arrived. They know where she is."

Jack gazed up at the lawyer who had edged his way across the room to them. "I've got to go."

He grabbed the package, and made a dash for the door. Damn, civilization was ten times more dangerous than the jungle.

***

As he dashed up the rickety hotel stairs, he heard scuffling in the hallway above. His feet hit the dirty green carpet, running toward the girls' room. Adrenaline shot into his blood stream as he imagined Maggie fighting off menacing Arabs with wicked daggers. He rounded a corner in time to see Moktar gut an Eastern-looking assailant with a long knife. Two henchmen disposed of the body.

Moktar looked up at Jack, grinning as he wiped his weapon on his trousers and replaced it in its sheath. "Foolish Saudi. He was no match for the son of a whore from Bangkok."

"One of Ahmed's men?"

Moktar nodded. "I have disposed of the traitors. This is the last. You had better get the missionary out of here as soon as possible. I do not think Ahmed is such a good loser. I myself am taking a long trip."

Jack tossed him the package. "Here's your traveling money. May you never have a day's luck with it."

He opened the door to Maggie's room. The danger had passed for the moment, but he wanted to bug out as soon as possible. "G'day girls. Ready to push off?"

Maggie turned from the window, sunlight poured through her red mane in gleaming sparks. She'd traded her khakis for pyjams that enfolded her body in soft emerald cottony drapes. By God, he was happy to see her. All in one piece and irritated as hell. His Maggie.

From the look on her face he knew she was about to go into a tirade —*where have you been? Do you know how long we've been sitting here?*

He winked at Hannah, who sat on the bed with Lorelei perched on her shoulder. He crossed the room to Maggie. Just as she opened her mouth to launch into her spiel, he grabbed her shoulders.

Her eyes widened. "What…"

He kissed her thoroughly, completely, joyfully. He was so flaming glad to see her alive. Her melting response warmed him. "Miss me?"

She blinked and stammered.

Moktar's laughter broke their spell as he stood in the doorway. "So the Hollywood gossip is true about the power of Jaguar Jack over women."

Jack winced, knowing Maggie would not take kindly to that remark. Sure enough, she snapped to attention and broke their contact, pushing his chest. "Nice try, Jack. I'll give you a piece of my mind later. Right now Hannah and I are ready to check out of this Helliday Inn."

Moktar leaned against the door jam. "I hope you will tell the authorities you were treated well by Moktar. I saved the missionary from that fanatic Saeed."

Maggie rolled her eyes. "Oh, sure, we'll tell everyone what a swell guy you are, for a kidnapper and murderer."

Hannah stood and approached Moktar. "What will happen to Amelia? Is she being ransomed?"

His expression turned to stone. "She is in the power of Saeed. The men I left behind on the island are all in his control. Forget about her, as I have forgotten about them."

Hannah turned to Maggie with soulful eyes. "She's just a teenager. I feel responsible for her."

"I'm sorry, kid. Like the fella said, you can't save the world," Maggie replied.

"I know. But Amelia was special."

Moktar lifted his meaty hand in farewell. "Until we meet again, Jack."

"So long, mate. Hope you don't take offense when I say I never want to see your ratbag face again."

The swarthy face smirked as he stepped back into the hall. Suddenly, the rat-a-tat of assault weapon gunfire erupted. Moktar's body jerked as bullets slammed his body.

Hannah screamed and shrank back.

Jack kicked the door shut. Maggie reached protectively for Hannah. The thumping of approaching feet rattled the room, followed by the sounds of Moktar and Saeed's men doing battle in the hallway.

"We need another escape route," Maggie said.

Jack's eyes lit on the wooden table beside the bed. He grabbed it and bashed into the wall. Instant doorway. Maggie dragged Hannah through. Jack smashed four more walls through adjacent rooms before they lit out into the hallway just as Ahmed's men busted down their door.

Chapter Twenty-Nine

Elegant elevator doors opened onto the sparkling marble and brass tenth floor of the Jakarta Grand Hotel. After a mad excursion through the twisty maze of streets in a variety of conveyances from rickshaws to doorless taxis, Jack led the way to the posh high rise section of the city.

Maggie gave him points for resourcefulness. And humor. He worked his Jaguar Jack magic on Hannah to put her at ease. While Maggie tensely looked over her shoulder for the bad guys, he relaxed in his seat and offered a cockeyed tour, observing the people they passed along the way.

"See that wizened old woman over there? She was Miss Fish Head of 1942."

Now, the trio headed down the hall to Hannah's parents' room. Dressed in her native garb, sweaty from their hasty departure, Maggie felt more like a war refugee than a Marine. Hannah had covered her blond hair with an indigo headscarf. Two Secret Service types stood planted before the designated door.

Jack halted before them. "Afternoon, mates. Would this be the room of Senator and Mrs. Smith?"

The men stared with stony expressions and offered no reply.

"Let me handle this," Maggie said, pushing Jack aside. "Major Maggie Savannah, United States Marine Corps. We have a delivery for the Smiths."

She pushed Hannah forward, and yanked the scarf off her head.

The men moved like lightning, pushed them against a wall and executed a thorough frisking.

With his face plastered against the vinyl wallpaper, Jack struggled to turn his head toward Maggie. "Whatever I was supposed to be paid for this mission has just doubled."

"Wimp," she said, and then squealed as the guard squeezed her breasts. "Watch it, buddy, those are for real."

No concealed bombs or weapons were found, just one insulted cockatoo hidden under Jack's vest. After matching Hannah's photo to her face, the security men eased up and granted them entrance to the hotel room.

Compared to treading the rocky mountainous floor, the threadbare carpet of the Rat and Roach Motel, and running across the asphalt jungle of Jakarta, the plush knap under Maggie's feet felt like she'd entered heaven. Exquisitely decorated in beige and maroon with huge flower arrangements on the teak wood tables, the room featured a million-dollar view of the city.

Hannah's parents and assorted assistants occupied the living area. A television murmured an episode of *NCIS*. Hannah's mother, Rita, sat in a chair, dressed in a navy blue suit, glittering stud earrings in place. She appeared the epitome of a senator's wife, though her blond hair appeared a bit flat to Maggie's eye. Silver-templed Senator Smith stood facing the window, lost in his thoughts.

Hannah stepped lightly into the room, so quiet she remained unnoticed by most. But Rita noticed her. She slowly rose from her chair, as if she couldn't believe her eyes, perhaps afraid she saw only a mirage. Emotions played across her face from shock, to recognition, to tearful relief.

Hannah stood frozen in place, tied-up in her own knots of emotions. "Hello, Mother."

The dam burst. Rita Smith ran to her daughter, shameless tears coursing down her cheeks. "Thank God, thank God."

The other occupants' boredom and gloom gave way instantly to joy and exultation. Hugs, tears, smiles…a million questions. Touching, kissing, laughing.

Hannah turned in circles answering questions, reassuring everyone of her well-being.

Senator Smith silently crossed the room. People parted like the Red Sea. He placed trembling hands on his daughter's cheeks, looking deeply into her eyes through his own blurred vision.

"You're really here. I tried to stay positive but…"

She covered her hands over his. "It's all right, Daddy. I had my doubts, too. I'm sorry I put you through this. But I'm okay."

Then that eloquent, polished statesmen, that stern steely-eyed politician, pulled his daughter to his chest and wept, beyond words to express his pain, relief, and joy.

Maggie just about lost it herself at that moment. Her stomach turned somersaults while her chin quivered. She blinked and blinked to stem the tide of tears threatening to turn her into one big puddle.

A strong arm curved around her shoulder. "A bit of a cry is in order, Red. Have at it."

Jack's kindly gaze did her in. She turned into him and enjoyed female tears of relief. They felt good. Nothing to be ashamed of. Jack seemed to be drawing out facets of her personality she didn't know existed.

She wiped her face on her dangling sleeve. Slightly embarrassed, she drew away from him. "I always was a sucker for a happy ending."

Jack hugged her, and tried to ignore the foreboding feeling that the end was nowhere in sight.

***

Global newspapers reported a rash of suicide bombers: a police station in Iraq, a shopping mall in Jerusalem, a school in Afghanistan. Most surprising was the first suicide bomber in the United States, a disgruntled employee took out himself, the factory owner, and ten workers in a textile factory being closed for the cheaper labor market south of the border. Fear, greed, and bloody retribution continued to spread like a virus across the globe.

An unusual storm swirled in the Pacific, mystifying international weather watchers. It didn't follow the usual patterns, seemed to come from nowhere. The Indonesian city of Jakarta lay directly in its path. All air flights were canceled; fishing boats took storm precautions.

Swirling purple mounds of black clouds, whipped by gusts of angry winds, rotated above the city. Slaps of thunder pounded windows; fingers of lightning struck and sizzled. Fistfuls of hail dented and destroyed windshields and roofs.

Chapter Thirty

Jack gazed out his hotel window, a damp towel hung around his neck. The storm seemed to have a personality, nasty and noisy. His mood matched the turbulent weather. The terry bathrobe failed to warm the bone deep chill, a chill that had nothing to do with temperature.

Shut it down, Jack, shut it down. You're off the bloody island. This is just a freak storm, nothing more.

Images loomed in his mind, a lion's head, Hannah's innocent face, his mother… Maggie. A sense of calling; a fate he refused to meet. He was a lightweight television star, nothing more. A man with a ready wit, a sense of adventure. Good time Charlie. That's all. When you got down to it, Jaguar Jack Campbell was a fake--only a celluloid hero, not the real thing. A man who played with ancient weapons...a pretend warrior.

Hannah and Maggie were more courageous than he. Hannah, in her quiet manner, had faced deprivation, captivity, and mental assault. Brought from the brink of destruction, she had been the one comforting her mother and father that afternoon. He'd been amazed at her inward calm, her core of inner strength.

And then, there was Maggie. My God, what a woman. There were layers and layers to her. He'd only scratched the surface. Tough and sassy on the outside, but filled with courage and heart beyond his comprehension. She'd been wounded emotionally, but he sensed a healing taking place that would render her even stronger than before.

She couldn't be taken lightly. Not his usual sort of bird at all— those cute and cuddly chippies kept things easy, no fear of attachment. Maggie was tall and sinuous with a sharp gaze that saw beyond his winning smile. While he'd glimpsed beneath her exterior to the incredible woman beneath, she'd also tuned into his secret side. The one he kept hidden even from himself, most of the time.

Another clap of thunder, followed by a flash of lightning, shook the walls. Blue light charged the air.

Fear gripped Jack's chest. Ugly, powerful, raw. He tried to laugh it off. Jaguar Jack scared of the storm, scared of the boogie man. Or in this case some strange mythical creature he'd conjured in his head. There couldn't really be a Beast. He just had an over-active imagination.

Or the delusions of a mad man.

He sensed the window of his mind opening. He slammed it shut. He didn't want the unbidden images, the knowledge beyond comprehension. *Bloody, fucking psycho.*

He needed a drink.

***

Maggie blew her hair dry in the luxurious hotel bathroom. Oh yeah, money had its rewards. Senator Smith was footing the bill for a three-room suite. Jack had one bedroom; she had the other. The adjoining drawing room matched the elegance of the Smith suite, only this one was done in stunning dashes of blue and gold against the off-white walls and carpet.

She was probably being stupid to use an electrical appliance during a minor typhoon, but she lived dangerously, right? She peeked into the bedroom, gazing at the queen size bed. Usually, Major Savannah would be planning a night of room service snuggled in the myriad of pillows, alone in the bed watching whatever American program she could find.

But tonight, tonight was different. She wanted to celebrate, kick up her heels. An hour nap followed by a hot shower had rejuvenated her body and spirit. Maybe she and Jack could trip the light fantastic. Her mother had insisted on dancing lessons years ago. Many a night in secret, she would put on her favorite music and dance and dance. Twirling, dipping, leaping in a solitary apartment or motel room, wherever Uncle Sam had sent her. Maggie the Marine released her alternate self, Magnolia, for a few short hours of femininity when no one could see.

One of the Senator's female aides had been dispatched to the lobby dress shop with Maggie's size requirements, and delivered an array of clothes. One shimmering cocktail dress in particular caught Maggie's fancy. The top could barely be called more than two wide criss-crossed straps and it had no back at all. Her breasts would bobble under the shiny golden material for all the world to see. The skirt flowed to the floor from the gathered waist, but the slits up the side revealed plenty of leg. And if there was anything Maggie possessed, it was legs. Stunning legs, Jack had called them.

She held the dress up before herself in front of the full-length mirror. Could she do it? Did she have the guts? Could she put this dress on and wear it like a second skin? Or would she feel like a Marine out of uniform?

Why did it take more courage to put on a slinky evening gown than face enemy fire?

She needed a drink.

***

She fortified herself with two of those little bottles of bourbon from the wet bar. *Wonder what they would cost the Senator?* Maggie put the finishing touches on her make-up. Yes, mascara, eye shadow, the works. She took one final look at herself in the mirror. Maybe it was just a boozy haze, but her eyes beheld a goddess in slinky gold. The material enfolded her curves worthy, of a Cosmo cover. Not bad, not damn bad. She walked toward the mirror and watched her boobs jiggle. My God, she looked great!

Suddenly, she had the urge to rush to Jack's room and get his approval.

Practicing a sensuous swivel, she crossed through the suite, reached his door and knocked.

"Jack? Are you decent?"

She knocked again. No answer.

"Jack?"

She turned the knob. The room was dark, except for the illumination through the plate glass window overlooking the city. Flashes of lightning added to the neon glow from the signs blinking on the neighboring high rises.

At first she thought he was gone, but then she noticed an arm rise with a drink in hand, facing away from her in a chair near the window. The arm was white and she realized he was wearing one of the hotel robes. The large chair revealed only the top of his dark head, and that one listless arm.

Maggie crossed the room and turned on a lamp. "Hey, fella, want to go catch a bite to eat and maybe take a girl dancing?"

"Turn off the bloody light!"

Maggie quickly complied, then gingerly approached him, as one does a wild animal. She rounded the chair to look into his face, the window behind her.

His face appeared haunted; jaunty Jack had disappeared. With his mask of jocularity stripped away, he was a brooding gothic prince, a hero from one of those dark romances she had tucked away in her underwear drawer. Troubled, coiled in tension.

Flash! Light exploded and vanished. Jack gazed up at her, and slowly perused the length of her body. Heat seared her, as if he'd placed hot hands upon her.

"My God, Jack, what's wrong?"

His stare concentrated on her breasts, hungry. She responded with a sudden wave of yearning. The shimmering material of the gown seemed suddenly tight, restraining.

"Get out of here now, Red. I'm clucky company tonight."

Should she leave? Something told her if she stayed, she'd never be the same again. Well, would that be so bad? There was a lot of room for improvement.

As she looked down at him, staring into the night, she knew she couldn't leave, mustn't leave. He needed her. Whatever demon chased him tonight, perhaps together they could send it on its way.

The semi-darkness, the unconcealed pain of the man, the invisible bonds of attachment pulled her to him. "Remember the night in the jungle when you held me, Jack? You kissed me, touched me, caressed me. You did all the giving, I did all the taking. It was beautiful. It was healing. I'd been running away from my pain, but you made me give into it, face it. It wasn't as monstrous as I feared when I had you there to hold me."

She knelt before him; the terry cloth barely covered his thighs. She edged between them so she could reach up and cup his face between her hands. His skin felt smooth from a fresh shave, the smell of soap and man drew her, aroused her.

She whispered as her hand tenderly caressed his cheek. "Let me help you get through it, Jack."

He trembled with the need of wanting her. Did she know how beautiful she was? When she'd stood with the light behind her at the window, the diaphanous quality of the material made her look ethereal, otherworldly, an angel sent to save him from the darkness calling to his soul.

Now she knelt before him, utterly supplicating herself, openly sacrificing herself on the altar of his raging torment. The shadows played tricks, making her eyes seem bigger, giving, trusting. The golden material covering her breasts glowed. His fingers itched to hold them, stroke them, excite them. He wanted to bury his face in the valley between them, explore every inch of smooth flesh with his lips and tongue.

Did she know if they committed this ultimate act of unity, they might be bonded forever? Was it fair to trap a woman of such courage and power to a man who knew himself to be a coward? A man who quaked from inner fears?

He should send her away, set her free.

"Run, Maggie, run. I'm a bad bargain."

But she'd have none of it. She stretched her lovely, long body and met his lips with hers. Soft and sensuous, she tasted like sweet bourbon. She smelled like flowers, sunshine, and hope.

Ice cubes and dregs of his drink hit the carpet as he dropped the glass and reached for her, filling his hands with those bountiful breasts. The thin barrier of material only added to the pleasure of exploration. Round and round his thumbs edged the tips coming alive under his fingers. He felt her growing under his hands, hardening in response to his tender teasing.

Her kisses became more insistent. Maggie possessed a passion that had never been explored. He felt her opening to him and, by God, he wanted to take all she was willing to give.

"Please, Jack," she whispered between kisses.

He edged the material off her shoulder, releasing her breasts from their gauzy entrapment. Her nipples stood erect, waiting, wanting. He could no more stop now, than stop breathing.

He bent his head and took the offered flesh in his mouth. She tasted so good, all woman, primitive woman filling his needs so generously, so responsively. She moaned and held his head close, tenderly. Her fingers played in his hair as he laved and loved each puckered tip over and over.

Her head fell back, accompanied by little throaty sounds that sent his blood rushing. *Mmm...uuhh...mmm...*

His need grew stronger, rising at the center of him. She sensed it, dropping her hands to his thighs, running her fingers back and forth from knee to groin, raking nails against the sensitive inner flesh, bringing him to full erection.

Their mouths came together again, picking up a mating rhythm, as their bodies drew closer together. She unbelted his robe and explored his chest with hands and mouth. He unzipped her dress. It pooled around her knees.

They murmured appreciation, with both words and sighs. The storm swirled on beyond the glass, pounding in fury. But they were protected, dry and warm, in their own world of touch and taste, hard and soft.

Her hands found him, caressed him up and down, again and again taking him to the peak of need. Strangled noises rose from his throat, mingled with the rush of rain at the window. It took all his concentration to hold back, prolong the pleasure before giving into the desire to mate with this woman.

They tumbled to the plush carpet and he stripped away the rest of her undergarments. She lay naked, vulnerable, a shadowy vision of femininity. Her hair fanned above her head. She offered all the white flesh of her body, not withholding, not fighting or challenging.

"Oh Lord, Red, you're a work of art, a marvelous marble statue."

She stretched like a cat. "I don't feel like a statue. I feel soft all over, while you're…" Her fingers reached out, encircled him again, making him hard as stone.

He lifted her hand away, kissed it and then scooted down to her feet. He explored her legs with his hands and then his lips. He tasted; he traveled… higher and higher. She opened wider and wider. He found her with his mouth. Her scent, her saltiness filled his senses. Engulfed and elevated, the undulating movement of her hips matched the pulse of his blood, the flick of his tongue.

When she trembled and cried out, he felt the greatest joy. Pure joy on top of driving need. He rose over her and thrust himself inside, welcomed, wanted. Her long legs wrapped around him, pulling him deep. She desired this joining as much as he.

Hot…wet…tight, better than he ever imagined it would be.

They rode to the top together, climbing, climaxing, completing. Unity in body, bonded ever more strongly in spirit. This loving, beautiful woman chased all his fears away.

* * *

Jack eased up on the pillows, rising to a reclined position in the sumptuous king size bed. Maggie's languid body lay draped across his chest, her head rested on his shoulder, one arm limp on his belly. If scene one had begun on the chair and finished on the carpet, scene two commenced under the covers and was shot in slow motion.

Maggie, Maggie, Maggie. She moved over him like a warm wave, lapping again and again with increasing force. She was like a quiet lagoon that soon transformed into a Hawaiian beach, breakers crashing from twenty feet high, exhilarating and exhausting.

He glanced down and frowned. A sheet covered most of her body. He wanted to see it, drink in the view from every angle. He flipped back the white material. Ah, the rise of her bare back, bottom, and legs lay revealed before him in the muted light. Lovely. He indulged in his long-awaited five minutes.

He ran his fingers over her shoulder blades, feeling the sleek skin and firm muscles beneath. "By God, Red, you're a beautiful creature."

She snuggled a little closer. "Thanks, but you also think a beetle is a beautiful creature."

Her reply irritated him. He pulled the chain in the lamp beside the bed, pooling the bed with light. He tilted her chin and looked down into her face. "Listen to me, Magnolia. You are a magnificent woman. Dinkum all the way. You think because you're strong and lean and tall, you aren't pretty. And you're not merely pretty; you're bloody gorgeous. Miles of soft skin and legs that wrap around a man and send him out of this world. You have an innate sexuality that makes other women pale in comparison. And you're just getting started in that department. When I admire you, I see a female who can conjure erotic fantasies and live up to them. Believe what I'm telling you; it's the God's truth."

Maggie blinked. She gazed into Jack's face, as if seeking a joke behind his eyes, but found none. "You really mean it." Her mouth turned up in a half smile. She reached out and ran her fingers through his hair. "I meant to give you a gift tonight, Jack. But, it seems, once again, you're the giver and I'm the receiver. You make me feel beautiful. Not clumsy or awkward, but graceful, like a dancer. Making love with you is like participating in a choreographed dance, with a perfect partner turning and dipping at just the right moments."

How could you do anything but kiss such a woman? He leaned down and covered her lips, enjoying her rich response.

Then he pulled her against his chest. "That business of me giving and you taking is pure rubbish. Before you came in, my mood was as black as the tempest clouds. Look, I think you even made the real storm pass over."

Maggie glanced out the window. Though the rain continued, the lightning and thunder had ceased. She pulled the sheet back up, still not comfortable exposing her gorgeous body with complete abandon.

Turning her attention once again to Jack's profile, she said, "Storms really bother you, don't they?"

Jack pulled away from her and swung his feet out of the bed. He crossed the room to retrieve his robe and slipped into it. "Childish, isn't it? Downright cowardly, I'd say."

"Now who's talking rubbish? It doesn't take Sigmund Freud to figure out that you were traumatized by the violent death of your mother from that awful creature on the island. There was a raging storm that night, too, wasn't there?"

Jack froze, flashes of dreams or memories exploding in his mind, bringing on piercing pain to his temples. "I don't remember anything about my mother's death."

Maggie rose up on her knees, gathering the sheet around her. "Bull. Edith told me all about it. You've been trying to bury that memory for years, but it's been buried alive."

He couldn't breathe. A fog clouded his vision, everything in the room distorted. His heart raced in his chest, pounding as if he'd run for his life.

Coward, coward, a voice hissed in his mind.

Strong hands grabbed his shoulders and shook him.

"Snap out of it, Jack!"

Sharp green eyes came into focus. Maggie, dressed in a matching white terry robe stood before him, shaking him with determination. When had she left the bed and dressed? Lord, was he having blackouts again?

"You're not a coward, Jack. That's a lie!" She slowly released him and looked perplexed. "My God, I heard it. A voice inside my head saying 'coward, coward.' But that was coming from you, wasn't it, Jack?"

Oh, lord, he was afraid of this. He reached down and held her hands. "I'm sorry, darlin'. I think you just joined the balmy world of Jaguar Jack Campbell."

He expected her to turn away. Instead, she faced it head-on, a seeker of truth. "I know you spent some time in a psych ward when you were eighteen, but the records are sealed. What sent you there?"

Jack sighed. He seldom dwelled on that lost time. But Maggie deserved some measure of explanation. He crossed to the bar, poured himself a drink of water. "I was a freshman in college. First time I was away from the field, and thrown in the midst of a crowded city for a long period of time. The dreams started again--running, choking in the dark, a horrible monster. So, being tired, my ability to handle 'the gift' weakened."

Maggie sat at the foot of the bed. "What gift is that?"

"Seeing the dark side of people's souls; knowing their deepest secrets. What they've done and what they are capable of doing." He stared into his glass of water. "That year in college became a torture. I'd be sitting across from a mate, some bloke who appeared nice enough. Then, I'd flash to his moments of rage, see him beat the bloody hell out of another mate or, worse, rape a girl in the back seat of his car. It got so I couldn't sit in a classroom or move down a hallway without picking up the negative thought waves of the people around me. It was like watching one violent, hate-filled movie after another."

"That would be enough to send anyone to a psych ward."

"It got so I couldn't sleep for fear of the nightmares, wouldn't leave my room for fear of the visions." Jack crossed the room and sat next to her, taking comfort in the feel of her hip next to his. "I lost weight and, of course, flunked my courses. That's when Dad and Aunt Edith realized I was deeply in trouble and checked me into the Queensborough hospital. And thank God, they did."

Maggie reached for Jack's hand. "They didn't just pump you with a lot of anti-psychotic drugs?"

"No, Aunt Edith wouldn't let them. She found a therapist who did psychic research. Between the two of them, they taught me how to put up defensive mental shields. I learned how to avoid peering into people's souls. It's also very important for me to seek the beauty in life."

A smile graced her lips with the dawning of understanding. "That's why you stop at every butterfly, flower, and beetle you see. It balances out your ability to tune into the dark side."

"Exactly." His thumb circled the smooth skin on the back of her hand. "I've made a career of showing off all the wonders of creation and have steered clear of evil as much as possible."

"Except, you keep going back to Paradisio, the source of your worst nightmares."

Jack nodded. "Ironic, isn't it? It's been a personal challenge to overcome my fear. You don't know how many times I've stood on a cliff looking down at that valley, knowing something lurked, challenged me, but I never had the guts to venture in. I'd stand there and hear 'coward, coward' rolling through the air on the wind, thinking I was always a step away from madness."

She clutched his hand with a stab of guilty conscious. "Oh God, and I forced you to go there. I'm sorry, I had no idea. I've been incredibly insensitive. But, you must realize now you aren't a bit crazy. There *is* some strange creature that dwells on the island. You just made it bigger with your childhood memories."

"Did I? Or am I really crazy as a bed bug? For what could be balmier than thinking the source of all evil dwells on an island in the middle of the Pacific Ocean?"

Chapter Thirty-One

In a suite down the hall, Hannah Smith stared out the window, hypnotized by the storm, feeling—nothing. Except maybe like she'd been emotionally beaten by a baseball bat. She ran fingers through her clean hair. Well, that felt good anyway--clean hair, now so long it hung halfway to her waist in a long, blond curtain. Given the options of American jeans and a shirt or continuing to go native in some fresh turquoise pyjams, she still favored the pyjams.

When she closed her eyes, the smells, sights, and sounds of the jungle quickly filled her mind with its images. Any moment she expected Ahmed to enter her tent, speaking in his quietly intense manner with ideas that battered at her soul, ripped at her core beliefs.

Closing her eyes was a bad idea, but she didn't know what to do with herself. She'd spent time with her mother and father, but their emotional neediness had been draining. Good old Hannah had smiled her serene smile and allayed their fears as best she could. Her captivity hadn't been so bad. No rape or physical torture.

Just that constant mental erosion of her convictions. Rice to eat every day served with tidbits of doubt.

She wrapped her arms around her waist, a personal hug, needing human contact, even if it was only with herself.

I am with you always.

If that was so, why did she feel so lonely, so deserted, even in the midst of family and friends? She'd lost her bearings somewhere along the line. What was she supposed to do now? How did she sort it out?

There was a light tap at her door. "Hannah?" her mother asked.

She turned around, putting on her happy face. "Yes, Mom?"

"Honey, you have a visitor. An old friend. I didn't think you'd mind."

"Who…" Hannah's words froze in her throat as she recognized the tall figure standing behind her mother.

A vision of sun-tanned, fair-haired masculinity stood in the doorway, more filled out than the last time she'd seen him in Virginia Beach. Wearing his military uniform and a cautious expression, Chris

Matthews entered the room. "I had to see for myself that you're all right. I just had to, Sugar."

Rita Smith stood back and watched the drama unfold. Chris, a man who could carry out a military operation with cool dispatch, looked as nervous as a kid on prom night. Hannah stood stalk still, blinking with surprise. Her cornflower eyes filled with a bead of a tear.

"Chris…" she whispered. Her hand lifted up. "Is it really you?"

Chris entered the room, threw his cap aside, and cradled Hannah's cheeks in his hands. "I know we promised to never see each other again, that it would be better to go our separate ways. But, honey, you've had me worried half to death."

Hannah's face crumbled, the façade stripped away. Tears rolled down as she began to quake with emotion. "Chris, oh, how I've missed you."

She reached up as Chris bent to sweep her fully into his arms. Rita stepped back and pulled the door closed behind her. She'd known her daughter had been keeping up a false front. Rita hadn't been the one Hannah could trust to see her raw emotions. Hannah needed the strength of the man she loved.

Chris Matthews, the man she'd left behind for God.

* * *

Chris clearly remembered the first moment he saw Hannah Smith. She'd marched down the aisle of the Virginia Beach Metrochurch, trailed by a gaggle of pre-schoolers. Chris was on a much-needed furlough of R and R after a grueling turn in Afghanistan. Virginia Beach had seemed a good place to recharge before his next assignment in D.C. But after three days of wandering the beach, eating in fancy restaurants, catching up on movies, he still hadn't chased away the ghosts of war.

That Sunday morning, he'd found himself driving his rental car into the parking lot of a sparkling non-denominational church built on a hillside. From the looks of the crowd of people streaming into the modern building, this was a lively place. Chris needed the affirmation of life, after enduring the ravages of death.

He slipped into a long side pew, anonymous in the enthusiastic throng that stood clapping hands, raising arms, swaying to the contagious beat of the praise band. The sanctuary held at least two thousand people fanned out three-quarters around the wide altar area featuring the band, a baby grand, cheerful banners and a Plexiglas podium. So different from the stodgy brick and mortar church back home.

Chris stood with the others, enjoying the music, but not ready to raise his hands or shout "Halleluiah." The service spun along, lots of singing and then an up beat sermon from the young, charismatic minister. To end the service, the minister announced Miss Smith's pre-school class musical presentation.

His life forever changed when an angelic college student led the pre-school choir. Hannah's hair hit just past her shoulders, pulled back on the sides by pretty hair clips that glinted under the lights. Actually, everything about her seemed to glow—her blond hair, round cheeks, and sparkling eyes. His seat lay far enough to the side that he saw her in profile as she knelt before the children arranged on the steps. She waved her hands before the pint-size singers, mouthing the lyrics, smiling encouragement. The children sang in all different keys, some just shouted the words with great enthusiasm, while others hung shyly back. The congregation smiled and chuckled in appreciation.

For the first time in months, Chris felt the veil of heaviness lift from his shoulders. The weariness in his soul revived as Hannah freely poured out joy. Joy that seemed to exude from her fingers, through her smile, and out the top of her head. He was drawn to her like a man crawls to an oasis after a trek in the desert.

As the service ended, he made his way through the chatting women and dashing youngsters to where she released her charges to their parents. She hugged and praised the children as they were taken away. Chris stood quietly behind her until she stood alone.

She must have sensed him, because she turned around and looked up at him with a questioning smile.

"Miss, I just wanted to tell you, I really enjoyed your little choir. I'm Major Chris Matthews, United States Marine Corps."

He held out his hand. She looked down, hesitated a moment, and clasped his palm. "Thank you, Major. I'm just plain old Hannah Smith and I'm very pleased to meet you."

Their joined hands arced with magic.

Chapter Thirty-Two

Hannah had never been in love, except with the Lord. That relationship had been forged before birth, probably before conception. She had always known Him, talked about Jesus and angels when she was a toddler. By the age of eight, she knew she'd spend her life in the missionary field. Her goal through high school and college was to prepare herself for The Call.

Though she'd had plenty of attention from boys in youth group, they'd always just been friends. She'd witnessed a lot of her friends go boy-crazy. Girls gave themselves away to boys, who sampled the wares and then moved on. Crying teenagers called Hannah at three a.m., sobbing over being used and discarded.

She'd been given an innate maturity regarding relationships. She counseled, consoled, and cared. She also made up her mind she would never have sex before marriage. Not only was the Bible very clear about it, the wreckage of broken hearts around her confirmed the Biblical wisdom.

And in her twenty-one years, she'd never been sorely tempted. Love poured out from her for children and hurting people, but it had never zeroed in on one romantic relationship.

Until Chris Matthews.

They ate lunch after that first church service at a restaurant overlooking the water. Sitting on the deck, under a striped umbrella, waitresses came and went, other tables handled different parties. Hannah and Chris never noticed. They talked and laughed, dipping finger food in spicy sauce, munching through the afternoon.

Falling in love with a man on military leave telescopes the relationship. He may not be here next week, or next month or next year. Chris made it clear he was only on leave for three more days. By the time lunch ended, Hannah knew she wanted to spend every precious minute with him.

She skipped classes. Hannah always followed her instincts, secure in the knowledge that God was with her. Surely, if she felt such joy and love around this man, it had to be a God-deal.

The following Tuesday morning, he picked her up at her dorm and headed toward a historic lighthouse on Chesapeake Bay. The scenery rolled by. In the two days they'd known each other, they'd covered a lot of territory regarding past personal history, shared tastes in music, and family background.

So, it was pleasant to sit back and not talk, enjoy the soft music of a CD and occasionally steal glances at each other. In fact, Hannah couldn't help but smile every time she looked at him. Happiness bubbled inside. Everything about him captivated her—from his sandy hair, clean-cut features, and hazel eyes, to his respectful southern manners and the way he made her feel special, cherished.

He hadn't talked much about the military. She sensed his need to mentally break away for a while. Still, curiosity to know all about him brought her to the subject.

"When did you know you wanted to be a Marine?" she asked as she turned down the CD volume.

He shrugged his wide shoulders. "When didn't I want to be a Marine? I always played with military toys, read military magazines, loved the military movies—as far back as I can remember."

"But what exactly attracted you to it? It wasn't just getting to fire off guns, I hope."

"It isn't about the weapons, although they are integral to the job. It's about being part of something big and important. I know it sounds corny, but it's about making the world a better place, a more secure place. I wanted my life to make a difference and being a Marine seemed like the best way I could do it." His eyes remained on the road, but his conviction tightened his jaw.

Hannah sat back in her seat. He revealed a whole new perspective of the military. She'd always focused on the weaponry, the insanity of war, the endless escalation of violence.

She hesitated, but then asked, "Would you tell me a little about Afghanistan?"

Chris glanced at her, his eyes hooded, his mouth flat. Then he nodded and reached for her hand. "You have a right to know. If what's between us is headed where I think it's heading, you should get the full picture. It isn't all pretty."

He made a turn onto a gravel road leading to the lighthouse. The day blustered with wind, though the sun sparkled on the bay. He parked the car in the tourist lot, but they had the area to themselves. The old lighthouse could wait. They rolled down the windows, let the marshy smells and sounds of birds into their enclosure.

Chris turned his full attention on her. "It's like stepping back into Biblical times ruled by a culture that is based on revenge."

He told her about the villages of rubble. Senseless prejudices and hatred perpetuated generation after generation had wrought an endless cycle of violence.

Without realizing it, she reached out and clutched his hands as he recited some of the things he'd seen people do to other people. Tears rolled down her cheeks, though he remained stoic through his recitation.

She shook her head. "It's like some terrible spirit of evil has overtaken an entire region. It will never completely change until people's hearts are changed."

"I don't know about their hearts, but I do know the Marines can go in and make sure their behavior changes. Sometimes, the bullies of the world have to be stopped. Working in those areas is hard. It can be lonesome. You miss good food, a real bed, and the trappings of home. But, you know you're doing something worthwhile when villagers can start leading normal lives again. You know you've done something good when you see kids playing in the streets again."

Hannah felt her heart leap to her throat. Here was a man she could love. Oh, heck, here was a man she did love, probably from the first moment she'd laid eyes on him. Her expression must have given her away.

Chris' hands cupped her cheeks. He leaned into her. "I want to kiss you, Hannah. May I?"

Blood rushed through her veins; she trembled like a lost puppy. It wasn't as if she hadn't been kissed before. But she knew this one would be different.

She nodded her head slightly. Then, the soft lips of Chris Matthews molded to her mouth and changed her whole world.

Gentle, tender, holding her as if she were a treasure, he engulfed her senses. Small kisses at first, coaxing, exploring. Warmth enveloped her. Love swirled around them in blinding white light.

They separated, took a few deep breaths, and smiled into each other's eyes.

With the breeze in their faces and joy in their hearts, they explored the lighthouse and surrounding rocky terrain. They laughed, teased, and even tickled. Once Chris kissed her, they managed to find ways to keep touching. Holding hands, a casual tap on the arm, whisking an errant strand of hair behind an ear.

They raced up a flight of stairs to a lookout landing. He could have easily beaten her, but it was more fun to pretend to struggle and then whirl her around in triumph at the top of the stairs.

My God, she felt good in his arms. Soft…pliant… pure. Her herbal hair shampoo mixed with the scent of water and wind. Her laughter lifted his spirits.

After hugging her tightly in a playful spin, he settled her before him. Catching her breath from the dash up the stairs, she loosely held onto his forearms. He couldn't seem to let her out of his embrace. She tilted her head up, all smiling, blue-eyed innocence.

He gazed down on her. "Oh, honey, you're the sweetest thing I ever saw."

He didn't ask permission to kiss her this time. It happened as natural as rain, as right as robins singing on a spring morning.

They held hands sitting on a bench overlooking the bay. Huge white birds glided against the pewter sky before diving into the water.

Chris circled his thumb over the top of her hand. "What are you planning to do when you graduate? You're getting a teaching degree, right?"

He pictured her teaching on base, wherever he was stationed. That would be good. She'd be well-occupied when he pulled duty that kept him away from home for months at a time. He'd seen too many marriages fall apart when the wife was bored at home.

He blinked, realizing how far his thoughts had come in such a short time. He'd read about this, heard about it from his buddies—knowing when you met The One.

Hannah nibbled her lip. "Yes, I'll have a teaching degree. It seemed practical and I love working with children. But, I've always pictured myself in the mission field somewhere. I've been waiting for the leading."

"Sugar, do you think it's possible that you've been led to me?"

Her big blue eyes gazed at him, tremulous. "It's possible."

"I think I love you, Hannah. I know it's only been a few days since we met, but I've never felt like this with anyone before. It feels so *right* with you, sweetheart. Do you understand what I'm saying?"

Hannah blinked back a few tears. "I do understand. This is all so overwhelming. I've always thought girls who told me they were 'in love' with some guy after one date were foolish. But Sunday night, as I laid in my bed thinking about you, I wondered if I was falling in love with you. I couldn't get you out of my mind."

An unexpected sense of desperation hit Chris like a wave. He placed his hands on her arms. "I really want this. There's one thing I've learned from serving in war-torn countries. You've got to grab opportunities when they come by. I want you to be part of my life, Hannah Smith. Our time together hasn't been nearly long enough. For the first time since I signed up, I hate the thought of having to leave. I don't want you to forget me."

He pulled her close and kissed her passionately, possessively. Her arms flew around his neck, eagerly responding to his ardor, matching it with her own.

"Oh, Chris, I do love you. I could never forget you."

"We'll make this work. I'll get away whenever I can. I'll be stationed in D.C. for a while."

"I'll drive up every weekend."

"I'll get a cell phone only for calls from you."

"We'll talk every night."

And they did. With distance and commitments keeping them apart, they managed to become best friends through lengthy phone conversations. Being physically separated became a constant dull ache, but it forced them to communicate without being distracted by desire.

Though Chris couldn't always go into great detail about his work, Hannah came to realize how intense his work must be. He was involved in terrorist counter-intelligence, a growing global threat. When he sounded too serious after a tough day, she tried to come up with an amusing story.

As time went by, it became obvious that Chris saw them living a married military life. He would go off and perform his important business. She would stay behind and keep the home fires burning. They'd have babies and build a life together.

At night, she'd lay awake and try to visualize the future. Was she meant to be this man's life partner? She knew she loved Chris. But try as she might, she couldn't conjure up the vision of herself being the good little wife, making brownies, and hauling the kids to soccer practice.

Once the spring semester ended, Hannah would leave for a mission trip to Nicaragua to work in an orphanage. Chris received orders to

Germany for several weeks of training. They had one weekend before they'd be going their separate ways.

He drove down early Saturday morning. As the sun was just peeking through the tall trees and shades of pink swirled in the sky, she came running out of the dorm to greet him. He'd barely stepped out of the car as she launched herself into his arms.

"Hey, Sugar, you sure smell good," he said, burying his nose in her hair.

"It's cinnamon rolls. I just popped them in the oven."

He kissed her soundly. "Now I *know* I love you."

Arm in arm, they walked up the uneven, old sidewalk around to the kitchen entrance. They enjoyed an early breakfast as half-dressed college girls wandered in and out ogling Hannah's beau.

They sat over coffee and rolls at the old, scratched table planning their day. Their glorious day all to themselves. They were in accord about pursuing leisurely activities until they got to the evening's agenda. Chris had a steak dinner in mind at a nice restaurant.

Hannah had another idea. "There's a really great speaker coming to church tonight. He's a Bible translator. He spent decades working in Asia."

Chris' less-than-enthusiastic expression didn't faze Hannah. "Come on. I sat through a military banquet last time I visited you. And, I promise this will be much more interesting."

He chuckled. "Okay, but don't expect me to want to run off and teach a bunch of Aborigines the Lord's Prayer after hearing this guy."

They enjoyed lunch at an Italian restaurant, marred only by a couple of cell phone calls that forced Chris to move out of earshot for a private conversation.

She worked at raising his spirits when he returned. "Don't look so serious, soldier boy. This isn't your watch."

Chris smiled. "You're right. Seems like there is always an emergency."

"You should try to let go and let God."

"Sugar, I really admire your faith. But, I've got to tell you, I believe in that scripture, 'God helps those who help themselves.'"

Hannah wrinkled her brow. "That's not scripture." It bothered her that they didn't seem to be in the same place spiritually. "How important is God in your life, Chris?"

"God's real important. I think He's given me a job to do and I'm trying to do it. I read my Bible. Then I get to work."

"And the work you do involves tracking down terrorists and sometimes going in and killing them, doesn't it?"

Chris hadn't given her the details of his work. But she was a smart girl. Her father was a Senator. She knew about covert operations, national security.

His mouth tightened. "Yes, sometimes I've had to kill people when I've come under fire. I don't enjoy it, but when I'm assigned a mission, I follow through."

She reached out and held his hand. How hard must it be to kill another human being, even when you knew you were probably saving the lives of innocent people by doing so? How must that eat away at your soul? If Hannah married this man, she would be playing a supportive role in the military missions he was required to carry out. Was that God's plan for her life?

She placed her hand over his. "I admire your courage and strength."

He shook his head. "I'm just doing my job. But sometimes I feel empty inside." He squeezed her hand. "You fill up that emptiness, honey. I need your warmth, your joy for life. It radiates out of you like a beacon of light. It was the first thing I noticed about you."

"That's the Lord. It isn't me."

"I know I'm not as close to God as you are. But, you see, having you in my life brings Him closer."

Hannah smiled, but his comment troubled her. Was being his spiritual strength her calling? Didn't he have to find that connection on his own?

***

Chris showered and changed in his motel room in the late afternoon. Hannah waited on the queen size bed, feeling a bit self-conscious. A picture of Chesapeake Bay hung on the beige wall. The paisley bedspread of blue and gold felt starchy against her palms. His aftershave scented the air. An undeniable sense of intimacy enveloped her. This was the first time she'd come into his room during one of their visits. She knew Chris would never force her to do something she didn't want to do. But the truth was, she liked his kisses. She liked the way he touched her and the warm, melting feeling in his arms. She knew where it led.

If I give myself fully to Chris, it will be a lifetime commitment. Am I ready for that?

He emerged from the steamy bathroom in a fresh shirt and slacks, hair still damp, his chin stubble-free from a shave. My gosh, was there ever such a handsome man?

Chris smiled, then froze as he stared at her reclining on the big sapphire throw pillows.

Hannah's face warmed. "This seemed like a comfortable place to wait. That side chair has a nasty bite to it."

She swung her legs over the side.

"Wait," he said.

She gazed over her shoulder at him as he sat on the other side of the bed. He reached across, twisted a curl resting on her shoulder with his finger, gently tugging her toward him.

She could have easily pulled away, gotten up from the bed, grabbed her purse and coaxed him to safer ground. But, this was their last chance to be together for a long time. How could she deny him? How could she deny herself, when she wanted to feel his arms around her so very, very much?

"Oh, Chris," she whispered.

They reached for each other like two streams joining together, melding and merging. He smelled of aftershave and soap. She was all softness and pliant femininity.

They kissed and hugged and ran hands over clothing, exploring textures and contours. He'd never touched her breasts before. He couldn't resist now, not when she arched into him, making little moaning noises.

Even through her blouse and bra, he felt the sweet mound of flesh and a responding tip came alive under his caressing hand.

Kissing her temple, he said, "Sweetheart, you make my heart burst."

He knew she was a virgin. She intended to stay chaste, but he'd been aching to hold her, feel all her warmth cuddled against him. She may have been inexperienced, but she wasn't unresponsive. Unbridled passion laid only a few strokes away. And he was tempted, oh, so tempted.

He pulled slightly away, trying to keep his head. "Honey, you remind me of cotton candy at the county fair. You're so sweet, you just melt in my mouth."

Her heart shone in her eyes. "I love you so much."

"We could stay here all night." He stroked her hair. "I'll make love to you and then we can get married in the morning. How does that sound to you, Sugar?"

She nearly went for it. She placed her hands on his chest, had the words ready to say, ready to launch her life in a certain direction. A journey through life with this worthy man. She could never love any man more.

But then she had what she called "a check in her spirit." A quiet voice that whispered... *wait.*

She gave him a quick kiss and pulled away. "We'd better hurry, or we'll be late."

Chris relaxed against the pillows and sighed.

She hurried into the bathroom to refresh herself and get a grip.

***

The church was packed. Chris marveled that so many people would give up a Saturday night to hear some missionary from Timbuktu or someplace. He held her hand, walking to a spot on a middle pew about half-way to the back.

Pop-Christian music bounced from the praise band, electric guitar, and drums, thumping a beat to pump up the crowd. Hannah stood beside him, clapping her hands and singing along. She gazed at him, those cornflower blues twinkled and urged him to loosen up his military demeanor and go with the flow. She exuded contagious joy. Soon, he clapped along with the throng, caught up in the mass praise.

The service proceeded casually. The young pastor, dressed in jeans and a sweater, addressed his flock, garnered a few chuckles, shared prayer praises and concerns from the congregation. Then, after considerably more singing—this was the singingest church in the world—the main speaker was introduced.

If Chris had known the effect a white-bearded, raspy-voiced old man would have on his life, he'd have dragged Hannah out of the sanctuary the moment John Wesley Monroe set foot on the raised platform.

Monroe had spent thirty-five years translating the gospel into the native tongue of an indigenous people group living in a mountainous region near Afghanistan. The sect was tiny compared to the Hindu-Muslim population that surrounded them. They suffered increasing persecution in the face of growing modern tensions. Members had been martyred, tortured by religious police. Still, they persevered and grew in numbers. Monroe had dedicated his life to these people.

A video captured the foreign living conditions, the exotic women and thin, dark-skinned children. Chris had traveled through similar regions on military missions. Memories of hurried crowds, hungry palms begging for handouts flooded his mind. Then, he took a closer look at the pictures. Monroe's video depicted people choosing a different lifestyle than their neighbors—a culture resisting the cruel caste system or rigid religious totalitarianism.

Monroe's piercing, blue eyes shone above a mass of wrinkles and a snowy-white beard. Traces of his New England childhood still colored his speech. At one point he flashed a picture of himself as a teenager, a North Eastern affluent schoolboy similar to all the others in his class. His confident smirk made him look like a future lawyer, not missionary.

He gave a brief testimony about his resistance to The Call as a young man, and his ultimate surrender to his destiny. Chris chafed at this philosophy. Chris wanted to determine his own destiny—not be driven into a fate of some deity's whim.

Monroe told the stories of his friends and foreign family—the people he devoted his entire life to. Smiling faces flashed across the screen. Children saved from the streets; women escaping from slavery prostitution; men choosing a peaceful lifestyle in the midst of violence. Monroe's people didn't have it easy. But they had a Christian vision, and now they possessed a Bible they could understand within the terms and language of their culture. And Monroe insisted the living God—worked in their midst through the Holy Spirit.

He revved the crowd with his missionary zeal. "Amen's" and "halleluiah's" popped up from the congregation. Chris jiggled his foot. The whole tone of the evening turned him off. Believing in God was one thing. Knowing right from wrong and living by the Ten Commandments all made sense. But this guy was over the edge.

He nudged Hannah, hoping to ease out and maybe go get a snack and drive to the lake. He turned and studied her profile.

She gazed transfixed at the video, tears streaming down her cheeks. Monroe's talk had turned into a full-blown sermon with prophetic words.

Resembling a modern-day Moses, Monroe admonished the crowd. "Open yourself to the call of God in your life. You may have one plan. But He has a better one. There is someone here at a crossroads. Your life could go in two directions—one step either way will influence your entire life. Listen to the voice within your heart. Follow your true path, the one pre-ordained since your conception. It may not be the easiest course. Like Peter, you will go where you do not want to go. But those who make the greatest sacrifices bring forth the greatest blessings for the kingdom."

That's when Hannah completely broke down. Alarmed and perplexed, Chris wrapped his arm around her. She cried into his shoulder even as they exited up the aisle. What had her rattled, he had no idea. Certainly no one else in the auditorium appeared so overwhelmed.

Hannah, his sweet Hannah, obviously had a tender heart—too sensitive to hear stories of starving children and abused women. He'd have to protect her from the uglier sides of life.

He settled her into the passenger's seat of his car and found the box of tissue in the glove compartment. "Here, Sugar."

She wiped her face. "Thank you. I'm sorry. I don't usually get so emotional."

"Want to take a spin down by the lake?"

Hannah nodded and stared straight ahead. "Yes, that a good idea. I think I have something to say to you."

***

Parked in a deserted beach lot facing the black lake against the star-shot sky, Hannah and Chris stared out the windshield, each wrapped in their own thoughts. When he reached for her hand, she stiffened and withdrew it into her lap.

He turned his head toward her, eyebrows knit in concern. "That fella back there sure knew how to stir up the congregation. We left before he could put the squeeze on them for money. I'm sure that was coming next."

Hannah's face whipped around. "That's a very cynical point of view."

"He was playing on your emotions, sweetheart. Surely, you realize that."

She took a deep breath and roved Chris' face, as if memorizing it in the moonlight. Her eyes glistened with unshed tears. Her hand reached up and cradled his jaw.

"I'll never love another man except you. You've given me a wonderful experience, one that I know I'll treasure my whole life. I'll never stop thinking about you, remembering you, praying for you."

Fear seized his gut. "What are you talking about? We're getting married, aren't we?"

"I can't marry you." Her sad face tore at his heart.

"We belong together," Chris said, fighting confusion and panic. "I need you. You're the one I want waiting for me at the end of a tough assignment. I promise it will be a fulfilling life. We'll have children. We'll travel. You can teach at bases all over the world."

She slowly shook her head. "I'm sorry. You'll never know how sorry. I can't be your wife, and serve the Lord the way He wants me to. I'd always know I'd taken the selfish path—the one that placed my happiness over the call He has for my life."

"This is ridiculous thinking. You've been brainwashed by a bunch of fanatics. You've got no business traipsing around the world, wasting your life on people who will only reject you and break your heart. I love you. I want to take care of you."

She twisted the tissue with her fingers. "You don't understand. I heard the Voice tonight speaking to me--*You are the Saint. Send Faithful away. He's not for you.*"

"You're speaking in riddles, sweetheart. You're confused and easily influenced by that old man. You didn't hear anything but your overworked imagination."

Tears welled in her eyes. "I heard the Voice loud and clear. So loud it drowned out much of what Pastor Monroe was saying. I don't know what it all means. But I know you're Faithful, and I'm supposed to send you away. I can't deny it."

Chris clutched her by the upper arms. "Don't do this to us. Don't throw us away."

Desperation made him kiss her too hard, hold her too tight. She didn't fight; she endured. Tears trickled down her cheeks. He tasted them when they reached his lips.

He released her. "Oh, Jesus, I'm sorry. Did I hurt you?"

A sad ghost of a smile rested on her swollen lips. "You could never hurt me, Chris. But you need to take me home now."

Her incredible calm, her immovable resolve, defeated him.

He pointed the car toward her dorm, driving on automatic pilot, as his emotions churned.

This can't be happening...She'll come to her senses in the morning...I'll call her and everything will be all right again...

After insisting he stay in the car, she walked away from him on the uneven sidewalk toward the lighted porch of the old dorm house. The image of golden hair resting on slim shoulders, as her sweater swayed above curved hips burned in his memory.

Chris slapped the steering wheel in frustration. He loved a girl who obeyed The Voice. How could a mere man compete with that?

Chapter Thirty-Three

Now, five years and a lifetime later, Chris held a weeping Hannah in his arms, clasping her tightly. Cleansing tears ran their course, as the couple stood near the plate glass window. Rain pelted the glass pane in tandem with her personal downpour. His hands soothed her back with lazy circles. He frowned at the bony shoulder blades poking through the cotton shirt. Captivity had taken its toll in many ways. Thin, tired, wrung out—Hannah needed serious R and R.

Looking down, he recognized the same cornflower blue eyes over sharper cheekbones and, something he'd hope to never see in Hannah's eyes—fear.

He stroked the side of her head. "Want something to drink? They might even have a genuine Coke in the wet bar."

She sniffed and offered a watery smile. "Sounds great."

She sank onto the love seat near the windows. Two small cushioned chairs and a table filled out the area. Chris found a couple of Cokes and poured two glasses.

Crossing the room with the drinks, he said, "Sugar, you sure are a sight for sore eyes."

"You look pretty good yourself, soldier." A trace of the old Hannah twinkled in her eyes. She took the offered drink. "Cheers."

Chris settled next to her. "This is sort of an official visit. We'll need to spend time tomorrow in debriefing."

Worry shadowed Hannah's face. "Of course. I'll try to be as helpful as possible." Her gaze swept over the insignia on his shirt. A smile tugged at her lips. "You've been promoted since I saw you last. Congratulations, Colonel."

"Thanks. I know it won't be easy for you to have re-live the events of the past few months, but I'll be there with you. If you get tired, just send me the signal. But, tonight, anything you say is strictly off the record. I want you to know that. Anything said in this room is just between the two of us."

Hannah leaned back, relaxing into the sofa. "It's a wonderful surprise to see you. I never forgot you, Chris. I know I hurt you and--"

He placed a finger on her lips. "You made the right decision. Well, at least in not marrying me. I'm not so sure about living with a bunch of natives, and getting captured by fanatics." Jiggling the ice in his glass, he continued, "We wouldn't have had any kind of life together. I've been traveling constantly, always at risk, never knowing where I'd be from one week to the next. I couldn't expect a wife to put up with that. It wouldn't have been fair to you."

"I guess we've both been leading solitary lives." Hannah cocked her head. "Have you been happy?"

He frowned. "My life has never been about pursuing personal happiness. It's been about serving a purpose."

"Yes, that's the one thing we always had in common. We wanted our lives to count for something. Only we used different paths." She ran her fingers through her hair. "But, now I feel like I've lost my way."

Chris reached out for her hand. "Your joy is gone. I can sense it. You've been robbed of the peace you used to wear like a cloak."

Hannah clutched his fingers. "You're right. Oh, Chris, you know me so well. I'm scared all the time. Fear sits in my chest like a heavy weight, always pulling me down. The slightest noise makes me jump."

"Honey, that's normal. It's called battle fatigue. You've been under fire for months now. Even trained soldiers come back from battle jumpy. You'll get over it."

"It's more than that. I have doubts. Doubts about everything I ever believed. What if I was truly just brainwashed as a child in church? What if my faith is nothing but a bunch of fairy tales and wishful thinking? Oh, Chris, have I been looking at the world through rose-colored glasses my whole life? Are my beliefs mere myth—a do-gooder's illusion for a wicked world?"

Chris didn't have any answers. And, he didn't think she wanted to hear calming platitudes. All he could do was lift her hand to his lips, and offer a caring kiss of tenderness.

That small gesture pierced her weak defenses. "Will you hold me, Chris? I need your strength tonight."

Wordlessly, he wrapped his arm around her, brought her to the crook of his shoulder. She felt as fragile as a kitten. "I'm here, Sugar."

She released a small shudder. "I've had to be strong for so long, fighting the good fight. Keeping Amelia's spirits up, pretending to be the Christian Superwoman. I'm so tired."

"They can't touch you now."

She didn't seem to hear him. "I've seen evil. I've smelled and tasted it."

His arm tightened around her. "I hate to think of you at the mercy of those bastards."

"I'm not talking about my captors. I'm talking about myself. I've seen the blackness in my soul. I've hated and wished revenge. I've denounced God in my heart. He deserted me. That's what it felt like. I was left to battle the enemy alone. Then, the more Ahmed talked, the more I came to wonder who the enemy really is. Ahmed kept telling me about the Master, being held captive on the island by a jealous God. All I had to do was worship the Master, and he could be set free. It sounded wonderful. Finally, a way to bring peace on earth through the power of this Master."

Chris frowned at the turn of the conversation. What kind of crazy mind-bending had she experienced?

Hannah's eyes glazed over; her body trembled. "I thought I served the true God. But Ahmed told me it had all been lies. Over and over, he called the Scriptures lies." She buried her face in his shoulder. "Oh, I'm so confused, I don't know what I believe anymore. His words sounded so convincing. Speaking of the new world, with the power of the Master restored, sounded like heaven on earth. *Come to the Master of your own will.* He repeated it again and again. His voice could be so soothing, hypnotic." Her voice dropped to a whisper, colored with guilt and humiliation. "I almost did it. In that airless tent, with only Ahmed and myself in the space, I fell on my knees and nearly submitted to Ahmed for baptism to dedicate my life to the Master. I came so close."

Hannah froze at the memory.

Chris tilted her face toward him. "What happened?"

"I looked into his eyes. His voice had deceived me, but his eyes could not."

"What did you see in his eyes?"

"Death...murder...and total destruction."

***

Somewhere around the witching hour, Chris sat in a chair watching Hannah sleep. Emotional depletion and physical exhaustion had knocked her out. However, he was wide awake, pumped with the adrenaline that comes from anger and confusion.

Ahmed's bizarre brainwashing attempts had obviously shaken Hannah to her core, stolen her calm serenity. Something more was going on here than a kidnapping and a demand for ransom. The Arab's greatest goal appeared to be destroying her faith. And what was this "Master" business? It didn't sound like any form of Islam he recognized.

Chris stood and paced the carpet. Something about that island disturbed him. What secret did it hide?

Hannah stirred in the bed, mumbling in a fitful sleep.

Chris knelt at her side and smoothed her hair. "Quiet, honey. It's just a bad dream."

She opened groggy eyes and smiled when she recognized him. "Hey, soldier, you still hanging around?"

"I don't want to leave you, Sugar."

She slipped her hand into his. "I don't want you leave."

"But we need answers about what happened to you."

Thunder crashed again outside the hotel. "I know. This doesn't feel like it's over."

Chris pondered his options. One person knew more about Paradisio than any other. Jaguar Jack Campbell.

"Put on your slippers and robe, honey. I think we need to pay a visit to some folks down the hall."

Chapter Thirty-Four

In a nearby bedroom, Maggie smiled in her sleep. Floating just under consciousness, she knew exactly where she lay. Next to the warm, naked body of Jaguar Jack Campbell. Jack, the mystery man, the jocular jokester of animal adventures, the man who made her feel like a woman. Compelling, complex, and compassionate. A triple threat. And there was something else. He needed her.

Tonight when he'd spoken of his nightmare, his sense of cowardice, she'd known he needed her. Whatever Jack's nightmare entailed, they could face it together. Already, they were in it together, whether she liked it or not.

Jack's body jerked, startling her fully awake. When she touched his chest, the dampness of sweat slicked her palm. His ribcage heaved in uneven, tight breaths, as if he struggled for air.

From seemingly nowhere, images flashed through her mind—jagged teeth, bared claws, dark green razor-sharp palm fronds, running…running…

Maggie blinked away the images and shook Jack's shoulder. "Jack! Snap out of it."

Keep away, you ruddy bugger. Jack's voice echoed in her mind.

"Wake up. I mean it, Jack."

She knew he dreamt about the island. Was he just dreaming or was he tuning in on something? Had Jack taken a trip to the Twilight Zone again?

He thrashed on the bed. She had to bring him back. She didn't try to understand it. Didn't know what was really happening here, but she followed her instincts. There was only one way to pull Jack out of the vortex of fear and destruction.

Sliding over him, she grabbed his flailing hands and slid her fingers between his. She rested her head on his heaving chest and whispered, "I've got you, Jack. Red is holding on and won't let go."

Then she closed her eyes, released her mind, and freed her emotions. Reaching out into an unseen dimension, she called out to him with her thoughts. *I'm here, Jack…*

His thrashing continued unabated, the choking worsened.

She silently screamed, *It's Maggie! Find me!*

Nothing…She sensed herself hanging onto an emotional cliff, afraid to let go and take the plunge. But she'd never find Jack until she released her grip, and dropped into the unknown depths of her psyche.

Jack's voice whispered in her mind from farther away. *Oh, God, help me…*_

She was losing him. Panic seized her. *Don't hold back or you'll lose him forever.* Struggling and scared, Maggie surrendered her pride, her fear of emotional attachment, her self-centered ego, and allowed the truth of her emotions to burst forth.

Love poured out of her. Pure and true and strong. And, just as Maggie could throw herself into battle for the country she loved, now, she could fight the forces of evil for this marvelous man. This man she loved—a crazy, civilian TV star.

Heartbeat to heartbeat, Maggie rode the wave of Jack's distress, falling in sync with his breathing. Eyes closed, she willed him to feel her love, hear her beckon him back from the brink of hell. Time lost meaning. She yelled into a tunnel of darkness, calling to Jack through the abyss—*Come back to me.*

The bed seemed to spin, sucked into a speeding tube, a wild ride through time and space.

Jack knew he was suffering another bout of insanity, but couldn't pull out. Caught in another dimension, his astral body faced the Beast in the island lair. Jack fought his lifetime conditioning of terror, holding firm where he stood, not giving into the desire to cower. The Beast bellowed; he roared; he rose high on his hind legs, huge claws mauling the air.

"Run, Warrior, run before I tear you apart!"

Jack's courage crumbled. He was eight years old again, running in terror, dashing away with unspeakable fright. His feet jumped over roots and rocks, higher and higher up the mountainside. Sulfuric fumes wafted in the air, growing stronger and stronger. Vegetation gave way to uneven volcanic ridges. Roars of the Beast grew closer and closer, louder and louder, driving him to the rim of the volcano.

Sprays of molten lava shot from the mouth of the opening to the earth's core. Jack halted.

"Jump!" the Beast commanded. "Choose the easier death. Otherwise, I'll rip you slowly to shreds."

Confusion muddled Jack's reason. He hovered on the brink, caught between a burning underworld, and a monster. Heat seared his face, the undulating red magma churned in the mountain's depths. He glanced over his shoulder at the Beast, in all its hideous power. Fright punched Jack's gut, quaked his limbs. He gritted his teeth and forced back the irrational fear. Something didn't add up here. He stood frozen between two kinds of hell.

Maggie's mind zoomed through the netherworld, searching for her missing man.

Spinning, spinning…the whirling wouldn't stop. She couldn't find him. How to find him? Sulfuric smoke obliterated her vision and fear slammed her chest like body blow. Only Maggie's years of mental military training kept her from retreating.

Don't stop. Find him. Find him.

How? How?

Then she knew. She possessed a force stronger than evil, stronger than fear and intimidation. *Don't just admit you love him, use the power of that love.* She pictured her love as a beacon of light. Into the darkness she imagined a laser beam of love blasting through the black hole.

I love you, Jack…See the light……Follow the beam…Seek the light…

No more words, just love, that's what she sent Jack. The force from her heart unfurled through the tunnel like a glowing rope, a life-saving cord for him to grab and be reeled in.

Standing on the precipice, waiting for the Beast to attack, Jack heard Maggie's thoughts. *I love you, Jack…See the light……Follow the beam…Seek the light…* They calmed him, centered him. Gave him courage. Made him realize something.

Jack spoke to the Beast. "You're bloody good at scaring the bejeezes out of me, and making me feel like a child again." He swaggered a step toward his foe, issuing a challenge. "Come on, Beast. Give me your best shot."

The Beast charged him. Jack had two choices: jump into the churning pit or hold his ground. He held his ground. The Beast stopped just short of attacking him.

Jack locked onto the Beast's red eyes and for the first time, he glimpsed the truth. The Beast was afraid of *him*!

A glowing rope dropped between Jack and the Beast, like a rescue line from a helicopter.

Maggie's voice rang in his mind. *Reach for it, Jack...Hold onto the shining rope...Hold on, hold on...*

Jack grabbed it and held tight. Fear immediately vanished. Jack sensed Maggie in the laser-like beam. She reeled him back to reality and sanity.

The world stopped spinning, the blackness receded. Maggie re-entered real time and three-dimensional space. The hotel room...the king size bed...lying on top of Jack.

She waited, knowing he was coming back to her. Finally, his breathing calmed, the struggle ceased, his eyelids fluttered and then opened.

Maggie lifted her head and smiled down into his face. "Welcome back, jungle man."

He lifted a hand, and ran it through the lush red mane that dangled over her shoulders. A croaky rasp rose from his throat. "You entered my nightmare and pulled me out. How did you do it?"

The words dammed up in her throat—*I love you.* She'd only just discovered it, only understood an inkling of its power. This much she knew, her love had brought Jack back from the Twilight Zone. But she wanted answers. He'd been evasive long enough.

"I want to know what's going on, Jack."

"Yes," a familiar southern drawl said from the doorway. "I'd also like to know what exactly is going on."

Light poured into the room from the opening door. Maggie glanced over her naked shoulder. She blinked. *Cripes, Chris Matthews.* She scrambled off Jack, and yanked the sheet up to her chin.

Jack casually stretched his hands behind his head. "Crikey, Maggie, you didn't have to call out the bloody Marines."

Chapter Thirty-Five

Standing atop the volcanic peak, the Beast roared in frustration. He'd nearly captured the Warrior's soul! So close, so close. A mere leap away from being trapped in the underworld and separated from his mortal body. A body that would soon die without its spirit.

What force had plucked the Warrior from his clutches? He'd been blinded by the flash of light, momentarily weakened, reminiscent of his collapse after losing the last great war.

The Beast paced furiously; his steps caused the earth to tremble. He refused to become a defeated, scrawny weakling again. He glanced at his haunches, now bulging with taut muscles. He smiled in satisfaction. Spiritual strength poured into him across the cosmic waves as his followers grew in numbers. Only the Saint and Warrior stood in his way.

They must not discover their true identities. The Warrior with his power to throw the Beast into the underworld. The Saint with her power to keep him there. But the Beast had two weapons he used with cunning. Fear and lies. So far, both of his nemeses had failed to overcome the wall of fear or see through his veil of lies.

And everyday, more mortals came under his control. In the West, he'd unleashed the harlot of Babylon to spread sexual bondage and the deadly AIDS virus; millions now sought only sexual pleasure and drug-induced oblivion, remaining spiritually shallow. In the East, terror and intimidation reigned. The Beast purred with glee, picturing the thousands of believers suffering behind bars, tortured and ridiculed.

Every mortal that followed the path of darkness made him a little stronger every day. No kindness, no compassion, no charity. That's what he loved to see. Oh yes, he had only to destroy the spiritual power of the Warrior and the Saint, and he'd be free!

Free to roam the earth and fulfill his voracious appetite for souls.

***

"Damn it, Campbell," Matthews said, "you're evading my questions. I'm not leaving until I get some straight answers. I want to know why Mokar needed you to get Hannah off the island. Why wouldn't Ahmed cooperate in securing the ransom?"

Sitting wrapped in a hotel robe across from Hannah and Chris, Maggie listened to the conversation swirling around her. After barging into their suite, Chris grilled Jack about the events on the island. A verbal game of cat and mouse.

Seated beside her, Jack gripped Maggie's hand. He sounded cavalier and casual about the rescue, but she sensed his trepidation. He avoided any mention of the Twilight Zone. Fear from the other realm stalked Jack. Constantly, relentlessly. Psychically connected now, she glimpsed his torture. He acted the daredevil to prove he wasn't a coward. But the specter of fear always loomed in his mind like a shadow.

And it was a lie. Maggie knew it, but Jack did not.

She squeezed his hand. "Look at me, Jack."

He cocked an eyebrow. "What?--"

She stared at him with steely intent, trying to emblaze her words into his mind. "You're not a coward. Nothing is farther from the truth."

He stared back, dumbfounded.

Chris exploded with frustration. "What's really happening on that island?"

Hannah spoke for the first time. "You're reciting the outward facts, Jack, but I need to understand the underlying forces. This experience has been more than a hostage being held for ransom. Ahmed battled for my soul. And I don't know why."

Jack ran his fingers through his hair and muttered, "Lordy, I wish I was back in the jungle facing a ten foot anaconda." He sighed. "Listen, I have a lot of crazy thoughts. Delusions you might call them. If I tell you what I think is going on at Paradisio, you'll be calling for the men with the white coats."

"Jack! Don't do this anymore." Maggie jostled his shoulder. "You are not crazy. You're certainly not a coward. Don't buy into those lies anymore. Tell us what you know. Trust us with your secrets." She squeezed his hand. "Trust *me*."

He gazed into Maggie's steady green eyes and took courage. Her touch grounded him. Her small smile of confidence empowered him.

He turned to Chris and Hannah, and decided to take the plunge. He'd tell them what he knew or, perhaps, merely imagined. "All right, mate, at the risk of sounding totally balmy, here's what I think lives on Paradisio—the bloody Beast from the Book of Revelation."

Hannah gasped.

Chris frowned. "You mean there's some sort of religious cult on the island that worships the Beast? Hannah kept talking about the Master. Is there some high priest on the island that has everyone under his spell?"

Jack shrugged his shoulders. "See, Red, nobody's going to believe me."

"I believe you. I've seen the Beast, remember?"

Hannah nodded. "Please, Jack. I really need to understand."

Chris grunted, "Just spill it, Campbell. Anybody who's watched your television show already knows you're half crazy."

Jack lowered his head. Letting go was hard. He'd worked so many years at keeping a lid on the Pandora's Box in his mind—the memories, the images, the fears. What if he let them all out and they destroyed him? What if he dissolved into the balmy coward he knew himself to be before these people?

Once again, Jack took courage in Maggie's strength. Her steely nerve never wavered. With her at his side, he could open his mind and search for the truth. A twirling vortex widened in his internal vision. Like a picture show flashing on a movie screen, the events of his past played in the theatre of his mind. He unleashed the images screaming to burst forth from his subconscious.

"My Mum died protecting me from the Beast." Jack gripped Maggie's hand and allowed the memory to focus. "My father had gone off in search of specimens as Mother and I made camp. I was eight years old, searching for a bit of tucker to contribute to dinner when the wind came up suddenly; the sky went blue to black in a matter of moments. Even as a young boy, I knew it wasn't natural. Neither was the smell." He turned his head toward Maggie. "Red, it's the most horrific stench. Beyond imagination, really. Trees quaked at his approach. Leaves and branches hit my head. I fell to the ground and covered my face. Then I heard his roar and looked up."

He gazed toward the ceiling, reliving the fateful day. "Oh, crikey, what a sight. A huge brown and black cat-head and body—but his broad legs and large claws were more bear like. His roar reverberated across the valley like a sonic blast, far louder than any animal could ever be." Jack's eyes stared off. "He was thinner then, his coat mottled and dirty. I gazed up at him from my knees, completely mesmerized."

He stopped for a moment, lost in memory. Maggie spoke up. "But you weren't really scared, were you, Jack?"

"No, Red, you're right. I wasn't scared. In fact I stood up and held my ground, a defiant little eight year old boy, full of piss and vinegar. I spoke to him. *I'm not scared of you, you smelly old bugger.*"

Maggie smiled, "That's my Jack."

His eyes darkened. "Then the Beast spoke. *Not scared of me? You will be. You shall be terrified of me for the rest of your life.* A bolt of lightning struck the ground and knocked me off my feet. But I jumped back up. *I'll never be frightened by the likes of you.*"

Jack stood and paced the carpet, as if trying to put pieces of a puzzle together. "I'm just remembering something. When I stared into his red eyes, he seemed frightened of me. Yes, I've seen that look in hundreds of animals' eyes. Fear before they either run or attack."

"Is that when he attacked you?" Maggie asked.

Squinting as he endeavored to recall, he said, "No, he spoke to me. *So, Warrior, we meet at last.*"

Hannah leaned forward. "He called you Warrior?"

"Yes, I remember now, he called me Warrior, whatever that means. Then the storm broke out in full fury. Lightning strikes, hail, whirlwinds. *Run, coward,* he yelled. Still, I wasn't afraid until my Mother came through the bushes searching for me. The terror on her face…her screams…the Beast's hot breath on our back as we ran. Then I was bloody scared all right. Mother grabbed my arm as we fled through the sharp palm fronds. Trees struck by lightning crashed in front of us. She cried *God help us* over and over. We reached a small hill where an animal had dug a burrow. She shoved me inside. I crawled as far back as I could, but there wasn't room for her, too. She turned and faced the Beast, protecting me. Dirt and roots fell down, choking me. I couldn't see her anymore, but I heard my Mum's cries mixed with the Beast's roar."

Jack's hands drew into tight fists at his side as he gazed out the window, unseeing. "I hear the sounds in my dreams. Terrible, terrible noises of rage and destruction. Then I hear my Mum no more—only the words of the Beast. *You're a coward. You allowed your mother to die for you. Coward!"*

A fine sheen of sweat covered Jack's face, caught in the echo of his memory. Watching him from the love seat, Maggie trembled for him. Her gaze traveled to the other sofa. Chris's arm was protectively wrapped around Hannah's shoulders. Quiet tears tracked down her cheeks. His knit eyebrows reflected his difficulty believing Jack's story. Maggie didn't blame him for being skeptical. Until very recently, Maggie the Marine would have declared Jack a candidate for the loony bin and left it at that. But she knew better now.

Jack continued, "I stayed huddled in that hole until my father found me, too afraid to venture out and try to help my mother."

Maggie rose and joined him by the window, placing a hand on his arm. "I've seen the Beast. There's no way an eight-year-old boy could have fought him off."

"Perhaps not." He offered a wan smile. "So, that's what I've kept inside me for thirty years. Feels kind of good to let it out, even at the risk of being dragged back to the nut house. The Beast exists; he isn't just a figment of my imagination."

Maggie nodded, and the truth of her life became suddenly clear. "We've been busy fighting the visible enemy, when an invisible one has been in charge all along."

"I don't see what any of this has to do with Hannah," Chris said.

"I think maybe I do." Hannah spoke quietly, pensively. She rose, glided into the bedroom, and returned with a Gideon's Bible in her hand. Flipping back to Revelation, she searched for a passage as the others silently watched her.

"Here it is," she said. *"I saw heaven standing open and there before me was a white horse, whose rider is called Faithful and Truth.* The passage goes on to describe a battle between the warrior on the white horse, and the Beast and his false prophet. One night on the island, I was taken to a ceremony. I drank some drugged wine and had a strange vision I didn't understand at the time."

Sitting on the edge of the love seat with the Bible open in her lap, Hannah frowned. "My brain is still so fuzzy. I'm trying to remember the details."

Maggie tugged on Jack's hand and brought him back to their couch. She nodded at Hannah. "Just tell us what you remember."

Hannah pulled the memory into focus. "I saw a fighting arena. A winged white horse descended out of the sky carrying a warrior on its back." She looked sharply at Jack. "I realize now, that warrior was you. He had the same dark hair and piercing blue eyes. There were two attendants who made him ready for battle. A woman with red hair and a fair-haired man."

Hannah gazed down at the scripture again. "It says here the rider is *called* Faithful and Truth. But perhaps the translation isn't quite correct. Perhaps the rider is *with* Faithful and Truth. Remember, Chris, when I heard the Voice tell me I had to send Faithful away? I knew it was speaking about you."

Chris lifted a skeptical eyebrow. "I'm having a real hard time buying all this, Sugar."

Maggie lifted a hand. "Hold on, Matthews. As crazy as this all seems, it's beginning to make some sense to me."

Hannah smiled. "That's because you're Truth. You have the gift of discernment. Haven't you always been a seeker of truth? Someone who always gets to the heart of the matter?"

Maggie blinked. "That's right. My not-so-nice nickname is Maggie the Mouth because I'm so blunt. And you're saying that's a gift?"

Jack stroked her hand. "Take it from someone who knows, Red. A gift can feel like a curse."

She gazed into his cobalt eyes, sharing a penetrating moment of perception. They each possessed "gifts" they'd been fighting their whole lives.

Maggie turned back to Hannah. "Okay, so I'm 'Truth' and Matthews is 'Faithful.' How exactly did we get Jack the Warrior ready for battle?"

Hannah excitedly flipped through the Bible again, seeking another passage. "I just realized, you were fitting him with the armor of God from Ephesians." Her finger moved down the page. "Here it is: *Stand firm then with the belt of truth buckled around your waist, with the breastplate of righteousness in place...Take the helmet of Salvation and the sword of the Spirit.* I saw you equip Jack with all those things. They were magnificent."

"Then what happened?" Jack asked, leaning forward.

"Then the Beast stepped out of the shadows. Only everyone was calling him Master and chanting 'Master...Master...Master' over and over. The Beast and the Warrior fought hand to hand. It was loud and fierce and bloody. Round and round the arena they went, slashing and tearing at each other."

When Hannah failed to continue, Chris placed a hand on her shoulder. "Who won, Sugar?"

She shrugged. "I don't know. I must have passed out entirely before the battle ended."

Maggie sat back, tapping her leg in thought. "Okay, I'm Truth, Matthews is Faithful, and Jack is the Warrior. Who the heck are you?"

Hannah shook her head. "I have no idea."

Chapter Thirty-Six

At 0900 hours the following morning Chris, Hannah, and Derby gathered in her sitting room at a round table, debriefing. Derby typed with astonishing speed into his laptop, recording the questions and answers volleying back and forth between the man and woman.

Chris purposely dressed in uniform to remind himself that today he was on the job, gathering intelligence information from a key witness who'd spent hours with one of the most-wanted men on the planet, Ahmed Saeed. For her part, Hannah appeared a bit stronger and more alert than the night before. Dressed in a Western pale blue blouse with yellow flowers and a soft skirt, she could almost be that college girl he'd fallen in love with in another time and place.

He fought to keep his emotions in check, keep a professional detachment as Hannah's tale of capture, deprivation, and brainwashing unfolded. But it was damned difficult watching her fragile face recall moments of terror. Even before Ahmed Saeed appeared on the scene, she'd had more than her share of gun battles, and an arduous march through an insect infested jungle. She reluctantly showed him a place on her leg that had ulcerated and healed roughly. He could only imagine how that infection had throbbed during relentless marches.

"How did you treat it?" he asked.

She smiled that little turned up way when she was embarrassed. "On a day it was really bad, we entered a village and a medicine man looked at it. I felt like maybe I had been led to him, so I let him treat it."

"Did he use native medicine?"

Now, she truly grinned. "Maggots."

Derby quit typing at that. "Maggots!"

"Yeah, he had them in his hut with all his medicines. He carefully placed them in the wound and covered it up. They actually tickled as they ate up the infection."

Derby made a face and pushed up his glasses. "Gross."

"Hey, whatever works."

With anybody else, Chris might have found the anecdote amusing, but the thought of his pure Hannah walking around with an infected, maggoty leg filled him with impotent rage.

Hannah must have read the angst on his face because she reached out and patted his hand. "It wasn't that bad, honestly."

Chris recovered his cool, and asked her questions regarding Ahmed Saeed. Hannah's recitation of Saeed's continual assault on her faith turned her face ashen.

"He kept talking about the Master. The Master could save the world, stop all conflicts, bring about world peace if everyone would just worship him. All I had to do was deny my faith, come to him of my own free will. He made it sound so logical, so attractive."

"What held you back?"

"His eyes. The words that flowed from his mouth could be as sweet as honey, pouring over me. But, when I looked into his eyes, I glimpsed darkness that chilled my soul. I never would have forsaken my faith on Saeed's words alone. But, I almost gave in for another reason. If Maggie and Jack hadn't arrived when they did, I would have gone with Saeed to the ceremonial place and surrendered myself to the Master."

"Why?"

"Amelia. He knew how protective I felt toward her. I could see the relationship blossoming between her and Felipe. Given a chance to get away, they might have had a future. Amelia and I secretly clung to our faith, whispering together whenever we could. I thought, perhaps, God had sent me to be a sacrifice for Amelia's sake. *Greater love has no man than when he lays down his life for another.* I kept trying to make sense out of why I was there and thought maybe that was it. But then, I was rescued. So now, I don't know what it was all about."

"Sugar, sometimes people just get caught in the crossfire. It isn't always part of some grand plan."

She sighed and ran her fingers through her hair. "Maybe you're right. I used to be so sure of things, and now I don't know anything anymore."

If she'd been anyone else, Chris would have hammered her for more information, but Hannah looked tired. "Let's take a break. I'm sure you want to say good-bye to your father before he leaves for the states."

She nodded. "Yes, Mom's going with me for the medical check up in Germany, and then we'll meet him back home."

As she headed down the security-tight hallway to her parents' room, Chris paced the elegant hotel room. Derby muttered in the background, fiddling with his computer.

Regret poured through Chris, bitter and achy. He never should have walked away. He should have stuck like glue to Hannah, despite her protests and visions. She'd needed his protection, whether she'd known it or not, and he'd let her down by allowing her to break away.

Well, it wasn't going to happen again. This might be a second chance, and he wasn't going to let it pass by.

***

A ruckus in the hall commenced when one small monkey, dressed in a snappy paisley cap and matching vest, dashed out of the elevator. Four security guards drew weapons, scaring the monkey into screeches and a panicky attempt to escape between their legs. The men hopped around, attempting to catch the elusive critter.

Edith Campbell scampered out of the elevator, wearing a mad print tent dress featuring red and blue hibiscus flowers. "Mr. Jiggs, you naughty boy, stop right this instant."

Auntie Edith waddled to a crew-cut Marine and removed a frightened Mr. Jiggs from his back. "Sorry about that, young man. The sight of pistols disturbs him." She patted her monkey like a baby. "That's all right, Mummy's got you."

A stern guard spoke up. "You'll have to leave, ma'am. This is a restricted area."

"Oh, twaddle. I'm looking for Jaguar Jack Campbell. I know he's up here. I'm his Aunt Edith."

A younger guard recognized her. "It's Auntie Edith, from *The Adventures of Jaguar Jack!* I love your show."

Edith patted his cheek. "Aren't you a sweet boy?"

Mr. Stern Guard clamped a hand on Edith's shoulder. "You'll have to leave ma'am."

As he began herding her toward the elevator, Mr. Jiggs responded with a needle-like monkey bite.

"Aahhh!" the guard yelled.

"Mwooock!" Mr. Jiggs replied.

A room door opened. Maggie peeked her head out, followed by a flapping of white wings and a squawk of "Crikey, mate!"

Lorelei flew into the fray, responding to the distress call of her favorite playmate, Mr. Jiggs. Auntie Edith dithered in the chaos, trying to placate Mr. Stern Guard, who cursed a blue-streak. "He's had his rabies shot. I'm terribly sorry."

Jack and Maggie took a step into the hallway from their room, drawn by the commotion.

He cocked an eyebrow. "Looks like the start of another typical Jaguar Jack day."

He stepped forward and took command of the situation. Dressed in a flashy tropical design shirt and dark slacks, his hair still damp from a shower, he embodied Jaguar-Jack-on-vacation. As Maggie watched him charm the guards, control his animal psychic aunt, and end up with a bird on his shoulder and a monkey in his arms, she marveled at her change of emotions.

The old Maggie would have cynically witnessed the hallway circus as a lot of TV hero hoo-ha. Now, she gazed at Jack with starry eyes, taken by his good looks and easy charm, protective of the complicated man beneath the surface. No doubt about it, Maggie had turned into a genuine Jaguar Jack groupie. And, she had the love bites to prove it.

When she'd gazed at Chris Matthews the night before, all the Magnolia Savannah fantasies had disappeared. Chris was just another Marine, a good guy to have at your back. What had Hannah called him —Faithful? Yeah, Chris lived up to that title, a true blue straight shooter. And, he appeared to be carrying a burning torch for one blond missionary.

Hannah had quietly explained to Maggie while Jack and Chris had been hashing out some matters, that Chris was the boyfriend she'd left behind. No wonder Matthews sometimes seemed more than a little edgy about the mission.

Auntie Edith opened her arms to Maggie as she approached down the hall. "My dear, I'm happy to see you looking so well."

Maggie leaned down into Edith's cushiony embrace, inhaling her flowery scent. "It's good to see you, too."

Arm in arm, they strolled into the room, soon followed by Jack and the pets. Auntie Edith talked a mile a minute, catching them up on all the happenings with the crew. Jack had evidently made contact with them while Maggie had been holed up at the Rat and Roach Hotel.

With Mr. Jiggs and Lorelei contentedly eating fruit at the table, the three humans sipped hot drinks in the seating area. Jack and Maggie didn't try to conceal their easy intimacy sitting on the brocade couch. For the first time in her life, she felt feminine. He casually held her hand, sometimes unconsciously playing with it as he visited with Edith.

"So, when do we leave here, Jack?" Edith asked. "That nasty squall has both our plane and your helicopter grounded at the moment."

A shadow passed over his face as he glanced out the window. "Yes, this storm has been a ripsnorter, all right."

"A new shipment of those old antique weapons you like arrived. Looks like they followed us halfway around the world."

"Really? I wasn't expecting anything. I guess old Nicodemus came across something special and knew I'd be good for it."

"I stowed the package on your helicopter. You can look at your goodies later. We've scheduled the next shoot in the Galapagos Islands three days from now. I'd hate to postpone."

Jack's eyes lit up. "That's right." He turned his gaze to Maggie, all afire for another adventure. "Have you ever been to the Galapagos Islands, Red? You're going to love them."

Reality smacked Maggie in the face. "I can't go with you to the Galapagos Islands."

"What? Why, not?"

"My mission here is over. Even though we all have questions about what dwells on that damned island and how to deal with it, technically, the mission was accomplished." An invisible thud hit her solar plexus. "I have to report back, and then be given a new assignment."

Jack slumped in his seat. "The bloody Marine Corps."

"It's what I do, Jack."

He stood and crossed to pour himself more coffee. "Sure, sure. Maggie the Marine fighting for truth, justice, and the American way."

"Don't belittle it. There are thousands of troops with their asses on the line every day for the very things you're mocking."

Edith peeked over her tea cup. "He's just jealous of the Marine Corps. He wants you for himself. Don't you, Jack?"

He turned around, his face an impassive mask. "Don't be ridiculous. Maggie's right. She has her own life. She wouldn't want to go traipsing around the world with a whacker who's balmy half the time." He strode back and cupped Maggie's cheek with his palm, his indigo eyes piercing her soul. He towered over her as she remained on the couch. His wide shoulders blocked out the rest of the world. The touch of his fingers burned. "Just remember, Red, you're a stunning woman. It's been an honor knowing you."

He bent down and touched his lips to hers, a soft farewell. He offered a sad wink as he turned on his heels and scooped Lorelei into his arms. Then he strolled into his bedroom and shut the door.

Maggie sat motionless on the sofa. She should get up, pack a bag, and shove off. Track down Matthews and Derby and figure how to get off this soggy island. But she couldn't move. Leaving Jack Campbell felt like cutting off her own arm. When did this happen?

Edith jarred her out of limbo. "I think you've taken a fancy to our Jack. Am I right? I knew when he met the right girl, she'd be very special. Someone with a strong heart and spirit."

Maggie pushed to her feet, feeling the need for some kind of action. "This is crazy. I can't stay with Jack and live in his unreal, Hollywood world, all tinsel and pretend. I'm used to being on the front lines and fighting for what's important."

Edith raised an eyebrow. "Maybe you just don't have a true picture of what Jack is all about or what's really important."

Maggie hated feeling confused, and at the moment she was confused as hell. "I'd better go pack."

Before she could escape to her room, the phone rang.

It was Chris Matthews. "Mag-Pie, I need you and Jungle Jim to come down to Hannah's room to finish the report."

"Okay, sure. We'll be right there."

Maggie crossed the room and tapped on Jack's door before opening it. "Jack, we need to report to Matthews."

Rather than being busy packing, he sat on the edge of the bed, petting his white feathered best friend, communing again in the Twilight Zone.

With blank eyes, he looked through her. "He's laughing at me, Red. I can hear the laughter."

"What the hell are you talking about?"

"He's getting so much stronger. I can hear the Beast, even off the island. Until now, I'd sensed him being imprisoned there. But, his influence feels like it's spreading."

"You're wierding me out, Jack."

"I want to walk away and leave the bloody thing where he lies, but I'm caught up in something I can't escape. I don't know what's coming, but it's coming as sure as an inevitable train wreck."

The intensity of his otherworldly voice made her blood run cold.

Aunt Edith toddled in and tapped Maggie on the shoulder. "I'm going to go find the crew. Don't be rushing off yet."

Staring at Jack in his bizarre state, Maggie knew she couldn't leave him yet. "Fine, Auntie, I'll--"

Boom! The hotel rocked from a powerful explosion. Shattered glass flew across the living room, as windows imploded. Maggie instinctively threw her body over Edith and hit the deck. The lights died, pitching them into darkness. As she glanced over her shoulder into the living room where they'd sat earlier, she thanked God they'd moved into the windowless bedroom. Shards of glass spiked like miniature daggers in the sofa and chairs.

Jack crawled across the room and folded his arm around her back. "Are you all right?"

Ceiling pieces rained on their heads as curls of smoke rose through the gaping window spaces. While the three humans regrouped, Lorelei flapped around the room squawking, "Crikey, mate!"

Chapter Thirty-Seven

As smoke plumed into the room and the building continued to tremble, Jack knew the time had come time to meet his fate. If it meant he went completely crazy, lost his mind and spirit forever in the maze of the otherworld, he'd have to risk it.

He dropped his mental shields. A cacophony of images and sounds hit his brain like hundreds of radio stations turned up full blast. They swirled in a noisy fog mixed with the smoke. Then Maggie grabbed his hand and everything came into focus.

"I've got to get to Hannah's room," he said.

Maggie hauled Edith up as Mr. Jiggs came running from his hiding space and jumped into his mistress' arms.

Edith hugged him. "There you are, dear boy."

Jack grabbed Maggie's arms. "Get Auntie out of here. I've got to go."

"How will I find you?" she said, hustling Edith into the hallway.

He gazed into her clear, sea green eyes. "Just keep your mind open and listen."

Without even a hint of skepticism, she nodded and disappeared down the hall with Edith and Mr. Jiggs. Lorelei rode away on her shoulder. A bonzer woman indeed, Jack thought.

Chaos reigned in the smoky hallway. People screamed and ran wily-nily. Jack pushed against the panicked tide of humanity. He had to reach Hannah's room. As he rounded the corner, he found the door standing wide open.

In the smoke, he tripped over the body of a guard. Lord, he was too late. The lifeless figure lay in a pool of blood. Poor sod had his throat slashed from ear to ear.

Jack regained his footing and crouched as he ran into the room.

Hannah's room wasn't nearly as smoke-filled as the hall. Furniture lay over-turned, whether from a struggle or the blast, he couldn't be sure.

Then Jack's heart sank.

On the floor, a pair of man's shoes and trousers protruded from behind the sofa. He walked around to see Chris Matthews laid out. Dropping to his knees beside the Marine, he breathed a sigh of relief when he found a pulse. No blood. The worst injury appeared to be a nasty bump on the head.

The bedroom door creaked open. Derby cautiously peered out.

Jack sat back on his haunches. "Come on, the coast is clear. Where's Hannah?" he asked. In his heart, he already knew.

Derby took mincing steps into the living room. "After the explosion, a bunch of terrorists burst into the room, including Ahmed Saeed. I ran into the bedroom, where I have my communication equipment, to send a distress call to command."

Jack stood and made quick work of improvising an ice pack at the wet bar. "Your mate is lucky to be alive."

He returned to Chris and gently placed the ice bag on the angry, swelling lump on the side of his head. The Colonel moaned and regained semi-consciousness.

"That's it, Marine, wake up." Jack checked his pupils. "We need to haul our arses out of here."

Chris tried to push up on his elbows. "They took her, didn't they?"

"I'm afraid that ratbag Arab nabbed her. How is it you're not dead?"

Chris struggled to get up. "She wouldn't let them. It was almost as if she'd been expecting them. She bargained her freedom for my life. She looked Saeed calmly in the eye and said, *I'll go of my own free will if you don't harm him.*" He winced as he gained his equilibrium.

Jack hooked an arm under his shoulder for support. "Easy does it."

"I tried to stop them. The last thing I remember is holding her against my chest. Then they must have bashed me in the head. God, Jack, you've got to tell me. Why do they want her so badly?"

Jack gnawed his lip, still trying to piece together the fragments of information in his mind. Pieces of the puzzle were coming together, but he couldn't make out the full picture. Yet, one thing gnawed at him.

"I think she's the key to the Beast's release from the island."

***

After leaving Auntie Edith safely in the hotel with the Jaguar Jack crew members a few blocks from the blast site, Maggie ran back toward the scene of chaos. Her feet jarred in her flimsy civilian sandals. Lorelei's talons dug into her shoulder. Leaving the bird behind with Edith just hadn't felt right. No doubt about it, Jack's balminess *had* rubbed off.

Emergency vehicles, fire engines, and police cars pushed through the congested streets. She looked for a familiar face, but saw only a sea of frightened humanity. *Think, Maggie, think.* Where would they go? How would they secure Hannah? What had Jack said? *Open your mind and listen.*

Standing on the steamy sidewalk, amidst the relentless flow of foot traffic, she sought to open her mind. Nothing. Too much confusion and people jostling her body. She spied a niche between two shops and backed into it, out of the crowd. The cockatoo inched along her shoulder.

Open your mind and listen.

She closed her eyes. *Nothing, nothing, nothing.*

"This psychic stuff is a lot of crap."

Then, Lorelei cooed in her ear--that little love song she sang to Jack in their quieter moments. Maggie raised her arm, and Lorelei strolled toward her elbow. "You know where he is, don't you, girl?"

Lorelei preened her feathers while Maggie stared into her beady eyes. And, that mind-opening thing actually worked; the image of the airport flashed in her mind. *Of course.*

She hopped a taxi, took a wild ride to the airport, and dashed through the corridors. The Jakarta security was a joke, even in light of terrorists and hijackers.

On the tarmac, she spotted the Jaguar Jack helo warming up. The worst of the storm had moved off, leaving clumps of pewter clouds in its wake. Her feet pounded the asphalt; the silly sandals slapped through puddles. She banged on the door of the helo, not believing for a minute that he would leave the ground without her.

Jack opened the cockpit door and yelled over the noisy rotors. "Wait for us, Red. This is between me and the Beast. I don't want you in harm's way. The Colonel will be my stand-to man."

"Bull. Let me in. I'm part of this, too."

"It's going to be dangerous, *real* dangerous."

"You bet your ass it is. You need me, Jack. We're in this together."

With a frown and a grunt of resignation, he extended the door and she thrust herself and the bird inside. Scrambling to the back seat, she strapped in.

Chris Matthews looked over his shoulder at her from the passenger seat. "That madman Saeed has Hannah."

Maggie placed her hand on his shoulder. "We'll get her back."

Chris nodded, granite-faced with concern.

Jack pushed the throttle. "Hold on, mates. Up we go."

She gazed out the window. The crowded concrete jungle gave way to groves of swaying green palm trees. The land shrank smaller and smaller as they headed out over open sea. Her eyes focused on the competent hands of their TV hero pilot as he set his course.

She reached out and squeezed his arm, needing to make physical contact.

Without his uttering a sound, she heard his voice. *You're my girl, Red. Don't ever forget it.*

A bolt of distant lightning flashed his hair black silver. The invisible cord between them pulled taut. Connected, so connected. She couldn't deny it, wouldn't fight for independence anymore. Somewhere in this crazy adventure she'd more than fallen in love with Jaguar Jack Campbell, she'd bonded and welded. Soul to soul, spirit to spirit. Her heart squeezed.

She leaned back and gazed at the two male silhouettes before her-- one dark, one light. Fellow warriors gathering inner strength to do battle. She'd been in this place before. But never had the enemy been so momentous, never had the stakes felt so high. Her hands rested on the torn and filthy cotton outfit she'd donned earlier that morning. Glancing at the feminine sandals strapped to her ankles, she missed her sturdy boots. She closed her eyes to conserve her energy for what was to come.

The cliché is true. There are no atheists in foxholes. Her thoughts drifted to Hannah and she prayed to the missionary's God. *I don't know you very well. But, if you're out there, send us all the help you can. Don't let me screw this up. Amen.*

She dozed until a dip of turbulence jarred her awake. Though still midday, the air had filled with a dark purple cloud. Bits of grey ash hit the windshield. Visibility was almost zero.

She leaned forward and squinted into the curtain of haze. Tension rolled off the men.

"What's going on?" she asked.

At that moment, the smoke cloud parted, revealing an island ahead.

An island with a live volcano.

Chapter Thirty-Eight

Hannah climbed the steep incline, coughing from the fumes and stench that encased the churning mountain. Ahmed Saeed alone accompanied her on the final ascent. The Arab guards had dropped them off, and departed again from the island that quaked from the eruptions of the awakening inferno.

While lava poured off the west lip of the crater, Hannah and Ahmed approached from the east. She climbed the mountain, strangely at peace. Her sense of destiny had returned. What lay in store remained hidden, but she found a tenuous connection to God again. Realizing that Jack, Maggie, and Chris were part of a grand scheme had calmed her. If only she understood what her role was supposed to be.

Female screams rolled down the mountain. Terrorized high-pitched alarm increased Hannah's speed toward her unknown destination. Pushing razor-sharp palm fronds out of her way, she moved toward the frantic female voice.

She entered a volcanic grotto, a shelf of solidified lava in the shape of a large bowl on the side of the mountain. The air sizzled with blue light as a strange electrical storm hovered over the grotto. She nearly gagged at the smell of death and brimstone.

Across the expanse, the Beast stood on his hind legs, roaring with his front paws lifted toward the sky. Two figures sat bound together on the jagged lava floor before the raving monster.

A jolt of recognition hit Hannah. *Amelia. Thank God she lived.*

Amelia and her guard, Felipe, struggled against their ropes. The Beast's display of might sent the girl into hysterics.

Hannah broke into a run, her protective instincts overrode any sense of self-preservation. Despite the menacing figure of the Beast, Hannah threw her arms around Amelia and Felipe. She shielded them with her body from the wicked claws of the monster.

Amelia's sobbing shook Hannah's shoulder as she tried to calm the captive down. Felipe fought bindings on their limbs.

Hannah gazed up at the Beast. "Let them go. I'll come to you of my own free will, if you let them go."

Greater love has no one than he lays his life down for a friend. The scripture crossed her mind, but she wasn't sure it came from the Voice.

The Beast sat back on his hind legs, a smile on his lips as he licked a paw like an ordinary cat. He glanced at the prostrate figure of Ahmed Saeed crouched in worshipful abeyance. "You have done well, Saeed. The Saint comes of her own free will."

"Your day is almost here, Master."

Hannah wasted no time working loose the ropes binding the two young natives. They struggled to their feet, stomping the circulation back into their limbs.

Amelia gazed at Hannah with tear-tracked cheeks. "Gracias."

Hannah hugged her. "Vaya con Dios." The ground quaked with another volcanic explosion. "Hurry! Run!"

Felipe grabbed Amelia's hand and pulled her away. They disappeared into the foliage.

Hannah wondered what special purpose would be carried out in their lives through her sacrifice. Surely, they were the reason she had been called to this destiny.

She gazed into the Beast's red eyes and suddenly nothing made any sense. The embodiment of evil stood before her, so strong her knees buckled. Her mind fogged.

The Beast crouched low on his mighty legs, bringing his massive head to her level. He whispered in honey tones. "You have done well to surrender, little Saint. Your life will set me free and the world will know true peace. No one will dare wage war while I am in power. They will fear me too much. Mortals should never have been given freedom. They don't know how to handle it. From now on, there will be no more dissension, no more political parties, no more hunger. Those who obey and worship me shall enjoy my favor."

His voice worked like a drug, dulling her senses, painting a picture of a peaceful world bowed down before statues of a Lion-Bear god throughout the world.

The Beast's hypnotic voice continued. "Hold Ahmed's hand. He will take you to your destiny. Remember, *There's no greater love than one who lays down his life for his friends*. And you are laying down your life for the entire world. Go, go in peace, go in joy…"

Ahmed's cold hand assisted her to her feet. With a dazed mind, believing the words of the spellbinder, Hannah took a step toward the top of the smoldering mountain.

Ahmed continued whispering in her ear the same litany she'd heard from the Beast, or the Master, as Ahmed called him. "The Master will be free. The Master will bring peace and harmony. The Master will obliterate hunger and suffering."

Higher and higher they climbed. Her feet stumbled on the rocky slope, but Ahmed held her up. The fumes grew denser, her head lighter.

"The Master will provide for all. The Master...the Master...the Master..."

Finally, almost sleepwalking, Hannah found herself at the brink of the churning volcano. Rivers of lava poured down the other side of the mountain. Red, smoking liquid rock from the bowels of the earth spewed in geysers. Immense heat radiated. Her body instantly dripped with perspiration, and she nearly fainted.

Ahmed stood behind her. "You must jump. Jump of your own free will. Save the world with your sacrifice."

Mesmerized by the Arab's voice, the pull of emotion and dulling of senses, she readied herself to jump and meet her fate.

One step, then two. Then...

A new sound vibrated the air, a rhythmical beating of the wind. She turned, breaking her concentration from the volcanic activity. She gazed into the sky.

"Jump!" Saeed commanded.

The vibrating sound grew louder and louder, followed by the emergence of a helicopter. Grey blades whipped the smoky air. From her vantage point on the hillside, she gazed down over the hardened bowl of lava surrounded by the ring of palms and jungle foliage. The Beast stood on his hind legs, roaring in indignation.

It all seemed so familiar—and then she remembered—her vision the night of the occult ceremony. Instead of a horse, a helicopter descended into the natural fighting arena. Before the blades quit churning, the cockpit door opened. A white bird flew out first. Of course —Lorelei, the winged companion of the Warrior. Only now a cockatoo, not a horse.

Saeed jerked her arm. "You must jump! The Master must be set free!"

Clarity came to Hannah. "Your Master is the Prince of Lies and Deceit. I need to learn the truth."

Hannah broke out of his grip, and raced back down the hill.

***

Jack turned knobs and switches bringing the helo to a safe landing.

Chris shouted over the dying engine noise. "How did you know where to go?"

He quirked a small smile. "I could get here in my sleep, mate."

Maggie gazed out the windshield at the Beast, ferocious and huge. "Cripes. You can't face him bare-handed. Did you bring any fire power? Like a small nuclear device?"

"Guns and knives won't touch the Beast, Red. It'll take weapons much more powerful than that. Open the duffel that's stowed under your seat."

Maggie grabbed a heavy bag. Chris helped her lift it onto the seat beside her. She unzipped it and peeked inside. An ancient sword and shield, relics from another age.

Chris lifted a skeptical eyebrow. "You think you're going to take down that creature with these museum pieces? Listen Jack, Hannah's life is at stake here. Hell, all our lives are at stake. Why don't you sit it out and let Maggie and me take it on. I've got my weapon. I'll take out the Beast while Maggie secures Hannah. You be ready to take off."

Maggie reached into the bag and pulled out a tarnished silver belt. The raised inscriptions seemed somehow familiar under her fingers. Her mind flashed back to the sword she found in Jack's closet that first night. Her hand curled around the hilt of the age-blacken sword. A buzz of electricity shot up her arm. What was even more remarkable, the tarnish faded before her eyes.

"Where did you get these?"

"I've collected them through the years. A sort of crazy obsession. Biblical artifacts. Always searching for the ones that felt right. My contact in the Middle East sent them. Just in time, wouldn't you say?"

A shiver went down her spine. An unseen hand seemed to be playing a part in this drama.

Chris lifted the sword. "Didn't Hannah refer to these when she spoke of her hallucination after she'd been drugged?"

Jack nodded. "The belt of truth, the breast plate of righteousness, the helmet of salvation and the sword of the spirit."

Maggie looked at her two companions, sensing that all their lives had always been heading toward this moment. "Hannah called me 'Truth'. I don't understand how I know this, but we have to let Jack battle the Beast with these weapons."

The helicopter shook from a sudden gust of wind. A bolt of lightning struck the ground. The Beast paced his area, his massive tail whipping in anger.

Chris stared at the contents of the duffel, and shook his head in disbelief. Then he studied the determined expressions on his companions' faces and came to a decision. "All right, Jack. We'll do this your way, as crazy as it seems. I'll cover your back as best I can."

Jack raised his arms and the trio formed an unbroken circle with a warrior's handclasp. "Come on, mates, let's go."

They exited the craft. Hot wind wafting off the volcano hit them in a wave. The sky swirled in a surreal mix of purple and red. Thunder rolled in a constant hum of rumbles. Maggie covered her nose against the onslaught of the horrific odor. She fought the urge to gag.

Unlike herself, Jack seemed oblivious to the elements, almost trance-like staring at the pacing Beast. She recognized the look—somewhere between the Twilight Zone and the deep blue sea. He stood arms akimbo. His muscular triceps and biceps bulged with pent-up tension. The two Marines worked quickly to protect him with the Biblical weaponry. Her hands trembled as she fastened the buckle around his waist. Chris worked with tense efficiency, helping her strap on the rest of the equipment.

Never taking his eyes from his waiting opponent, Jack spoke with deadly calm. "Matthews, follow the path up the mountain for Hannah. I can see her in my mind's eye with Saeed."

Without questioning, Chris scanned the landscape and broke into a run.

In the grotto, the Beast paced and hissed. His red eyes glowed with challenge.

Maggie took a stand beside Jack. "I'm with you all the way."

He faced her, his gaze smoldering. "No, Red. This is as far as you go. Whatever happens, I want you to know you're the most magnificent woman I've ever known, and a piece of my soul will always be with you."

She longed to wrap her arms around him, pull him to safety. Run far, far away. But he had to go and meet his destiny. And if he didn't come back he had to know one thing. "I love you, Jack."

His eyes sparkled as he whispered. "You have my heart, Red. Take good care of it."

He motioned her to stay, and took a step toward the monster.

The soldier within her rebelled at standing idly by. She scanned the arena for a good fighting position to aid Jack in his quest. But this sort of battle wasn't in her training manual. What in blazes was she supposed to do?

A still voice seemed to whisper, *Watch, wait, listen.*

As Jack approached the battle ground, his armor took on a fresh sheen. The old sword lost its battered appearance and became a lethal weapon of justice. The helmet glowed golden above the glistening shield protecting his chest. He stalked toward the center of the arena, a shining warrior in precious metal and jewels. A gladiator ready to fight to the death.

Step by deliberate step, he approached the Beast.

The creature's laughter echoed across the grotto. His voice rumbled low. "You're coming against me in that old tin? Armor does not a warrior make. Bow down to me now, and I won't do to your lady friend what I did to your mother."

Jack growled. "You're bloody right you won't rip her apart like you killed my mother. I'm not an eight-year-old child any longer."

"You're still a coward under all that metal." The Beast's sharp teeth appeared brown and jagged and utterly deadly. "You were born a coward, and a coward you will always be."

Jack hesitated. Maggie sensed his doubt. She yelled, "He's playing mind games with you. You were never a coward. He's a liar."

She sent a mental message of love and confidence. *You are the Warrior. The power is within you, only doubt can defeat you.*

Jack lifted his chin and pointed the blade toward his nemesis. "Prepare to return to the gates of hell, Beast."

With a fierce battle cry, the Warrior charged the creature and the combat commenced. The Beast roared and lashed out. Using both arms for power, Jack swung the sword and gashed the Beast's belly. The abomination howled, and answered the assault with a bolt of lightning and a back-handed blow to the shining shield. Maggie gasped as her man flew backwards. Undaunted, Jack rose and charged again, this time drawing blood from the monster's hind quarters.

"I've never believed in cruelty to animals, but in your case, I'll make an exception," Jack said as he got close enough to deliver a strong kick.

Don't get too cocky. Maggie winced. The Beast slashed Jack's arm with curved claws. Trickles of bloods hit the rocky floor.

The opponents took measure of each other. Tension in Maggie's spine grew as she watched them go round and around. Jack used his speed and dexterity to deliver punishment, and then avoided a killing blow in return. Still, the Beast had size and weight to his advantage. Every blow he inflicted jarred Jack's body.

Her attention diverted when she heard Hannah's voice ring out from the hillside. "Let me go!"

She glanced over her shoulder to see Chris reach the incline where Hannah wrestled with Ahmed Saeed. Chris punched the Arab and sent him rolling down the hill, white robes tangled and tearing. Ahmed managed to stop his fall. With his face and hands gashed from the jagged lava protrusions, he gained his footing and started a stumbling run down the hillside.

Matthews clutched Hannah in his arms and obviously had no intention of chasing the Arab. Maggie turned back toward Jack and the Beast, still engaged in their dance of death. God, what should she do? Jack might need her. Then, that small voice whispered. *Don't let the minion escape. The Beast's mouthpiece to the world can't be free to spread his spellbinding lies.*

Maggie broke into a run. This time Saeed wasn't getting away. No cold-blooded smiles as he took off in a helicopter. She tripped twice in her lousy sandals and scraped her hands on the ground, but she kept the dirty white tunic in sight.

He edged around the lava floor toward a break in the palm barrier —a path she'd not noticed before. Grunts and roars from Jack's fight continued behind her, but she pressed on toward Saeed before he dissolved into the jungle.

He slipped into the path and disappeared. *Damn, damn, damn.* Maggie plunged forward, pushing the sharp fronds out of her way. Ahmed glanced over his shoulder, his eyes two black coals of evil.

Maggie yelled, "Stand and fight like a man, you baby-killing bastard."

Instead, he ran faster. But it's hard to dash in a dress. She sprinted with her long legs and jumped on his back to bring him down. Together they fell on the jungle floor. They tumbled and tussled.

Ahmed grunted. "Worthless whore."

Lying together on the ground, he gained position over her and hit her hard with the back of his hand. A heavy ring gashed her cheek.

With tears smarting in her eyes, she used her elbow and knee. Keeping emotion in check, her training took over. Power surged into her limbs as she did her job. An upper cut to his chin shot a resounding crack through his jaw. Her strategically placed knee jab had him curled in pain. She rolled away and struggled to her feet.

She spun around. To her surprise, he recovered quickly, standing hunched over in pain. He grimaced and panted.

"You stupid bitch. You can never defeat the Master. He is eternal, don't you see?"

"But you're not eternal, are you, Saeed? You were born and you will die, just like the rest of us. He's been using you—just like he's used greedy, heartless men throughout history—all the way from Attila the Hun through Hitler. But their domination was always temporary, just like yours. Because it's over for you. Right here. Right now."

Ahmed let loose a blood-curdling war cry, pulled a long dagger from his robe and attacked. His face became a hideous mask of hatred.

Oh, shit. Maggie assumed a defensive position. She twisted to deflect his lethal blade as his body slammed into her. She slid on the slick jungle ground. *Frickin', flimsy sandals.*

He grabbed her hair and yanked her head back. An image of spurting blood flashed in her mind.

I don't think so. She elbowed his gut and broke loose.

He lunged again and they grunted in their struggle for control of the knife. Maggie's arms shook.

Saeed's eyes blazed, only inches from her face. Sweat trickled down his swarthy temple. His fetid breath assaulted her nostrils. *God, what an ugly bastard.*

He backed her into a rough tree trunk. Her spine jarred against the punishing wood. Her two hands gripped his wrist that held the knife. The damn tree kept her from delivering a good ball-busting kick.

With his free hand, Saeed punched her stomach. *Oh crap.* She doubled over and gasped for air.

The son of a bitch can't win. Not this time.

She wheeled around the tree trunk and caught her breath. Saeed's knife slashed downward, grazing her forearm. Pain blazed like a flash fire. He stalked her around the tree. She gulped in the acrid, ash air.

Come on, Maggie, pull it together.

Digging deep into her dwindling reservoir of strength, she leaped up to grab a tree limb, tucked her feet up and busted Saeed in the chest with both legs. Caught off balance, he stumbled backwards. She fell to the ground and used round house kicks to pound him.

"That's for Al…that's for Hannah." One more kick, "And that's for me!"

He tripped in a tangle of his torn tunic and landed on his knife. The blade impaled his belly; blood coursed onto the jungle floor. He panted and groaned, trying to rise, but too stunned and breathless. He struggled to pull out the knife, which only made the bleeding increase. His body began to convulse.

She stood over him, trembling with the adrenaline that pumped through her veins. God, how she wanted to beat the holy hell out of him. Her hands formed fists at her sides. She beat down her emotions and summoned her military control.

If she'd had a revolver, she might have executed him then and there. But that seemed too damn easy. He deserved a slow death. Even that wouldn't be payback for the prisoners he'd tortured. The smell of his blood and guts assaulted her nose. Everything about this island had a bad smell.

A rustling of leaves caught Maggie's attention. A pair of familiar yellow eyes in a black feline face edged through. Jack's jaguar girlfriend. She undoubtedly scented fresh blood.

Maggie gazed back at Saeed, relishing the poetic justice of the moment. "So long, Saeed. One less bad guy in the world."

He gurgled in pain. "Wait, you can't leave me alone like this."

Saeed would meet his fate with a creature that resembled his god. "Oh, I'm not leaving you alone. I think you'll be well taken care of."

She grabbed his dagger and trotted back toward the grotto.

Behind her, she heard a cat's howl followed by a man's scream.

Chapter Thirty-Nine

Jack and the Beast fought their way up the mountain, an ancient sword wielded against lethal claws. The combatants drove each other toward the final battle ground--the mouth of the volcano. The twisty path felt familiar under Jack's feet, although he'd never been here before—in the flesh. Yet he knew he'd been chased up this mountain many times. Astral memories collided with the physical plane. A lifetime of buried fear emerged. Fear of the monster. Fear for his sanity.

In the smoky, purple haze the scene seemed too bizarre. The Beast's hideous magnitude couldn't be real. Jack's eyes smarted and everything blurred. Was he asleep? Was he awake? Had he gone completely mad? Was he on an island or living out a delusion in a padded cell? He stared up at the monster, trying to focus. Scarlet eyes glowed down with hypnotic power.

The familiar voice hissed. "You're crazy. Utterly insane. Lay down your silly toys. You're locked up in a hospital again. Give up the fight. It isn't real."

Jack's arms suddenly felt weak and impossibly heavy. So sleepy. He must be hallucinating.

Suddenly Maggie was at his side, grabbing his shoulder and shaking him. "You're not crazy. He's lying. He's the Master of Lies."

The Beast howled, "Bitch!" His forearm whipped out and punched her backward. Her head hit the ground hard, knocking her unconscious.

Jack snapped out of his confusion. The surroundings came into focus. The island was *real*. The bloody Beast all too real. "Liar! No more lies!"

He raised his sword and drove the Deceiver toward the brink of the volcano's fiery edge. Molten rock spewed from the cavity, flaming yellow and red.

The final stony ascent to the burning opening sapped his strength. Besides parrying blows from the Beast, he had to keep his balance in the skittering rocks and dodge hot cinders falling from the sky.

When Jack tripped, the Beast wrapped both front legs around him in a monstrous version of a bear hug. The stink of bloodied fur gagged him. He strained to break the creature's hold, but instead rose from the ground like a dangling doll. Oh, Christ, he was about to be flung into the sea of lava. He braced himself for destruction.   Instead, the Beast howled and dropped him.

Jack stumbled backward and bumped into Chris, who stood with his rifle drawn. "The bastard isn't entirely impervious to bullets. I think you need some back up, son."

"I think you're right, mate." Maybe between him and good old Faithful, they could pitch this Beelzebub back to hell.

So it was two against one, but it still wasn't enough. Chris discharged his weapon on the Beast. The shells affected him like nasty bee stings--annoying, but not lethal. Jack's sword carried more debilitating power, but the opponents reached an exhausting stalemate at the volcano's edge.

Standing before them, now mauled and mangled, the Beast panted. "You little men will never defeat me with your puny sword and gun. Feel the power of fear and lies. You have nothing to compare."

Then he howled and blew a mighty breath from his diaphragm. The stench of it knocked Chris and Jack to their knees, blinded their eyes. The sword and shield slipped from Jack's fingers. With one blow of his paw, the Beast could send the two mortals cartwheeling into the abyss. Jack gasped and tried to scramble away from the precipice. Sweat poured off his brow and his limbs hung lethargic and heavy. His strength was drained, nearly depleted.

His mind sent out one last message. *Oh, crikey, I'm going to lose. I'm sorry, Red. I let you down.*

Down the hillside, Maggie struggled to reach consciousness. Jack's words echoed in her head *I'm sorry, Red…I'm sorry, Red.*

A smooth hand rubbed her brow. "Maggie, Maggie, wake up!" Hannah's voice wavered with urgency.

Maggie forced her eyes open. Damn, her skull throbbed. Her head lay cradled in Hannah's lap. The missionary's face came into focus. "Cripes, I feel like I've been hit by a truck."

For a moment she couldn't recall what happened. Then it all flashed back and she tried to push up. "Jack…"

"The Beast has the men trapped at the volcano's edge." Hannah supported her up.

"We have to help them, but I'm not sure exactly how."

"I've been sitting here praying while you've been unconscious. I think I have it figured out. Come on." Hannah tugged Maggie's hand.

Strength from the missionary's grip poured into Maggie's system. As they strode together up the twisty terrain, she glanced at the young woman's profile. In the midst of imminent catastrophe, Hannah exuded tranquil determination. My God, where did she get such peace? But, of course, she knew the answer. From faith.

And in that moment, truth flashed in Maggie's mind. A panorama unfolded in her mind of the events at hand and everyone's role.

At the brink of destruction, the men and the Beast savaged each other. As if sensing the escalating battle, the earth quaked. Hannah's foot slipped over the edge of the path. Maggie grabbed her arm and hauled her to safer ground. The women struggled to keep their footing.

As they reached the summit, Maggie's heart twisted to see Jack's condition. Gashed, bloody and grimy, the Aussie hefted the sword with weakened arms and lumbered toward the Beast. Beside him, Chris pulled the trigger of his rifle, but nothing discharged.

The Beast looked battle worn also. Red oozed down his matted fur. He dragged one hind leg. Yet, strength still rippled his muscles. His teeth bared in a grisly smile as he drove the men toward the churning lava. His voice held strong with monster resonance. "It's over, Warrior. This time the victory is mine!"

He raised his bear-claw, ready to cast Jack and Chris into the inferno.

The women thrust themselves between the Beast and the men.

"Stop!" Hannah's powerful authority rang through the air. "In the name of the One who sent me, the source of your power is extinguished. The bonds of your spiritual slaves are severed."

The Beast moaned. "No...No..."

"Your reign of evil is over for now," Maggie said. "I know the Truth. I am Truth. The Saint is your gatekeeper. As long as she holds her faith, you will remain imprisoned in the bowels of the earth."

Hannah spoke with unearthly calm. "I realize now you were using scripture against me. I wouldn't have been sacrificing myself so that others would be free. You used lies to confuse me. Now my constant vigilance will keep you locked behind the gates of hell."

The Beast raised his forearms to the sky and howled. Lightning blasted the ground, but the women stood firm, shoulder to shoulder.

Barely managing to keep upright, Jack marveled at these incredible women. Such courage, such quiet power. Maggie turned her back on the Beast. She held her hand out to Jack.

"Time to finish the job, Warrior," she said.

He clasped her palm. Strength filled and renewed him like rain replenishing parched soil. Her green-eyed gaze transmitted infinite confidence. Despite a nasty cut on her cheek, she was the most beautiful thing he'd ever seen. The other half to his soul. Unspoken understanding passed between them.

"All right, Red, let's send the devil back to Hades."

Chris and Maggie flanked Jack as he stalked his quarry. Hannah stood vigilant to the side and uttered a strange, otherworldly language. Her words rolled across the air. Though he didn't understand their exact meaning, Jack absorbed their power.

The Saint and the Warrior joined forces.

"No!" The Beast crumbled before their eyes. He groaned a baleful cry. The millennium of his true age instantly deteriorated his body. He crouched on all fours. His eyes watered and his legs trembled like the most decrepit of creatures. Fur dropped off his hide in motley balls.

Jack raised his shield and sword. Step by step, with his partners beside him, he edged the Beast to the brink of the burning pit. Tongues of fire singed the mangy fur.

The Beast pleaded, "I can offer you the world. Pleasures and power beyond your imagination can be yours. A never-ending harem of virgins for your enjoyment."

Jack laughed. "Sorry, Beast, that promise of virgins you've been using sounds quite balmy and totally exhausting."

In a last desperate attempt, the Beast lunged and grabbed Jack's body armor. Lifted off his feet, Jack slashed the hairy arm. He dropped near the torso and drove his blade into the rotting flesh. Again and again he plunged supernatural steel into the belly of the Beast.

Enraged roars ripped through the atmosphere. The air crackled blue and violet as the Beast's last connection to his power disintegrated.

With a firm whack of his shield, Jack plunged the embodiment of his nightmares into the sizzling crater. Revelation's monstrosity tumbled into the depths.

Jack backed away from the searing opening of the volcano. Energy spent, he leaned on his sword. His lungs filled with the sulfurous air. Still, it was better than breathing the body odor of the Beast. A warm hand wrapped around his arm. Maggie, his bonzer woman. He glanced to his side and smiled at his three companions, now gathered around him.

Though Matthews looked fairly banged up himself, he offered Jack a salute of respect. "Well done, my friend. You're a true hero, not just the TV version."

"Too bad the camera crew wasn't here. We would have sent the ratings through the roof. Of course, who would believe it?"

"I believe you." Maggie gazed at him with smiling eyes. "I believe everything you ever said."

"Ah, Red, you've come a long way."

From the depths, the mountain quaked and shuddered. A deadly cloud of volcanic ash belched from the pit.

Jack faced his companions. "I suggest we make tracks, mates."

He heard no objections.

The Warrior, the Saint, Truth and Faithful scrambled down the hillside, just ahead of a bubbling wave of lava.

Epilogue

Chris Matthews approached the Acaban village. Except for a dusting of ash and a series of earthquakes, that side of Paradisio had escaped effects of the volcanic activity.

He passed native homes built on stilts that rode above seasonal flood waters. They looked idyllic under the swaying palm trees. A group of dark-haired children played with a small dog, throwing a stick. Squatting women worked on meal preparation, and glanced up from their tasks. They nodded, recognizing the tall mainlander.

Hannah's laughter tinkled out of the missionary hut. "You're just making fun of my bad accent."

Chris smiled as he climbed the steps up to the platform that served as a porch for her home. He peeked through the doorway. She stood before a chalkboard filled with phonetically spelled Acaban words. Dressed in colorful garb, she'd gone native, except for her shoulder-length blond hair. A group of natives sat before her—the translation team.

Her face lit up when she spotted Chris. Her companions peered over their shoulders and rose to their feet. Ysway, the leader, greeted him in proper Acaban tradition, and then guided the team out of the hut.

Hannah's home had a few amenities not seen in the native huts—like a couple of chairs with padded cushions and a round table. Her "kitchen" was a series of shelves against the wall holding canned goods.

Chris walked in and reached out for her hands. "I had to stop by and see you before I leave for D.C. Jack let me hitch a ride in his helicopter."

Hannah smiled. "Good old Jack."

"The terrorist network seems to be breaking down, but I'm being assigned to work on the Palestinian-Israeli Peace Accord. I hate to leave you, Sugar."

"I know." She tugged his hand. "Sit down, soldier, and have a drink."

They sat at Hannah's little table. In the center, she had placed a bunch of wild flowers near a pitcher and cups. Her slender fingers poured juice made from some mystery jungle fruit.

She gazed at him with her cornflower eyes, once again with their hint of mischief. She smiled and he recognized the return of her deep-seated joy.

He sighed in resignation. "As much as I'd like to see you safe in the states, you shine here."

"The Voice has been very clear since I've been back. I'm to stay here for a season, translating the Bible for the Acabans and praying a vigil to keep the Beast in the underworld. It won't be forever. Another gatekeeper will be chosen."

Chris held her hand, enjoying the softness, memorizing the moment. "You know I'll be waiting for you whenever you feel you've been released from this place."

"Even if I'm a withered old hag?"

"Even if you're bald and lost all your teeth."

She threw her arms around his neck. He pulled her onto his lap. One last time, he had to hold her. She snuggled her head against his shoulder. "I do love you, Chris. You brought me back from despair. You gave me strength when I needed it most. My mistake in all this was thinking I had to carry on alone—Hannah, the super-missionary girl."

Chris hugged her tight. "Whenever you need me, I'll come running."

She gazed up into his face. Her fingers ran through his hair, sending warmth down his spine. "I was wrong to cut off all contact with you. We both have our jobs to do, but I know we'll be together someday."

"I'm counting on it, Sugar."

She lifted her lips to his in the sweetest of kisses. Oh, yes, someday this woman would be in his home. But until then, she would live in his heart.

Their intimate moment came to abrupt end by an invasion of one spider monkey, dressed in a safari jacket. He jumped on the table and helped himself to some fruit.

Auntie Edith clomped up the stairs. "Oh, you naughty boy! You shouldn't just barge into someone's hut."

Edith panted as she stood in the doorway dressed in a bright yellow-floral shirt and matching slacks.

Hannah winked at Chris as she slid off his lap. "Auntie Edith, come in. I'm so glad you dropped by. Please sit down and have a drink. Where are Maggie and Jack?"

"Oh, they had some secret place they scurried off to. You know how honeymooners are—always wanting to be alone."

Chris chuckled. "They weren't exactly alone for their wedding. I read fifty million viewers tuned in."

"The highest ratings we ever had. Maggie was such a good sport about having her wedding at the San Diego Zoo. Training that orangutan to be flower girl was no small trick, I'll tell you."

***

Jack stared down at the valley. Lorelei perched on his arm. His fingers petted her soothing, downy feathers. How many times had he shaken in his bloody boots on this very spot?

The rocky precipice hovered above the placid, greenery below. He waited for the old feeling to roll over him—fear from echoes and taunts blasting his brain. He sniffed the air for the stink of mangy fur and rotting flesh. He braced for the chill of cowardice to tremble down his backbone.

Instead, warm hands slid over his shoulder blades, reached under his arms, and hugged his chest. Maggie's scent wafted around him; her touch centered him. Her love cast out the old demons. Jaguar Jack felt whole and utterly sane.

"A penny for your thoughts, Mr. Campbell."

He lifted his arm and Lorelei lit into a nearby tree. Then he turned around and pulled Maggie into his embrace. "I don't think they're worth that much. Of course, if I concentrate on you, my thoughts become priceless, Mrs. Campbell."

She snuggled like a contented cat. "That name has such a nice ring to it. So much better than Maggie the Mouth."

"What about Maggie the Marine? Have any second thoughts about signing up for my crew and giving up the Corps?"

"No. Not a moment, not an instant." Her head eased back so she could look him in the eye. "Somewhere between Jakarta and the blast of the volcano, I realized my place is with you. It's a lifetime assignment."

Warmth whooshed into his belly and he nearly gushed with love talk. But he didn't want to sound like a sentimental jackass. "You'd be miserable without me."

"Your ego is obviously still intact." Her fingers trailed up his chest. "But let's face facts. I'm nuts about you and you'd be lost without me."

A gust of wind shot up the side of the hill, a minor dust devil swirled around them. Jack thought of the evil below, always waiting for its chance to ascend.

He tightened his grip on her. "You're bloody right I'd be lost without you. Why do you think I hustled you into a whirlwind marriage? I didn't want to give you time to back out. You're not only my heart, Red. You're my peace of mind."

"It's funny, isn't it? I've brought you sanity and you've made me a little bit crazy." She whispered into his ear. "Don't tell anyone, but I'm beginning to understand what Lorelei is thinking."

"Crikey, mate!" The bird squawked on cue.

Jack lifted an eyebrow. "Welcome to the loony bin. What's she thinking right now?"

"She thinks a lot about food. I'm going to surprise her with some fresh pomegranates."

Jack laughed. "By God, Red, you're turning into a blinking animal lover!" He spun her around. "Oh, the things I'm going to show you. We'll leave this spooky island behind us forever. No more Beasts or bogeymen. I'll show you all the wonders of the world."

"That sounds really good." Maggie pulled away and gazed down over the valley. "There's only one thing, Jack."

"What is it, darlin'?"

"I sort of *know* things now."

"What things?"

"Well, you're the Warrior and I'm Truth. And while the Beast is now under control, there's still a lot of evil in the world. Still too many bad guys."

"Oh, Lord." Jack groaned and in his heart he knew his wife would always be a Marine.

"That's right, Jack. I'm not sure exactly what our next assignment will be, but whatever it is, it's going to be dangerous. *Real* dangerous."

About the Author

Raised in the cultural crossroads of Southern California, Dana Taylor explores spirituality, healing, relationships, and multidimensional living in her writing. Her search for personal wellness lead to studying alternative medicine, essential oils, and energy healing. She is a Reiki Master.

Her books have won various awards including Golden Quill Awards Best First Book (Ain't Love Grand), and 2014 Independent Spirit Book Awards – Energy Medicine Category (*Ever-Flowing Streams: Christ, Reiki, Reincarnation and Me*). She has frequently been on the Amazon Bestseller lists.

Currently, she divides her time between Hawaii, Missouri, and California. Visit her blogsite at SupernalLiving.com.

From Dana Taylor--

If you enjoyed *The Adventures of Jaguar Jack*, please consider posting a customer review on the Amazon book page. A shout-out on your Facebook page or other social media would also be greatly appreciated. I'm always happy to hear from readers. Feel free to drop me a message. My email is supernalfriends@yahoo.com

Bright Blessings—

Dana

www.ingramcontent.com/pod-product-compliance
Lightning Source LLC
Chambersburg PA
CBHW070818120626
46556CB00002B/554